Zenobia

This book is a work of fiction and any resemblance to persons, living or dead, or places, events or locales is purely coincidental. The characters are productions of the author's imagination and used fictitiously

Printed in the United States of America by Metacognition Press, Orinda, CA

ISBN: 978-0-9859707-3-4

A Novel of Lust, Conquest and Betrayal

ACKNOWLEDGMENTS

My thanks to Justin Beck, who originally conceived this story, and is a partner in the screenplay by the same title.

Don Maker

Zenobia

CHAPTER ONE

Zenobia watched the covers rise and fall several times—labored breaths that tore her heart and taxed her patience. Her mother had dozed off once again. She allowed her gaze to wander as she waited, knowing it would not be long. Thick red curtains added to the pervasive presence of death, but Zenobia's eyes were accustomed to the gloom. To think that only one year before her mother had looked young, strong, and as beautiful as any woman in the entire Eastern Roman Empire! Now here she lay, decimated from the wasting sickness like one three times her age, the smell of decay overpowering the perfumes intended to mask the odors. The tic of Zenobia's right hand, spilling a few drops of cool water from the silver ladle in her hand, was the only sign of the shudder that threatened to flash through her body like a flame racing up a bolt of silk.

The woman stirred, and Zenobia forced a smile to her lips. "Did you rest a bit, Mother?"

"I will rest eternally with the Rephaim very soon."

Zenobia's eyes flared at the mention of the gods of the underworld, but she held them steady on the drawn face of her mother. She forced the distress at her mother's words into anger, cursing her lack of control. The oppressive air of the darkened room helped fuel that anger.

"Of course not, Mother. As you often say, this trouble is only a stray camel passing across the face of the great desert."

"Pah!"

Zenobia knew her mother's thoughts: such pretense was another mark of weakness. The fetid body, wasting away to a shriveled hulk, made the inevitability of death clear. The only question was how long her mother had left.

"You have always taught me to fight through all adversity, Mother."

Her mother sighed, but the sound rattled as it came up her throat and passed her cracked lips. In spite of constant drips of water from the ladle, Zenobia could not keep them moist. When her breathing steadied once more, her mother continued.

"The blood of Cleopatra, the greatest queen the world has ever known, flows through your veins. You must not let this chance go to waste."

Her mother boasted Queen Cleopatra VII as an ancestor through Drusilla, granddaughter of King Juba II of Mauretania and Cleopatra Selene, the daughter of Cleopatra VII and Marc Antony. How much of this was true, if any? It didn't matter ... especially now. Zenobia opened her mind and her heart wide as she prepared to obey. "What must I do?"

Moments passed before the older woman spoke again. Zenobia was not certain if she were gathering her thoughts or her energy.

"You must know that, even now, King Shapur leads a mighty army against our wealthy neighbor of Antakya to the north."

With her free hand, Zenobia rubbed her fingers lightly over her lips. "No doubt Shapur wishes to make an impact after his father, Ardašir, proclaimed him co-ruler of the Persian Empire above his older brothers."

Her mother gave a tight smile, clearly pleased that her daughter understood the political implications. "Emperor Valerian will ride with Lord Odaenathus in two days to witness his destruction of the southern bandits."

Zenobia nodded. The Tanukh, one of the larger nomad Arab clans, had seized this opportunity to send a strong raiding party along Palmyra's southern border. But she did not see the connection.

"And then?"

Another pause as her mother once more gathered her strength. "It is said Valerian will grant him command of the combined armies to face the Sassanids if he is pleased with the result."

"Ah."

Now she understood. Since the rule of Tiberius, Odaenathus' family, the Septimii, had controlled the city of Palmyra in an uneasy truce with Rome. It seemed that Valerian now wanted to formalize the relationship, and viewed the current Septimii prince as the man to take charge of this desert city that acted as a buffer against the mighty Persian Empire. Quietly, it was rumored Valerian was getting old and wanted to spend some time in his villa in southern Italia. Before he handed over his legions, however, Valerian wanted to witness the vaunted leadership of Odaenathus using only his own Beduin cavalry.

"Yes. And you must go with them."

Zenobia's eyes flared once again, but she stifled an exclamation. She fussed with the ladle while she regained her composure.

"To what purpose, Mother?"

The woman inclined her head slightly on the beautifully made pillow, a sign she was pleased with her daughter's reaction. Before her illness she would have been more subtle, but now she came right to the point.

"The passing of Princess Lejka has left a gap that Lord Odaenathus must fill. When Emperor Valerian makes him governor—which he will—he must have both a wife and a mother for his young son. You must become that wife."

"Mother! He is still in mourning."

The exclamation slipped from her before she could catch it. Zenobia had forbidden the servants from speaking to her mother of the latest developments, not wanting her to exert herself over politics, but she should have known better. Dying or not, the woman's mind remained sharp and her strength of character like steel. Her mother's hand rose only slightly, but it was enough to dismiss the outburst.

"Lord Odaenathus must have a woman stronger than the one who died of the birthing sickness. You are strong, and have been trained since childhood for just such a position. You must not let this opportunity pass." Her voice cut through the silence of the household as she repeated the command.

Three years before, Prince Odaenathus had proudly held his heir aloft for the citizens to see: Hairan, named after his father. But Princess Lejka had died three days afterward. It had taken more than a year for the citizens to recover from the loss of the beautiful young princess, whose charity and kindness were renowned throughout Assyria. Only the presence of enemies to the north and south of his city had pulled Palmyra's prince out of his sorrow.

As Zenobia gazed around the large, richly-appointed bedroom, she reflected that she had indeed been trained for this moment. Her father, Zabbai bin Selim, had been a very wealthy minor nobleman of Palmyra. In keeping with the warrior queen tradition of Assyria, Zenobia had been trained from an early age in riding, hunting, and the use of weapons. When a trading caravan led by her father had been wiped out by bandits, her mother had focused all of her attention on preparing Zenobia for some great destiny, no doubt envisioning a rejuvenation of her glorious family heritage.

"And how am I to manage that, Mother?"

Her mother gave a slight smile, reminding Zenobia of the woman of only a year before. "It is already arranged. Lord Odaenathus will allow you to join the other young nobles who will get their first taste of battle. You must make certain to capture his eye, not just as the great beauty you are, but as a brave, strong warrior. When he is ready, he will think of you first."

Zenobia dipped the ladle once more into the cool water, giving her mother time to regain her breath. Lord Odaenathus was a great warrior, a splendid man, and no doubt soon to be second in Assyria only to the emperor himself. But he was old, at least twice her own age of seventeen, and now had a son and heir. How could she ever find happiness as the wife of such a man?

"Is it ... so important?"

"There is only one thing important in life." Once more, her mother's eyes gazed at her like those of a hawk about to stoop on its prey. "The only thing that gives one control of life."

"Yes, Mother."

Zenobia had been told that often enough by both of her parents. The only important thing in life was power, because only that could make you safe. As she dipped the ladle toward her mother's eager tongue, a sigh crossed her mind, but not her lips.

* * *

The early morning air was crisp, invigorating. The sky was cloudless, and not even the cry of a desert hawk broke the stillness. The morning was glorious, with shades of crimson complementing the yellows and browns.

Zenobia sat calmly on her horse, a bow in her left hand and the reins held loose in her right. A Roman *gladius* hung from a sheath at her side. She stared down a slight rise at the Tanukh camp. If she joined in the conflict, she would guide her swift Arabian with her knees to leave both hands free to use her weapons. The other young nobles, poised atop their mounts on either side of her, wore heavier armor, and each carried a spear and the longer Assyrian sword. To their left sat Emperor Valerian surrounded by his *turma*, a detached cavalry unit of thirty men from his Praetorian Guard.

Below, a few horses nickered and a handful of camels chewed their cuds. Some of the Tanukh stirred. Otherwise, the camp was quiet.

The bandits had found a large oasis only a few leagues from the village they had raided the day before. They slept on the ground with their horses tethered beside them. The camels, still weighted down with the booty from the Assyrian nomad camps they had attacked, stood at the center of the circle of Tanukh warriors. The guards posted along the rise and on the far side of the camp had been dispatched by stealthy Beduin, who had slithered across the sand under the cover of darkness, their long knives clenched in their teeth. When the first light of the sun broke the horizon, they had pounced as one to slit the throats of their assigned sentry.

A sudden war cry pierced the silence, and the main Palmyrene cavalry flew over the ridge toward the invaders. Odaenathus led the charge, the point of his sword circling above his head. The air suddenly roiled with the thunder of horses, the battle cries of men, and the dust that rose like steam in a cauldron.

With amazing speed, the Tanukh sprang from their bedrolls and grabbed their weapons. Some loosed arrows, while others leaped on the backs of their horses before the first wave of Palmyrenes swept into their ranks. Throwing their spears or shooting arrows, the Beduin horsemen wreaked carnage among their startled foe. Just as the Tanukh organized some resistance, a smaller band of cavalry swept from their rear, completing the trap.

From her vantage point, it looked to Zenobia that the battle would be over before she and her companions could enter the fray. Her brows furrowed and the corner of her mouth twisted, yet a sigh of relief fought to escape her lungs. Her mount pranced at the violent noise and motion of men in conflict, but she steadied him with a firm hand. At that moment something caught her eye: a group of Tanukh must have recognized Odaenathus as the opposition's leader and determined to exact some measure of revenge. Forming into a tightly mounted group, they charged the spot where the prince was already occupied by two of the bandits, his back to the half dozen warriors bearing down on him. Without thought, Zenobia kicked her horse into motion and raced toward the same spot.

At a full gallop, she managed to get off one arrow before she entered the melee. She felt a strange thrill to see the man fall, although there was no time to evaluate her feelings. As the distance closed rapidly, she drew her short sword and shouted a warning to the prince, who had killed one of his foes but remained oblivious to the greater danger.

Startled by her shout, the prince glanced up. In the time it took him to see both Zenobia and the enemy bearing down on him, the man below him gave a fierce grin and stabbed upward. His blow caught Odaenathus' horse squarely in the chest. With a scream, the horse reared violently, throwing his rider to the ground, the sword embedded in its muscular torso.

As though the flow of time had stilled to a mere trickle, Zenobia saw the attacker on the ground draw his long knife. At the same time, the rider now leading the pack raised his sword to cleave the prince with a mighty blow. Her warrior instinct still ruled her, an unconscious reaction to the unfolding scene. She pulled hard on the reins with her free hand, guiding her horse to a point in front of Odaenathus, who was just rising to his feet, one hand automatically reaching for the sword that lay on the ground beside him. The stench of blood, leather and sweat filled Zenobia's nostrils.

Just as the bandit began his downward stroke, Zenobia's horse rammed his mount from the side. Both animals went flying from the violent contact; the other rider slammed headfirst into the ground. The man's horse came down squarely on the assailant on the ground, crushing him beneath its weight. Zenobia had already launched herself into a dive, breaking her fall with both hands and rolling with the impact. Her shoulder smashed down even so, and the breath whooshed from her body. She just had a moment to see the other horses veer from the carnage in front of them before she tumbled over once more, slamming her heels hard into the yielding sand.

Dazed, Zenobia lay flat on her back for several seconds, amazed the sand had softened her fall enough so that she was not seriously hurt. Struggling to sit up, she saw Odaenathus already standing, swinging his sword ferociously at the riders who had regained control of their mounts to renew the attack.

But it was too late for them: more than a dozen Palmyrene cavalry had closed in, frantic to defend their prince. Within seconds, the Tanukh warriors were all dead or dying, while Odaenathus remained standing. He stared down at Zenobia with wide eyes, panting heavily.

Zenobia drew in great gulps of air, and suddenly realized that both of her arms trembled violently. Her heart beat as though to burst its way through the light armor she wore. Her head and shoulder throbbed, yet strangely she thought only of the concern and wonder that lay deep in the dark, soft eyes of Odaenathus.

Then the prince bent down and took her hand. Gently, he pulled her to her feet to stand beside him. His voice was deep, but flowed like a refreshing desert stream.

"Thank you … my lady."

Zenobia giddily had but one thought: her mother's command had been realized. The prince of Palmyra had definitely noticed her.

CHAPTER TWO

Sunlight filtered through the curtain, and the first faint rays dispelled the comfortable darkness. Zenobia stirred in her bed. Her eyes blinked twice, and she came fully awake. Throwing the covers aside, she stretched languorously, like a desert wildcat. She exhaled with unhurried satisfaction, joyful in her vitality.

Her glance went to her husband still sleeping beside her. As usual, he had flung most of the coverings off as he slept. Oddly, he always suffered during the hot summer months. Zenobia leaned over and kissed the skin on his back, which became more like leather every year. Odaenathus did not stir.

Zenobia flowed from the bed and stalked toward the light. She flung open the curtains and walked out onto the balcony, unconcerned with her nakedness.

Zenobia loved the sunrise. It climbed over a low range of hills to the east that broke the level plain of Assyria with irregular peaks. The light lanced through the air and spread itself over rocks and plants that dotted the undulating waves of sand. The natural hues of the land, enhanced and blended with the fire colors of the sun, gave the subdued tints an almost painful vibrancy. Her world revealed itself in clear, sharp contrasts. The shadows of objects impressed themselves firmly into the yielding sand, only to grow restless within the span of seconds and try another shape—equally clear-cut, equally firm in stamping it-self onto the ground. Even the smells of the desert were clean and pure.

The feeling of Life was as strong as the sunlight. The desert glared at her, stark and defiant, in almost the same way. Zenobia loved that palpable force. Each of the countless animals and plants fought with a fierce passion for its bit of territory and nourishment. She smiled at her favorite thought: when death is so common and so sudden, life is especially precious.

Zenobia lowered her gaze to the city of Palmyra. Her city. Where she was born, where she lived, and where she now ruled by the side of her husband.

King Solomon had settled here, on the edge of the Fertile Crescent region, because there were plentiful streams and wells of water, while in the upper part of Assyria water was scarce. The clear, sweet waters of Palmyra attracted caravans as a convenient stopping place before they started for their destinations in Asia Minor or on the coast of the Mediterranean. By becoming partners with Greece and then Rome, the city rulers had managed to enjoy much of the good those powerful empires had offered, but sacrificed little true independence.

Zenobia smiled and stretched once again. Then she turned and strode back into the bedroom.

She knelt on the edge of the bed, looking down at her husband. Contrary to her early fears, he was still in very good shape. He practiced regularly with his soldiers both on horseback and on foot. It was the only way an Assyrian commander could be respected. She stretched across the bed until her upper body lay across Odaenathus' back. She nibbled lightly on one shoulder and kissed him on the back of his neck until he stirred, groggy.

"Mmm...." He purred like a cat.

"You must rise, my lord."

"I think I'm rising."

"Not that way, husband!"

"Oh. Must I?"

"There is much to be done."

Odaenathus groaned. "Oh, right. Another battle with the damn Persians."

Zenobia moved back and Odaenathus propped himself up on an elbow. He rubbed his head and blinked several times. He licked his lips. "I must have had too much wine last night."

"A mighty feast." Zenobia had no sympathy in her voice. "Nevertheless, duty calls."

Odaenathus sat up, irritation bringing him to full consciousness. "Our best trade partners these days. And damn that Shapur! Why under Malak-bel's blessed sun did the man break Hadrian's truce?"

"I fear we've made ourselves too valuable, and perhaps look too vulnerable. Without the legions around to support our army, our neighbor now wants to own the Silk Road, not just travel it."

"The price we pay for having served Rome so well. The more they get, the greedier our neighbors become. Including Rome itself." Odaenathus shook his head in disgust. Again he stroked his forehead soothingly. He gave his wife a sideways glance. "Are you certain you don't want to lead a full-scale battle, not just a little border skirmish? Then I could be the one to laze in bed while you ride off to save our country."

"Oh, dear." Zenobia sighed in mock distress. She knew he would be forever shamed if he allowed her to lead the full army, but went along with the jest. Since the day they had met, her prowess as a warrior had been firmly etched in his mind. "I fear your men are not quite ready for a mere woman to lead them in an actual war. They only trust the great Odaenathus, the mighty hero of Ctesiphon and Emesa." She pointed a dramatic finger at his face. "Our army needs you, my lord!"

"Oh, my lord!" He lovingly mimicked her.

They both laughed and fell into a kiss. His was passionate, intense, while hers was as sensual as she could make it.

Zenobia no longer felt guilt over her lack of deep feelings for him. The tremendous respect she had felt from the first, the sincere affection that had developed over the years of their marriage, had been accepted as enough. She had done her duty to her mother and to his desires—and, in a way, her duty to Palmyra—and that would have to be enough. It certainly seemed enough for him, for he never complained, although he must certainly know.

A horn sounded. Zenobia bounded to her feet. "Come, husband. We must prepare."

Odaenathus rose with a sigh. "Yes."

The couple walked into their separate dressing chambers where their servants awaited them. Zenobia was helped into formal robes of state. When she emerged once again, her hair sitting like a crown on her head, Odaenathus waited in the bedchamber, dressed in battle armor, his helmet tucked under his arm. The couple walked together from the royal chambers into a large hallway. Their sons, Hairan, age twelve, and Vaballathus, nearly five, stood outside ready to join them. Royal guards flanked the family as they marched through the palace to the front entrance. Before he stepped out, Odaenathus placed his helmet carefully on his head.

As the group emerged from the palace onto the front portico, the full morning sun illuminated the huge courtyard. The palace had been built so that the sun was behind them, or they would have been blinded by its radiance. The citizens shaded their eyes as they waited to greet their leaders.

The royal guard stood at ease by their horses on both sides of the courtyard. As the family stepped onto the portico, the guardsmen came to attention. The crowd filled the remaining space and spilled through the gates into the main square of the city. A roar erupted at the sight of them.

Odaenathus raised his arms in greeting. The boys moved to one side of the portico. As Odaenathus walked to the edge of the portico, Zenobia descended two steps. After a slight wave to the crowd, she turned and gave her husband a Roman-style salute, one arm across her chest with a fist above her heart. Odaenathus pivoted from side to side, acknowledging everyone. After nearly two minutes, he held his fingers apart and lowered his hands slightly. The crowd gradually quieted. Zenobia dropped her salute, but continued to look up at her husband.

Odaenathus' voice rang clear and strong. "Fellow citizens of Palmyra, I salute you."

He gave them the Roman-style salute. The crowd cheered again until he raised his hand.

"Yet again, the Persians marshal their forces on our border." He looked around as a low grumbling came from the crowd. Then his voice turned mocking. "Our liege lords from Rome send us word that three legions, led by the new emperor himself, are on the way to help defend us." He paused as the grumbling increased. Then he held up his hand for silence once more. "We are descendants of the great Alexander. We are the children of Solomon the Wise. Do we need Roman troops to defend our borders from these greedy traders to the east?"

Shouts came from his audience.

"No!"

"No Romans!"

"We can defend ourselves!"

Odaenathus raised one hand. "Shall we cringe like cowards until these legions come to lead us? Or shall we march on our enemies like true warriors of the desert? Shall we hurl our wrath upon them like a storm sweeping away those worthless motes of sand?"

"March!" the crowd shouted back. "March!"

Odaenathus waited until the noise faded to a murmur. "I thank you my friends, my comrades in arms. During my absence, as brief as it may be, our worthy Queen Zenobia shall serve our people."

As he swept his hand towards her, she turned and bowed. The crowd shouted its assent.

"It shall be my honor to lead our army in this battle." Odaenathus put his hand on the hilt of his sword. "Are you with me?"

The crowd screamed its agreement, urging him to lead them in battle. He let the noise rise to a crescendo before he thrust both arms into the air.

"Then let us march!"

Odaenathus and Zenobia saluted each other, and the crowd went mad. Odaenathus slowly descended the steps, urging them on. As he passed by Zenobia, he spoke sideways so she could hear.

"They love me."

As she turned to watch him pass Zenobia rejoined, "As do I, my lord."

Odaenathus mounted his horse, a resplendent blue roan Nisean stallion. The most valuable horse in the known world, the Nisean was a slightly larger version of an Arabian; still fleet of foot with excellent endurance, but a slightly stockier chest and head that were desirable attributes for a war horse. The members of the royal guard, mounted on lesser breeds, followed suit. As the prince and his guard rode out of the courtyard and through the city to join the waiting army, the crowd followed, waving their arms and shouting encouragement.

"To victory!"

"Kill them all!"

"Slaughter the Persians!"

Zenobia waved and smiled confidently for the citizens as her husband rode off to battle. Their sons waved as well, although Hairan did not smile.

*   *   *

A lone horseman rode across the plains of Assyria. The rider, a Roman messenger by his insignia, moved at an easy canter so as not to kill his mount in the desert heat. He came from the direction of Palmyra as he approached the encampment of the Roman army. He walked his horse past the outer guards and headed directly for the tent which bore the flag of a Roman emperor.

Guards at the command tent stopped him. One poked his head into the tent to announce the messenger's presence. Within seconds Decius Cimbus, the *legatus legionis* who commanded the second legion and served as aide-de-camp to the Emperor Lucius Domitius Aurelianus, emerged from the tent. The messenger dismounted and saluted.

"Legate, my report as the emperor commanded regarding the Palmyrenes."

Decius nodded. "Good. He'll see you immediately."

The messenger entered, followed closely by Decius.

The messenger looked around quickly. The tent was spacious, but sparsely furnished. There was a small table and two chairs near one wall. A pennant with Aurelian's personal insignia stood on a pole behind the table. Several chests lined another wall. A curtain hung over a hole in the back wall, which led into a smaller tent where Aurelian slept.

The *imperator* Aurelian, supreme commander of the legions, sat at a table as he carefully studied a map. At the age of thirty-two, he radiated the confidence and strength of a man who had fought his way up the ranks to earn his position. His features were slightly squarish, but regular and chiseled in a way that reminded onlookers of a bust carved from marble. Never handsome, his presence still commanded attention. His stocky body, on a frame of average height, was well-muscled from the arts of his trade.

The emperor was surrounded by half a dozen officers. Foremost among them was General Mucapor. Beside him was General Domitianus, the *decurio equitarius*, commander of the cavalry unit. Procus, the *primus pilus*, or commanding centurion for the first cohort, stood respectfully to the side. Two other officers leaned over the far side of the table as they looked down at the map. Mnestheus, Aurelian's personal servant and scribe, kept in the background.

"Caesar," Decius said. "This man has news regarding Septimius Odeinat and his army."

It was another moment before Aurelian looked up from the map. "Excellent. Are they prepared to march?"

The messenger saluted. "Caesar, Septimius Odeinat marched with his army this morning to engage the Persians."

Aurelian frowned. "I presume this was after you informed him of our approach to Palmyra?"

"Yes, Caesar. I did so two days ago. He sent this message." The messenger took a scroll from a pouch and handed it to the emperor.

Aurelian accepted the scroll and noted that it bore the seal of the prince of Palmyra. He tapped it thoughtfully on the edge of the table before he opened it and read the message.

When he was finished, Aurelian leaned back and looked up toward the heavens. "So, Odaenathus declined our assistance, did he?" Aurelian had never met the man, but he had been told the Palmyrene consul preferred his Assyrian name to the Roman version. He wanted to practice it before their meeting.

"The arrogance!" Mucapor, commander of the Praetorian Guard, was only twenty-three. The son of a noble family with much power in the senate, he had been given the rank of *Praetor* quickly. In spite of looks that brought a statue of Adonis to the minds of many, he was a capable fighter with a temper that matched his pride. "He should be punished!"

Aurelian gave his general a sidelong glance. "Why, are only Roman generals allowed to be arrogant?"

"This nomad village princeling forgets himself, Caesar. Emperor Valerian appointed him consul and governor of the colony of Phoenice, not king of all Assyria."

"I would hardly call Palmyra a village." Aurelian sighed and rose to his feet, clutching the scroll in his hand. Sometimes, it was very difficult to be polite to this young pup who understood too well the art of arrogance. "Odaenathus gained Valerian's favor because of his many military successes. His titles were confirmed by a grateful senate. Rome needs all of its friends, General Mucapor."

They stared at each other for a moment, then Mucapor bowed.

"As always, you are correct, Imperial Majesty."

Aurelian did not press the issue. "Well, it seems there's no more need for strategy. Gentlemen, prepare your legions. We march at once to Palmyra."

All of the officers saluted and prepared to leave the tent.

Aurelian kept his voice as neutral as his expression. "Mucapor, a moment more." He turned to Mnestheus. "Go to my quarters and prepare my armor."

As the officers exited the command tent, Mnestheus bowed and disappeared into his master's personal tent.

Aurelian turned to his first officer, who had also been assigned to him by Emperor Valerian. Now he allowed his voice to show a hint of steel. "Remember, Odaenathus retains his position at our pleasure. As do you, General Mucapor." He thrust the scroll into the other man's hand.

Mucapor took the scroll and saluted stiffly. After one more glance, the emperor exited the tent. Mucapor stared after him, then crumpled the scroll in his fist.

"For the present, Aurelian," Mucapor said softly. "For the present."

*　　　　*　　　　*

Odaenathus set up his camp on the crest of a small hill, with his command tent at the center. The tent connected to one of equal size that served as his quarters. In addition to a large table in the center, there were several small divans and a few large pillows on the ground. A smaller round table held a pitcher of wine and half a dozen goblets. Two tapestries hung from the walls, one displaying the likeness of the great god Malak-bel, and another an expansive depiction of Palmyra.

Pennants with the insignia of the military units under his command also adorned the walls.

Artabanes, commanding general of the cavalry, which included heavy and light chariots as well as the traditional mounted horse, looked down on a map. In his early forties, Artabanes was short and slight, his muscles well-defined from spending more time on a horse or a chariot than he did on the ground. Odaenathus stood beside him, watching carefully as his general explained the enemy position. Four other Palmyrene officers stood respectfully around the table inspecting the map.

"Their chariots and cavalry are here." Artabanes pointed to a valley between two other low hills, which formed a neat triangle together with the hill they occupied. "More than twenty thousand. Their archers, perhaps thirty thousand, are on each flank, here and here." His bony finger poked the two other hilltops. "The foot soldiers are behind the cavalry. My scouts estimate sixty thousand, perhaps more."

Artabanes looked at Odaenathus expectantly, as did the rest of the officers. Zabdas, general of the army and second in command to Odaenathus, scratched at his full beard as though it were overrun with lice.

"So they outnumber us more than two for each one." Odaenathus ran a finger along his chin, which he kept clean-shaven in the Roman tradition. "And their archers are above on these two hills, which gives them excellent position should we dare to attack."

They all looked gravely at the map. Then Odaenathus grinned.

"They're in terrible trouble!"

"My lord?" Zabdas, a self-described "stodgy old soldier", saw nothing at all humorous about war. "Do you jest?" Now late in his forties, Zabdas was short and squat. He still looked as though he could lift a chariot in one hand and a flask of wine in the other.

"Not in the least." Odaenathus turned to his aide-de-camp and quartermaster. "Auzaina, what rations did you bring?"

Auzaina looked at his commander with a puzzled expression. "As you commanded, my lord. Provisions for three weeks. It took every wagon and nearly every beast of burden in the province to carry them."

"And what is in the caves at the back of this hill we camp on?"

"My lord, Afqa, the hot-water spring, as we all know."

"Yes. Thank you." Odaenathus turned back to Zabdas. "General Zabdas, how long would you say it took the Persian army to reach this point and set up their position?"

"A month, perhaps more." Suddenly his heavy brow shot up. "Ah, I see!"

Odaenathus nodded. "Exactly! Thinking we'd wait behind the walls of Palmyra, they would've brought only as many provisions as they thought they'd need for the march and a siege. That's why we marched out openly, to force them to either take defensive positions or to meet us where we chose—where we had the high ground. And the water."

Khalid, captain of the cavalry at the age of only thirty, was too excited to remain quiet before his superiors. "But we shall not attack, shall we, my lord?"

"Not at all" Odaenathus became serious. "We wait here, building up what fortifications we can. Eventually, the Persians will either get thirsty and go home or be forced to bring the battle to us."

"And then we shall have them," Artabanes said.

"Yes. Then we shall have them."

CHAPTER THREE

A roiling cloud of dust announced the approach of the Roman army long before they could be seen or heard. Zenobia stood on her private balcony and watched impassively as the cloud drew nearer. Knowing she would have to greet the new emperor alone, but not knowing what he would be like or demand from his new domain, she felt an unusual apprehension. Below, many of her soldiers and citizens also stood, not a murmur to be heard as the foreign army came into view. Not until she could clearly see the banner of a Roman emperor at the front of the column did Zenobia turn abruptly to enter her apartments. There was much to be done before the evening.

Inside her dressing room, servants helped Zenobia don ceremonial battle armor. With Odaenathus absent, it would not do for a woman to greet the new emperor in a gown, no matter how regal. In the mind of a soldier, greeting him in a dress would send a weak and feminine image. The gown would be saved for the banquet.

Zenobia smiled grimly at the thought of these elaborate preparations. She knew that, in every corner of the city, her subjects would be doing all they could to prepare a grand welcome for their new overlord. For the sake of her absent husband, the reception must be perfect.

*   *   *

The action was just as frantic inside the royal stables of Palmyra. The Royal Palmyrene Guard, attired in their dress armor, had already groomed their horses for a formal meeting. Many of them now braided the manes of their mounts, or cinched on saddles saved only for special occasions. They had been ordered to look more impressive than the Roman guards, and were determined to obey that command completely.

*   *   *

Inside one of the largest meat markets in the city, the butcher stood in front of his wife, a large cleaver dangling from his hand and an angry look on his face. The butcher's wife sat on a stool, calmly plucking a chicken. The butcher's teen-aged apprentice stood in the background, anxiously watching the two of them.

"Two sheep!" The butcher pointed the cleaver at his wife, as though it were all her fault. "Damned army took most of the salted meat, and now she wants me to butcher two good sheep to feed this foreign pig who takes half our taxes."

"Don't you curse our army!" Her eyes flashed at him, but she did not stop in her work. "They're out there in the desert protecting us from those devil Persians."

"Unless they fail, or we starve to death before they make it back."

His wife's glance was as sharp as his cleaver. The butcher knew when it was no use. He turned to the boy.

"Fetch me the skinniest sheep we have."

*   *   *

The head cook stood at the door to the pantry in the palace kitchen. His pastry cook wrung her hands as she anxiously surveyed her supplies.

"Do we have enough flour for a few pastries?" asked the head cook.

The pastry cook shrugged her shoulders helplessly. "I think so. As long as we make them small."

The head cook nodded fatalistically. "Put lots of figs on top. And a couple of olives."

"They'll taste terrible!" The cook made a sour face. "That's an awful combination."

"Do we have any dried fruits left?" the head cook asked.

"No."

"Then do it. I understand the Romans love olives."

*   *   *

The torches guttered from a slight breeze, and the major domo shivered. He was not used to being down in the palace wine cellars, normally leaving the choice of wines up to the official wine steward. This was too important an occasion to leave to chance. Thus he found himself down in the lowest levels of the palace, looking at huge jars of wine with the wine steward and pretending that he knew what he was doing. He was very aware that the wine steward knew better.

"How many amphorae you think we'll need?" The steward looked like a proud father being asked to give up some of his children. "It won't be a huge crowd, will it?"

"Not from our side, but a lot of Roman *sopios*. And they drink a lot. How much of the good wine do you have?"

"You think they'll know the difference?"

The major domo was not amused by the sarcastic reply. "No. But the queen will."

"Oh. Right. Only the best, then."

They both sampled the wine. This was one thing the major domo was good at.

*   *   *

Aurelian marched his army to the outer gates of the city before he pitched camp. They had actually encamped only a few hours away the previous evening, but he wanted to make an impressive show as they approached the capital of his new domain. Leaving at dawn, they made it to Palmyra just after noon. That allowed sufficient time for preparations before the formalities.

Aurelian turned to Mnestheus before he dismounted. "I want my personal tent set up before anything else. While that's being done, I want water heated for a bath."

Mnestheus bowed and scurried off to obey. Aurelian stalked around the camp, making certain all of his men knew what they must do for the ceremonies. He was the new master here, yet he felt as nervous as a raw recruit preparing for his first battle. After his bath, which served to relax him somewhat, Mnestheus helped him dress in a lavish suit of armor, a gift from the senate after one of his great victories. It would be useless in battle, but it looked splendid.

After erecting camp, the Imperial Roman Guard groomed their horses and cleaned their armor, determined to look sharp for the formal meeting. Fortunately, that did not include any of them being forced to bathe. While their servants prepared their horses and armor for them, General Mucapor, General Domitianus and Legate Decius were free to prepare to attend the banquet that evening. Everyone had their roles to play for the impending events, and all busied themselves in their tasks.

*   *   *

The two royal guards sat on their horses at attention on either side of the city square. By Assyrian standards the city was massive: nearly five hundred and forty hectares, filled with looming stone buildings in the Greek and Roman style as well as Assyrian, and walled all around with strong ramparts. Many of the walkways featured great columns, both Doric and Ionic, with massive arches above. On the outskirts of the city, an impressive amphitheater served as the main focus for formal entertainments. None of the Romans paid any attention to these details as they entered Palmyra.

Aurelian rode through the open city gates flanked by Mucapor, Domitianus and Decius. Zenobia rode toward him from the inner courtyard of the palace, alone. As they met in the middle, they turned in front of their own guards. For several seconds they appraised each other, probing with their eyes. Then Zenobia saluted and bowed from the waist. Aurelian returned her salute.

"Lucius Domitius Aurelianus, Emperor of Rome and its magnificent empire." Zenobia spoke loudly so all could hear. "In the name of my husband, Septimius Odaenathus, consul and governor of the *colonia* of Assyria Phoenice and Prince of Palmyra, I, Septimia Zenobia, bid you welcome."

Zenobia's voice was proud. A *colonia* was the highest rank of provincial Roman settlement. It was entitled to a Roman law court, a forum, and a major temple. While Odaenathus was a prince of Assyria by birth, he was also a Roman citizen and held the rank of consul and client king. Thus, her husband was an important man both in his native land and throughout the Roman Empire.

"In the name of the senate and the republic we protect, we thank you, Septimia Zenobia." His formal tone took on a slight edge. "However, I had expected that my consul himself would greet me on my arrival."

"I apologize profusely, Imperial Majesty, but he felt he could not wait for your army to join him before the enemy gained the advantage. He believed he must march immediately to prevent that."

"Ah, yes. Timing is everything—especially in battle. I quite understand."

Not knowing him, Zenobia could not tell if he were being sarcastic or sincere. She took the middle ground. "Then I pray you will forgive him, Majesty, as he only seeks to protect your domains."

Aurelian smiled, but with some irony. "Yes, of course. He is forgiven, I mean."

With the formal welcome over, they dismounted and approached each other. Zenobia knelt and bowed her head. Aurelian looked her up and down, then laughed.

Zenobia looked up sharply, glaring at him. "Do I amuse the emperor?"

"Forgive me," Aurelian said, only half sincerely. "I heard that many of the women of Assyria were trained in weapons, but I hadn't expected one to greet me dressed for battle. Especially not one so...well-armed in other ways. Arise."

She did so, struggling to curb her anger. "And yet the mighty emperor seems disarmed by the thought."

"By the thought of a woman dressed for battle? Oh, no. Women dress for battle in so many different ways. Who is to say which way is the most dangerous?"

Zenobia cocked her head. "Ah, so my imperial lord admits that a woman in battle could possibly be a dangerous foe?"

"That depends on the type of combat." Aurelian looked her up and down. "However, if you mean when attired for a more physical fray, such as we two are now, well...." He smiled. "That is an entirely different state of affairs."

She squared her shoulders defiantly. "Yet affairs of state often require both. And, armed as I am, I stand ready to be tested by my imperial lord in both."

"Oh, do you, now?"

Aurelian turned partially toward his guard with a smile, his hands slightly out to his sides as though to share a joke. Suddenly he drew his sword and whirled, swinging the sword upwards and down, obviously intending merely to swing it down by the side of Zenobia as if to frighten her.

Anticipating the motion, Zenobia had drawn her sword into a high defensive position. As Aurelian started to bring his sword down, it was met and caught by hers, the steel ringing loudly in the afternoon air. She could see the shock on his face, and they stood in tableau position for long seconds. Both guards instantly put their hands to their own weapons as they witnessed this action.

"Yes, majesty." Zenobia maintained her pose calmly. "I do."

Aurelian stood in surprise for one more beat, then pulled his sword away and laughed loudly. Zenobia lowered her weapon and stood straight once again. The guards looked at each other, then took their hands off their weapons as though suspicious they were being made the butt of some joke.

"By Jupiter, I would never have believed it!"

Aurelian held his arms out, sword still in hand, and turned to address those who were assembled. He spoke loudly so all could hear.

"I, Lucius Domitius Aurelianus, Emperor of the eastern provinces of Rome, do publicly acknowledge the error of my beliefs. The reports we have heard of the warrior queens of Assyria are no myth." He waggled his finger at his men. "My loyal and trusty guard, I give you fair warning: while we are guests in this fair land, do not trifle with these women on peril of your lives, if not your hearts!"

His men laughed at this speech, and Zenobia's cheered. He turned back to Zenobia and gave a slight bow.

"My lady, I fear I must beg your pardon."

"You admit fear then, mighty emperor?"

Again, everyone watching held their breath for another few beats of their hearts. Then Aurelian smiled broadly, and Zenobia returned the smile.

"The wise man knows there is always something to fear."

"Then pardon is freely granted."

Aurelian and Zenobia clasped forearms in the Roman manner. Their eyes locked for a moment, and they sized each other up in a more personal way. Then they smiled again and entered the palace.

*   *   *

As he entered the hall, Aurelian noted that all eyes went to the *paludamentum* he wore, the robe of a Roman emperor. Sweeping to just above the floor, it was a rich purple, the mark of nobility. Around the hem was a seven-inch band in gold depicting coiled snakes. On each front panel were intricately-woven tapestry pictures: on the left was Aurelian in battle armor atop his rearing stallion, and on the right Sol Invictus, the "Invincible Sun". While many generals made sacrifices to the bloody god Mars, Aurelian paid tribute to the cult of the sun god, who was as much a bringer of life as he was death. On the shoulders, also in gold thread, were two symbols: on the right the eagle taking flight, and on the left crossed swords encircled by laurel wreaths with the letters SPQR emblazoned across the swords. He fingered the material absently, thinking of the times not long before when he had been so below this finery that such a sight would have left him in awe.

The only jewelry he wore was his signet ring, which he used to seal the wax on documents. Even his head was bare of any mark of rank, a reminder to himself that he was a citizen and a soldier, and an emperor merely because of his skill in war.

Zenobia waited to greet him. Aurelian's eyes widened when he beheld her, but he said nothing as she guided him to his place. Over her tunic she wore a brilliant white *stola* of fine muslin. The long, full dress had a purple border around the neck, as befitted the wife of a man who held the rank of senator. The fabric was held together by a high belt made of woven gold, and gathered at the shoulder with a brooch of gold featuring an intricate pattern. The fabric swooped daringly downward, which served to accent the swelling of her breasts. Her armor had served to hide a tall, firm, fully curved figure, now displayed in all its splendor. Aurelian was shocked to find that his breathing had become heavier at the sight.

Matching earrings hung delicately, clearly visible as her hair had been plaited up into a crown, with a thin diadem of gold holding it in a circle. She wore a necklace of perfectly matched pearls, with plain gold bands on her wrists and her ankles. Each of these subtle bangles forced the eye to admire the exquisite shape of the limbs that bore them.

The banquet hall of the Palmyrene Palace was as sumptuous as any Aurelian had seen in Rome, although not at large as some. The decorations and furniture were quite different, so it seemed more exotic to his eye. While diners sat on cushions and divans in the normal style, small groups sat around low tables that held the dishes. Aurelian found it less messy than the Roman style of banqueting. Each person had a finely made tray on which he or she could place their desired portions from the serving platters. Used to sitting at the planning table in his command tent as he ate while studying some map or reading some scroll on the art of war, Aurelian forced himself to relax as he sat beside the beautiful woman.

*   *   *

Aurelian was seated next to Zenobia, no doubt in Odaenathus' normal place. Their table was on a dais, perhaps a foot high and in the center of the room. The dais was large enough to afford them some distance—and privacy—from those below. As he settled himself comfortably on a cushion, musicians began playing discretely.

There were several tables with Palmyrene officials and officers. Although all of the ranking officers were away with Odaenathus, Aurelian had been introduced to the officials. First among them was Nobonidus Zohan, the prime minister. Zenobia had also introduced him to her sons, who sat at a nearby table with a nurse and one of the queen's personal servants. Aurelian thought there was a strong resemblance with the younger boy, but could find nothing of her in the older son. A thin man with white hair sat with them. He was obviously Roman, although his wrinkled skin was darkened from the sun. Aurelian was told that his name was Cassius Longinus, a philosopher and poet who served as a confidante to the queen and a tutor to her children. Mucapor, Domitianus, Procus, and Decius sat at another table.

Aurelian's eyes were everywhere, but they frequently returned to Zenobia. After the customary invitation to partake of her hospitality, it seemed very difficult to make conversation. This close, it was easy to see that minimal makeup served to enhance her naturally fine features. There was a hint of some color that accented her dark, lustrous eyes within that velvety skin, but he was not so sophisticated that he could name it.

He noticed that she toyed with her food, but never drank from her wine cup, a golden goblet set with jewels. He also drank sparingly from a similar goblet. After eating enough to satisfy a new-born kitten, Zenobia ignored her plate entirely.

"Pray tell me, Imperial Majesty—"

"Please, Aurelian."

Zenobia bowed her head slightly. "Tell me, Aurelian, to what do we owe the honor of this visit?"

"You mean other than to witness the beauty of the Assyrian women, of whom we have heard so much?" Aurelian had long ago learned that it was best to flatter the wives of highly-placed officials.

"Yes, other than that."

Aurelian smiled. Naturally, this woman would be very used to flattery.

Zenobia maintained a pleasant expression, but her eyes bored into his. "You sent a message that your legions would support Odaenathus against the Persians. But surely not even your swiftest messenger could have sent you word of this invasion that you could march an army to our defense."

Aurelian nodded slightly. "Umm." He looked closely at her, reassessing her intelligence. "No, they couldn't." He took a sip of wine as he thought about what to say. "You may know that until recently I was a general under Emperor Publius Lucinius Egnatius Gallienus. A great fighter, Gallienus."

"I've heard Emperor Valerian speak of Gallienus. His son, I believe."

"Just so. You are also aware that the empire is fairly large." Zenobia frowned, and Aurelian sensed she was impatient with this explanation of matters well known to her. He reassessed her yet again. "Yes, well, when Valerian was confirmed by the senate, he asked that Gallienus share the crown with him. As they each had the title of Caesar, the legions were just a bit more, well, attentive to the command of both. Valerian watched over the prize outposts...." He waved his cup to indicate their surroundings.

Zenobia inclined her head graciously.

"Gallienus was given the great honor of keeping the Pax Romana in Germania, Gaul, Spain, and the Gallic empire. A bunch of damned barbarians, frankly, except perhaps the Spaniards." Aurelian shrugged. "Oh, well. Gallienus was young and full of energy." He drank more wine. "So was I, for that matter."

"I'm sure you still are, Aurelian."

Aurelian looked at her appraisingly, then laughed. "Yes, somewhat less than more. Well. When Emperor Valerian died in captivity under that damned Sassanid king, Shapur, Gallienus generously offered me the same title here." He touched his robe, self-consciously fingering the fabric. The band of color on her *stola* contrasted discretely with the ostentatious display of royal purple on his robe, and he grimaced at the thought. "He graciously presented me with this robe in front of the senate to confirm his choice."

"It's very beautiful."

"Yes, well. A bit ornate for my taste, but of course I was most grateful." He gave a slight shrug. "Never mind. When you greeted me earlier, you gave me too much credit. I only rule the eastern provinces, not all of Rome."

"Still very impressive for one so young...and handsome."

She smiled alluringly. He shrugged and frowned. She seemed to understand that he himself did not appreciate flattery, as she changed the subject.

"Are you disappointed in your new surroundings?"

"Why, should I be?"

"I've heard those places are very beautiful, while Assyria often looks quite harsh, even barren to many outsiders."

Aurelian put his cup down and leaned back. He looked at her frankly. "No, not at all. There are many types of beauty."

Zenobia gave an inscrutable smile.

He picked his cup back up and inspected it. "Yes, those places are lush, full of vegetation, practically infested with game. I confess, I quite enjoyed the hunting." He drank again, looking over his cup at her. "But, as I said, the people are barbarians. It was maddening to deal with them. Their dwellings are primitive and cold. And the music...well, it makes my head pound to think of it. The people I've met today are gracious, and quite sophisticated. And this city is beautiful. I can see why it's called 'the bride of the desert'."

Zenobia laughed lightly. "Well, you know your predecessors built most of it. It is quite Roman."

"True. Nevertheless." He put his cup to his lips again, but did not drink. "And the women…. Well, at least one is quite beautiful."

"Ah, you've met my sister?"

Aurelian widened his eyes. "You have a sister?"

Zenobia gave that same low, sultry laugh. "Yes. But my sister and I, we are one and the same. She is my passionate, adventurous side."

His brows knit for a moment, then he nodded knowingly. "I see." In spite of himself, he looked around to make certain no one was listening to them before he spoke again. "Well then, I look forward to meeting your sister."

Zenobia finally lifted her cup. "Then I'm certain you will. Perhaps quite soon."

They toasted each other and drank.

*   *   *

Zenobia was pleased the banquet had gone so well. Without her husband and his officers, there had been no tension that might have occurred between two groups of aggressive men meeting for the first time. Even though they were allies—well, technically subjects of Rome—the proud Assyrian warriors still resented first the Greeks and then the Romans flaunting their superior military to hold them in thrall. And the new emperor had been much more pleasant—much more charming—than she could have imagined.

All in all, a very good day. And it was not over yet.

Zenobia and Aurelian stood together on her balcony, enjoying the warm, dark desert evening of the summer months. After the heat of the day, the cool evening breeze was like wading in a mountain pond: cool, refreshing, energizing. She wanted to sink into its depths of inky comfort and let it embrace her. During the autumn and winter, the temperatures would drop to near freezing no matter how hot the day had been. Zenobia hated the cold.

They both had goblets in their hand, although neither drank much wine. It was enough to enjoy the night and the companionship of the other. Zenobia found herself surprised by this thought.

Zenobia raised her goblet in a toast. "To your new title, Caesar."

Aurelian lifted his cup as well. "To your adventurous sister."

Zenobia laughed. "Are you ready to meet her so soon?"

"Her, yes. But what of your husband?"

"Oh, he's already met her. Many times."

"You know what I meant."

Zenobia shrugged. He did not sound irritated at her teasing, but it was best not to take the chance. One of the great lessons she had learned from her parents was to never needlessly irritate those with power over you. In this case, she had even greater reason to please him. "This is Palmyra. We Assyrians accept the passions of the flesh as natural and enjoyable."

Aurelian raised his brow. "You think we Romans are not passionate?"

"I think you save your greatest passions for the battlefield" Zenobia pretended to take a sip as she considered how to be honest, yet cautious. "In other places you seem so...so cold, so reserved."

Aurelian looked at her, then threw his head back and laughed. "You wouldn't say that if you knew Caligula."

"Who?"

Aurelian shrugged. "Just one of our former emperors. Never mind."

Zenobia looked at him directly. "There is much I need to learn of Rome. Perhaps you could be my teacher."

"Then be my teacher also, Assyrian queen." He put his cup down. "School me in the arts of this passion of the flesh you admire so much."

Zenobia smiled slowly. "Yes. I think that would be my pleasure."

*   *   *

The night was still, with barely the screech of an Eagle Owl or the howl of a coyote searching for prey. They must have been frightened away by the massive presence of the deadliest hunters in world invading their territory. Unable to sleep, Odaenathus rose and wrapped himself in a cloak. It was colder in the hills than down on the floor of the desert.

He emerged from his tent and looked around at the camp. The

darkness was broken by a few campfires, most now down to glowing coals. The moon was not visible, but the blazing stars provided enough light to move about easily. All was still, but he was always restless before a battle. He did not know if it was dread of the slaughter to come, or eagerness to have it begin and then end. Either way, there was a constriction in his chest that could only be relieved by the swinging of a sword. The night before the battle was always the most intense: everything you had was still in your hand, but soon it would all be on the line.

Odaenathus walked slowly to the edge of the peak and looked grimly across at the many fires burning on both hills opposite, and below those even more in the valley. He could smell the sharp scent of the brittle desert wood from where he stood, reminding him of too many nights he had been in military camps far from the comfort of Palmyra, prepared for another battle on the following morning. He shook his head and swallowed bitter thoughts. He was damned tired of fighting with the Sassanid Empire.

For nearly two hundred years, Palmyra had been the ideal stop for the caravans that moved between China and the Mediterranean. They traded in perfumes, spices, ivory, glass and silk from the northern reaches of Mesopotamia to the Erythraean Sea, as far down the African coast as Raphta. As the trade became more prosperous, the Persians had coveted control over the mouths of the Euphrates and Tigris rivers. Aligned with the Romans since the rule of Tiberius, Palmyra decided that her interests lay with Rome. If the Persians gained control, they would make slaves of the Assyrians. The Romans were clever: once they conquered, they offered the possibility of citizenship to the people, and gave nominal control to the current rulers. The subsequent emperors treated Assyria's people well, so Palmyra's horsemen fought alongside the Roman armies.

When the Emperor Caracalla declared Palmyra a Roman colony, it exempted them from paying taxes on luxury items. At that time Odaenathus' family, the Septimii, controlled the city. Palmyra became one of the jewels of the Roman Empire. New construction abounded, and wealth flowed to both Palmyra and Rome. Odaenathus smiled, pleased at how his ancestors had brought both peace and prosperity to their land. But, like the sand dunes shifting position restlessly in a desert storm, that had changed quickly.

When Septimius Odaenathus was appointed by the Emperor Valerian as Consul and Governor of the province of Assyria Phoenice, the conflict between Persia and Rome reached its crisis. Shapur I of Persia marched a massive army against Valerian, who was defeated and captured. When Shapur put Valerian to death, Rome asked Odaenathus to avenge him. As a Roman general, Odaenathus won a resounding victory over Shapur and drove the Persians back until he threatened the Sassanian capital, Ctesiphon. When the new emperor, Gallienus, was threatened with an insurrection in Emesa, Odaenathus again brought the Roman Empire a great victory. Once again, there had been peace.

But that had been a decade before. Now, either because Shapur had rebuilt his army or he felt the Eastern Empire was vulnerable under its newest emperor, he had returned in force once more. Odaenathus sighed again. He was getting old, and this was getting very tiring.

A voice startled him. "Who walks here?"

Odaenathus was irritated with himself. He had not even heard the sentry approach. He did not turn. "It's only me."

He heard the sentry snap to attention. "My lord, forgive me. I did not know you were about."

"All is quiet, then?"

"Yes, my lord. Very quiet."

Odaenathus grunted. "Just give it a couple of days." He let another moment pass. "Carry on."

There was another brief pause, during which the sentry must have given him a salute. Then he heard the man walk on. Odaenathus continued to stare across the hills until the sun began to rise.

*　　*　　*

The thrusting and parrying was violent. Time became meaningless. Grunts, groans and cries filled the air with near palpable passion. Zenobia drew blood, and Aurelian left many bruises. It was almost like war. What had begun as an exploration had soon become uncontrolled desire. When their coupling was at last done, both lay back spent, their mouths open and gasping, their chests heaving. Another eternity passed before they could—or even wanted to—speak.

"That was...incredible." Aurelian struggled to get his breathing back under control.

It took another minute before Zenobia could respond. "I've never...never felt anything like that."

Aurelian turned his head to look at her. "Never?"

"Truly." She turned on her side and began to stroke him. "Will you be ready again soon?"

Aurelian laughed. "Again! Great Adonis, your husband must be a young man!"

"He has more than a decade on you, my wonderful lover."

"Well then, Odaenathus must be a powerful stallion, that's all I can say."

Zenobia started kissing his chest. "Aren't you desirous of me, Aurelian?"

Aurelian repressed a sigh of irritation. "I'm certain you could feel my desire. But I'm not Mars, indefatigable with Venus as well as on the field of battle. It seems I disappoint you."

"Not at all!" Zenobia raised her head to gaze directly into his eyes. "I was serious—that was the most wonderful experience I have had in a bed."

"But, your children...and what you said about passion...."

Zenobia sighed. "If it pleases you to hear it, you are much more virile and...enthusiastic than Odaenathus. He's not only much older, but he's...well, too polite in his love -making."

He frowned at her. "Am I not polite?"

Zenobia laughed throatily. "You were demanding. You were ferocious." Her smile broadened. "And that is what I enjoyed the most."

"I see."

"Oh, I respect my lord. He truly is a wonderful leader, husband and father. I'm extremely fond of him. As to the children, Hairan is the son of his first wife. Vaballathus is ours together."

Aurelian nodded slowly. "I had not known of this."

Zenobia propped her chin on her hand. She regarded him for several minutes. This was a great opportunity, but with every opportunity there was always an element of risk. He did not look away or flinch at the inspection.

"I think there are many things I want you to know." She spoke slowly. "When I was in my teens, I was introduced to Emperor Valerian. I was extremely naïve, and he seemed ancient, with hands of ice when he touched me once or twice. His gaze was just as cold. That is where I developed my thoughts of what Romans must feel about pleasures of the flesh."

Aurelian was quiet for a moment. "This is quite daring of you to tell me."

Zenobia shrugged her shoulders, and her breasts moved in a way that attracted his eye.

"I am a frank person. When his first wife died, I happened to be in a situation where I was noticed by Odaenathus. Soon afterwards, he did the emperor great service as a general, as you must know. Valerian granted him new titles, and urged him to marry again. Although he sincerely mourned, he knew his duty—as did I. It was not long before we were married."

Zenobia was tempted to tell him of the training she had received as a child, and about her mother's last wishes, but she had learned there were many things that a strong ruler must learn to bear in silence.

"I can well imagine." Aurelian allowed his eyes to travel her entire body. He leaned towards her, inhaling the natural scent of her skin, the strong odor of the sweat that was still not dry upon her body, even the musky smells of their mutual passions. It was like some strange, incredibly intoxicating perfume.

"And now I hope to learn much more of you—and of Rome."

Aurelian smiled. "And I shall tell you. Before that, however, I believe I may be capable of granting your desires in other ways."

Zenobia gazed happily at his manhood, which was once more turgid. "Oh, my lord!"

CHAPTER FOUR

It was early morning. Odaenathus, Zabdas, Auzaina, and a herald with a horn clustered on the bluff where Odaenathus had brooded several nights before. Once again he looked across to the opposite hills, but this time it was very different: the Persian army was on the march.

"Do you have an estimate yet, Auzaina?"

A huge fleet of chariots led the regiments of foot soldiers. First came the heavy chariots, each of which boasted four horses and two sets of wheels. The carriage carried a driver, a shield bearer who protected the driver, an archer and a spear thrower. Odaenathus noted that the Persians had modeled their heavy chariots after the ancient Assyrian design. Following them came the light chariots with two horses, a driver and an archer. The throng of Persian cavalry flanked both the chariots and the foot soldiers.

"I counted a dozen squadrons of heavy chariots, with three times that many light" Auzaina scraped long fingernails over his rough beard. "More than I thought." He shrugged philosophically. "But at least they're finally moving."

Zabdas spat on the ground. "I'm surprised it took them eight days to make up their minds."

"Shapur was never the most decisive of rulers," Odaenathus observed dryly.

Auzaina furrowed his eyebrows together. "Perhaps he waited until supplies were too low to return home so his troops would be desperate."

"Perhaps...but I think you flatter him."

Zabdas grunted. "Either way, I'm grateful he gave us time to make some preparations. We're more heavily outnumbered than we thought."

"Yes." Odaenathus hoped the wait had left the Persians thirsty and anxious, which might make the unusual tactics his staff had planned that much more effective. After a slight pause he asked: "How many mares did Khalid gather?"

"Only two score, my lord." Auzaina shrugged his shoulders by way of apology.

Odaenathus repeated the gesture. He could feel the tension between his shoulder blades, but kept his voice even and his face impassive. "Well, let's hope that's enough."

They watched as the Persian army continued across the open plain between the hills.

"No archers." Auzaina squinted as he observed the enemy. "Unusual for them, isn't it?"

"Same problem as we would've had. Firing uphill reduces range and accuracy." Zabdas pointed a stubby finger. "No doubt they'll wait on those hills to cut us down in case their first attack has to fall back. As usual, they send their heavy chariots first to break our ranks for their foot soldiers. And look at those magnificent stallions pulling those chariots!"

"Well, let's hope they're stallions and not geldings." The was no humor in Odaenathus' voice.

Zabdas grunted in agreement.

For many minutes the three were content to view the approaching army. It was very impressive, with the sheer numbers alone making the Assyrian commanders feel jealous. Their Roman armor was much better and, other than the Immortals, their army was much better trained and more disciplined. But all three knew this was somewhat like Thermopylae: if they were to win it would have to be on the strength of their tactics. Not being nearly as outnumbered as the Greeks had been, they hoped to have a much better result.

Zabdas cocked his head as though measuring. "Is that far enough, my lord?"

"Just a bit farther, I think." Odaenathus waited several more minutes. Then he turned. "The first signal, herald."

The herald gave one sharp blast on his horn.

*   *   *

Hidden in a gulley to the side of the marching army were half a dozen Palmyrene riders. They were led by Arum, one of Artabanes' most trusted warriors. Mounted on the cavalry's swiftest horses, they would need to rely on speed for their safety, as the group carried no weapons. They herded about forty mares in a tight circle, which became more difficult to control as the thunder of the marching army grew louder, vibrating the ground beneath their hooves. At the sound of the horn, they waved cloths and shouted to spook the mares, which charged out of the gulley towards the chariots. The timing was perfect.

The riders followed the horses until they were certain they would continue to flee towards the chariots. When he was satisfied the mares were on course, Arum screamed loudly and peeled off to race towards the side of the hill where the Palmyrene forces waited. Having watched him anxiously for this signal, the rest of the riders followed their leader. Some of the Persian cavalry saw them and gave chase, but most were distracted by the results of the diversion.

As the mares entered the chariot ranks, many of the stallions were attracted by them. As some stallions began to chase the mares, chariots begin to veer. Some crashed into others, and much of the heavy chariot corps became disorganized, with drivers having a hard time controlling their horses. Within seconds some of the light chariots and cavalry also became embroiled in the disruption. At this point, it was only an annoyance. Without further intervention, the experienced chariot drivers would have their steeds back under control within minutes.

*   *   *

Odaenathus and Zabdas looked at the action below dispassionately. Auzaina was grinning. When he judged the confusion to be at its maximum, Odaenathus gave the next command.

"The second signal, herald."

The herald gave two long blasts on his horn. Two groups of Palmyrene archers emerged from cover on each side of the hill and began firing arrows into the ranks of the enemy chariots. Because the chariots were moving about wildly, the shield bearers could not protect the drivers or spear throwers properly. The arrows therefore had a much greater effect than normal. As both horses and drivers were hit, confusion turned to alarm. Seeing the slaughter in front of them, the foot soldiers stopped advancing.

*   *   *

The three Palmyrene commanders stood still as they listened to the screams and curses of the enemy charioteers, and heard the crunch of wood as chariots crashed into one another or broke apart when they hit the ground. They saw the blood of the men and horses mix with the sand of their homeland, and were encouraged that each death meant one less foe their soldiers would have to face when the actual battle came.

As soon as the foot soldiers stopped, Odaenathus gave the next command. "The third signal, herald."

The herald gave three short blasts on his horn. Directly below the commanders, dozens of soldiers stood near the edge of a bluff. At the very edge were huge boulders, precariously perched on the precipice, having been chocked with smaller rocks in front of them. At the horn, the soldiers stuck the levers in their hands under the boulders. With great heaves, they set the boulders rolling down the hill. Neatly splitting their archers on either side, the boulders gathered speed as they hurtled towards the Persians.

Some of the chariot drivers saw the boulders and tried to turn their chariots away. Some were successful, but many others were smashed as the boulders rolled through their ranks. Alarm became panic. Most of the chariots and some of the cavalry turned to run. They fled without regard to their own foot soldiers, who stampeded as well.

Now Odaenathus allowed himself a slight smile. The gods must be smiling on them this day. "The fourth signal, herald."

The herald gave four long blasts on his horn.

The two groups of Palmyrene archers began moving down the hill, firing as they went. As they advanced, some of the arrows reached the foot soldiers. Within twenty minutes of the first horn, the Persian army was in full retreat.

Odaenathus waited until the foot soldiers were once again out of the range of his archers. "The fifth signal, herald."

The herald gave five short blasts on his horn. The archers ceased firing and moved back toward the hill. At last, Zabdas smiled.

*   *   *

From both sides of the hill, Palmyrene chariots charged towards the fleeing Persians. Artabanes led the heavy chariots from the left while Khalid led the light chariots from the right. Because there was still much milling and toppling of chariots within the Persian ranks, it was not long before both Palmyrene groups raced alongside the fleeing army. When they caught up, they fired at will into the tangle of chariots and foot soldiers. The Persian cavalry tried to regroup to fight them, but many were still in a panic and others were hampered by the chaos of their own forces. The cavalry on one side had little luck against the heavy chariots, and those on the other side did little better against the more mobile light chariots. The battle was quickly becoming a rout.

*   *   *

When his own chariots had cleared the plain, Odaenathus ordered the final attack. "The sixth signal, herald."

The herald gave six short blasts on his horn. Having moved up from behind the chariots, the Palmyrene cavalry now swept down the hill to join the fray. Most of them engaged the Persian cavalrymen who had rallied to their leaders. This allowed the Palmyrene chariots to continue to massacre the throng of Persian foot soldiers. A smaller group harassed the tails of the fleeing mass, ensuring that none were organized enough to reform and counter-attack.

Just when it seemed all was going their way, arrows start raining down on the Palmyrenes.

"Look!" Auzaina pointed to the far hill. "Their archers are firing into the melee, with no regard if they hit friend or foe."

"It seems Shapur is more worried about making his retreat than the safety of his army." Odaenathus was no longer smiling.

"The Persians never worry about running out of soldiers." Zabdas spat once again. "They breed like lizards. Other than the Immortals, it seems their king finds them all expendable."

Odaenathus nodded grimly. "Well, at least he'll have a long, hungry march home. And I have no wish to waste any more of our men when the battle is clearly won. Herald, sound the recall."

The herald sounded a very long blast, then two short, then another long blast.

Zabdas turned to his commander. "Shall I send Artabanes and his cavalry to harass their flanks as they retreat, my lord?"

Odaenathus hesitated, remembering his thoughts of several nights before. Then he sighed, ever the prudent commander. "No, let them go. Many of them will die on the road home no matter what." He cleared his throat roughly, wanting to hide the anger in his voice. "We shall camp the night, give the men a chance to rest. Have General Artabanes send out scouts to make sure the Persians don't try to regroup. If all is clear, we return to Palmyra in the morning."

Zabdas saluted. "Yes, my prince." Then he smiled again. "And congratulations on a splendid victory."

"Everyone did well. But let's save the celebration for when we return home."

*   *   *

The dawn was breaking. Aurelian stretched his entire body luxuriously, amazed at how tight some of his muscles were. Sometime during the night he thought he had become limp forever. As he moved to get out of bed, Zenobia placed a hand on his chest.

"Must you go so soon, Aurelian?"

"I don't want to cause any more stir in your court than we already have." Aurelian frowned, then shrugged. "Besides, my staff will be waiting for me. I haven't been in the camp for two full days."

Zenobia also stretched languorously. She exhaled in a long, contented sigh. "You could tarry just a little longer. You have still not taught me much of what I wish to know about Rome."

Aurelian's frown deepened. "Is it Rome you wish to know so much about?"

"Oh, don't be so childish. Who would know better about the empire than one of its emperors?"

"That's not the way to flatter your emperor, Zenobia. I begin to think you're only attracted by my power."

Zenobia sat up, not bothering to cover herself. She looked at him openly, with no sign of either irritation or embarrassment.

"Certainly I'm attracted by your power. Aren't all of us who seek to rule?"

Aurelian crossed his arms. Zenobia became seductive once again.

"But that's not all that attracts me to you, my imperial lord." She started to stroke him under the covers.

Aurelian looked away. "Which am I to believe, that you find me attractive because of my powers in bed or my power in the empire?"

"Well, you've certainly changed my mind about Roman prowess in bed. I know you are all invincible in the field; such big, strong warriors." Her tone was only half teasing. "And, of course, an emperor, even if it is only of half the empire! What is not to find attractive about you, my mighty Aurelian?"

Aurelian continued to frown, but his heart was not in it. He turned back to her. "That's better, then." Suddenly he threw his arms around her and kissed her fiercely. "Oh, I cannot remain angry with you for more than a moment! What have you done to me?"

"Which time, your majesty?" she asked coyly.

They both laughed. Zenobia became serious again.

"Won't you at least return tonight?"

"I don't know if I could survive another night like that. Especially not after the night before."

"The emperor is a god and he shall live forever."

"I think one part of me is already dead." He sighed dramatically. "I fear I shall never attain living godhood this way."

"You should know that, in this land, royalty are always resurrected in the afterlife, gods or not. I am a descendent of Cleopatra, you know, so I can grant you that power."

His eyes widened. "Are you? No wonder I'm so attracted to you. Can you resurrect me, child of Cleopatra?"

"Oh, I look forward to your resurrection, my emperor. It just depends on how devoted your worshipers are."

She ducked under the covers, and he could feel her mouth embrace his flaccid member. After a minute, he groaned in pleasure.

"Truly, this worship is miraculous. I feel myself stirring to life again already."

CHAPTER FIVE

The sun blazed down on the day that Odaenathus returned in triumph at the head of his army. Zenobia did not need to see beyond the courtyard of the palace; the sounds of the crowd told her exactly what was happening. Coordinating with her husband by messenger, she had overseen each detail of his welcome. The new emperor must be suitably impressed.

Every citizen of Palmyra—peering from the city walls, standing in the square, hanging out of windows, and finding any other viewpoint from which they might greet their prince—cheered and waved as Odaenathus and his staff, followed by his mounted guard, entered through the gates of the city. Pennants flew proudly both from the walls and within the ranks of the army. Following the royal guard were thousands of prisoners, who were closely watched by the infantry. Their legs were shackled and they were exhausted from the march, but none showed signs of abuse. Those important enough to be ransomed would be offered back to Persia; the rest would become slaves.

Zenobia and her sons stood on the left side of the portico; her personal guard was mounted at attention in the courtyard below. Cassius Longinus and other Palmyrene courtiers stood on the right side, with Aurelian's commanders and his royal guard below them. When the roar of the crowd reached a crescendo that announced Odaenathus had entered into the city, Zenobia and the boys descended the steps at a dignified pace.

She had timed it perfectly: just as his family reached the base of the portico, Odaenathus and his staff rode through the gates into the palace courtyard. The sounds of the crowd turned from cheers to jeers as Odaenathus disappeared from view and the prisoners were herded into the city. Many of the crowd tried to follow him, but were held back by guards. As they reached the middle of the two royal guards, the prince and his staff dismounted. His sons, no longer able to constrain themselves, rushed to greet him with loud enthusiasm. He bent to return their hugs.

A movement behind caught Zenobia's eye. Dressed in his imperial robe, Aurelian emerged from the palace onto the portico. He observed the scene without expression. Pretending she had not noticed, Zenobia approached her husband with more dignity than had the boys. Odaenathus stood straight to greet her; she hugged him tightly and gave him a quick kiss. His eyes went to the front of the palace, and she followed his gaze with her own.

She couldn't be certain, but it appeared that Aurelian frowned, then took a deep breath and forced a smile. The emperor slowly descended the steps. As he did, all noise quickly ceased.

Odaenathus disengaged from Zenobia and waved the boys back up the steps. He strode over to kneel in front of Aurelian at the base of the portico. Zenobia followed a few paces behind Odaenathus and knelt beside him. Odaenathus drew his sword and held it in front of him with both hands. He bowed his head.

"Your Imperial Majesty." He spoke loudly so that all could har. "In the name of the citizens of Palmyra I welcome you to our fair city. My sword and my life are at your pleasure."

"Have you avenged Shapur's defeat and disgraceful treatment of Emperor Valerian, Septimius Odaenathus?" Aurelian's voice was stern, almost challenging.

Zenobia looked up, a scowl marring her features. "Was this battle supposed to have been for revenge, Imperial Majesty?"

Odaenathus turned to her in alarm. "Zenobia!" He looked back up at Aurelian. "Caesar, I beg your indulgence for my queen speaking out of turn. She's not familiar with the protocols of Rome."

"Umm. Well, I've already noticed she's as quick with her tongue as she is with her sword."

Zenobia felt the color in her cheeks. A flicker at the corner of his mouth told her that Aurelian noticed, but she was certain her husband had not seen. For several seconds the two men looked at each other.

"Well, Septimius Odeinat?"

Odaenathus gave a slight nod at the use of his Roman name. "I regret I did not, Caesar. We destroyed nearly half his army, but under the cover of his archers King Shapur escaped."

Zenobia proudly observed no nervousness in her husband's face or voice. This must have also pleased Aurelian, because he nodded and placed a hand on his consul's shoulder.

"Given the circumstances, you did extremely well." Aurelian removed his hand. "Rise and sheathe your sword, Prince Odaenathus. Perhaps when your men have had time to recover we can march on him together."

Odaenathus rose and came to attention. "It would be my honor, Caesar."

"Well, we can talk of this another time." Aurelian looked around and raised his voice. "At this time, there is another honor to attend to." He waved to an attendant, who approached holding a wreath. "Septimius Odeinat, kneel and bow your head with humility."

Odaenathus knelt once again and bowed his head. "Caesar, as you command."

"We are informed you have won a great victory over the Sassanid king, Shapur. For this brave service, in the name of Rome, I place this wreath of laurel upon your brow." He gently lowered the wreath onto Odaenathus' bowed head. "In the name of the senate, I give you the title of *Orientis Maximus*, Great Victor in the East."

The Palmyrene guard cheered, as did the Praetorian Guard. Knowing what must have happened, the crowd echoed the cheer.

"Rise, Septimius Odeinat, *Orientis Maximus*."

Odaenathus rose and saluted smartly. "For the glory of Rome and your Imperial Majesty, Lucius Domitius Aurelianus."

They embraced, and Aurelian turned and presented Odaenathus to the crowd, who cheered again. Aurelian encouraged the tribute to go on for several minutes.

"We must celebrate the splendid victory you have brought us. We understand there is to be a grand feast in your honor tonight."

"To celebrate our victory, yes." Odaenathus swept his arm to include his subjects. "But much more to welcome our new emperor to his domain. It is in your honor, Imperial Majesty."

"Then I look forward with double pleasure to this banquet tonight."

Aurelian gave a slight nod. He looked at Zenobia, who returned his smoldering glance. "I look forward to many great pleasures tonight, and in the days to follow."

*   *   *

Because of the dual nature of the celebration, several tables had been set up on the central dais. There was little extra space and no privacy, but one of the intents was to enhance the camaraderie of the military leaders. Aurelian, Odaenathus and Zenobia were seated at one table. Zabdas and Artabanes were seated with Mucapor, and Auzaina was with Domitianus and Decius. The other Palmyrene officers, officials and courtiers, as well as the lesser Roman officers, had also been seated at mixed tables throughout the room. The boys were seated with a nurse and other ladies of the court at another table. Musicians played quietly in the background.

The air was redolent with the smells of freshly baked breads, platters steaming with roasted legs of lamb and braised chops, rice covered with a spicy goat stew, several types of fowl either roasted or cooked in pungent sauces, and other delicacies Aurelian did not recognize, and was too wise to enquire as to the contents. There were potatoes, cheese and vegetables in abundance. When the main dishes had been consumed to everyone's satisfaction, sweetmeats and more wine were brought out as other servants cleared the dishes away. As the servants moved silently to complete their tasks, Odaenathus described to Zenobia the diversion that began the battle. The others on the dais chimed in on occasion with some fond remembrance.

"You loosed mares to distract their stallions!" Zenobia laughed throatily. She enjoyed being the desirable mare in this corral of stallions. As it was necessary for anyone who held a position of importance to learn both Greek as well as the language of their overlords, she spoke in Latin.

"Damned clever tactic, you ask me!" To emphasize his point, General Artabanes banged his goblet—which had been filled often—down on the table, sloshing wine over the table and his robe. He took another gulp, not seeming to notice the stain or the glares coming from the head table.

General Zabdas did not seem amused by Artabanes' manners nor the tactic he had praised. "Yes. Isn't it pathetic what the thought of sex has on most males?"

Everyone laughed at his comment except Mucapor. Zabdas looked perplexed, as though not understanding how anyone could have found his remark humorous.

"You disapprove of your prince's tactics when they worked so well, General Zabdas?" Aurelian asked with a smile.

"Of course not, Imperial Majesty." Zabdas brought a heavy hand down on the table. "I merely disapprove of the fact that most males are so weak in resisting women when we are supposed to be the stronger sex."

Zenobia noticed Aurelian's smile become hollow at the remark, and immediately decided to turn the conversation away from that direction. "My lord, how did you ever think of such a clever ploy?"

"Actually, from one of your ancient Egyptian generals."

Domitianus looked puzzled. "The Lady Zenobia has Egyptian heritage?"

Odaenathus reached out to stroke her hand lightly. She smiled at him, aware that Aurelian's face became even darker.

"Yes. I heard tales of this tactic being used some hundreds of years ago. It's said some general loosed one mare amongst a fleet of chariots, and they all succumbed to her charms."

"So two score the number, two score the power, Consul Odeinat?" Decius asked.

Zabdas and Mucapor were again the only ones who did not join in the laughter.

"Exactly. Needless to say, he won the battle."

"As did we, my lord." Another large gulp of Artabanes' wine served as a solitary toast to his boast.

"Yes." Odaenathus smiled jovially. "I shall sacrifice three sheep to Malak-bel for granting us victory with so few losses."

Zenobia's laughter tinkled among the deep tones of the men. "So few, my lord, after receiving the laurel wreath and a new title? What will the gods think of us?"

She stroked her husband's hair, and Aurelian glowered at the gesture. She noticed, but this time chose to ignore him.

"Perhaps you're right, my queen. How about six large sheep and one small cock?"

Most of the others laughed, but Aurelian reacted as though he had been slapped. Zenobia saw Mucapor's glance slide from Aurelian to Odaenathus.

"Prince Odaenathus, was this victory then so small?" The general's voice was like fine olive oil. "Or was the emperor's reward not sufficient for such a feat, as it did not require the aid of the Roman legions?"

There was stunned silence for a moment as everyone interpreted the meaning of this comment. Before Zenobia could smooth the waters once again, it was unexpectedly Zabdas who played the peace maker.

"My lord Odaenathus is fond of jest, General Mucapor. But I trust in all of his modesty he does not make light of this important victory over our long-time enemy. Or perhaps others too much." Zabdas' voice was calm, but there was a steely cast to his eye as he looked at Mucapor. Then he stood and raised his cup. "Therefore, I propose a toast."

Zabdas' attempt at smoothing the waters seemed to have worked. Zenobia noticed that everyone on the dais took up their goblets, although Mucapor did so very slowly. Zabdas continued as though he did not notice his counterpart's slight sneer.

"In the name of the Palmyrene army, I welcome these honors bestowed on our prince by the noble Roman Empire. I drink to the defeat of the Sassanid army and their king. I drink to your wreath, Caesar, and I drink to *Orientis Maximus*."

The Palmyrenes toasted enthusiastically, and the Romans endeavored to follow suit.

"To *Orientis Maximus*," their voices chorused.

Zabdas sat. There was silence for another moment. Zenobia tried to decide whether or not she should say something else when General Mucapor stood.

"I, too, wish to express my praises for Septimius Odeinat. Such a clever diversion, and how charming to reach so far into history to think of it!"

He waved his cup in what Zenobia took as a dismissive manner. She decided she did not like the man at all, in spite of his beauty. He directed his gaze toward Zabdas as he continued.

"And yet, it would seem that the Persians merely lost a few horses and soldiers, as their king escaped unharmed and the borders of their empire remain unchallenged. Therefore, my lords—and ladies—I would suggest that one small battle has been won, but the war remains ahead of us."

The Palmyrenes looked at each other. Zenobia saw her husband's jaw clench, and knew well what that meant. Zabdas glared at Mucapor and Artabanes made a choking noise. Aurelian stared at him as well, looking as angry as Odaenathus.

"Surely not so small a battle, General." Decius glanced from face to face with a smile that was intended to mollify both his emperor and their allies. "They did defeat an enemy more than twice their own strength."

"So we hear." Mucapor continued before any response could be made. "Our emperor was gracious enough to grant the wreath and the title for this...magnificent feat, which was proof of the love he bears..." he paused briefly to glance at Zenobia, "...for our subjects and allies in this portion of the empire. No doubt, this is a worthy sign of respect from one great general and leader to another." He paused again, and swept the company with his eyes. A faint smile appeared on his lips, although it seemed more mocking than conciliatory. "And so, I too propose a toast. I drink to the generous nature of our new emperor, and to the strong ties that bind us all together, Romans and Palmyrenes alike. To Lucius Domitius Aurelianus."

"To Lucius Domitius Aurelianus." The combined sound was barely enough to reach the ears of those below the dais.

As Mucapor sat once again, Zenobia looked at the emperor. The speech had created a restive atmosphere in the group, and Aurelian scanned the entire gathering in a way that made it clear he knew he must do something about it.

The emperor slowly stood. "I thank you, General Mucapor, for those...kind words." He looked around again. "I believe you were both right." He turned to General Zabdas. "This was a significant victory. It stung Shapur badly, in spite of his escape. It opens up the gates to Persia should we decide to travel down that road." He pivoted toward Mucapor. "However, our mutual enemy still remains strong and dangerous." He paused as his eyes encompassed everyone, those below the dais as well as those on it. "In these days of unrest, the Roman Empire faces many challenges. The mighty Persians in the east. The many fierce tribes of barbarians to the north. The Gallic Empire still poses a threat from the west. And, it is no secret here, the endless political maneuverings from within the walls of Rome itself make all other foes even more dangerous."

Aurelian took a drink of wine. Zenobia gave him a small smile of encouragement, but she wasn't certain he noticed.

"Yes, many challenges." He paused again, and gazed as though seeing something in the distance. "Still, those challenges can be met, they can be overcome, but not if we succumb to petty jealousies and personal ambitions within ourselves." Once more his strong gaze captured the eyes of all who watched him. "Our enemies can only be defeated if we remain united, if we cling to our friends more closely than we cling to our desires, if we do not give in to the weaknesses that are inherent in all of us. So, Prince Odaenathus and Queen Zenobia, generals, court officials, I offer you one last toast."

Aurelian raised his cup. All of the adults in the room stood and held their cups ready.

"To all of us, united, as tiny pieces of rock in the wall that surrounds and protects the Roman Empire. To us! To Rome!"

"To us!" came the resounding echo. "To Rome!"

They all drank. The mood was lightened once more, but not nearly to the jovial atmosphere before Mucapor's speech. Odaenathus remained standing as the others settled back down.

"Caesar, in token of our unity, may I offer your majesty one small gift now, which I hope will bring you pleasure?"

"A gift?"

It was common to bestow presents on a new ruler, but Zenobia was certain that Aurelian was not yet used to being treated like an emperor.

He looked pleasantly surprised, which amused her.

Odaenathus waved his hand and a servant entered with a cloak, which he handed to his master. "I can never repay the honor of receiving the laurel wreath." Odaenathus held the robe up for all to see. "However, this cloak may remind you as long as you live of my undying gratitude. Please accept this cloak of a Palmyrene commanding general as a sign that we welcome your command of our armies and our city, and of our loyalty and fealty to Rome."

Odaenathus held the cloak out to Aurelian. The emperor stood and looked at it, but did not reach for it.

"This is a great honor." After a moment, he undid the fibula on his *paludamentum*, a clothing fastener which was decorated with a winged Victory emblem. Beneath he wore the basic garment of Roman men, a simple short-sleeved tunic tied around the waist with a belt.

"May I, Caesar?" Zenobia reached for his *paludamentum.*

Aurelian handed the purple robe to her, and she carefully folded it and placed it in her lap. Odaenathus held out the cloak, and Aurelian turned to allow his consul to slip it over his shoulders. It was a rich ocher color, with a small stripe of purple around the sleeves. The weave was not so perfect as Aurelian's robe, but heavier, made for warmth and durability, and with a hood. The hem had a plain pattern of interlocking blocks, signifying the strength of unity. On the left breast was a lion seated, guarding the gates of Palmyra, and on the right a circle with crossed pillars inside, which narrowed in the middle where they were encircled by the serpent; it was the symbol of Assyrian loyalty. Aurelian fastened the iron fibula, which had a circle with the symbol of Palmyra, but left the hood back.

"It fits me well, do you not agree?" He turned so all could see and held out his hands in invitation for a response. There was some laughter, although it was uneasy.

Zenobia reached up and lightly stroked the symbol of loyalty. "You wear it well, Imperial Majesty. Perhaps you could lead my husband's armies when General Zabdas retires?"

The laughter was more open, with Zabdas making a loud, half-snort of a chuckle. Aurelian smiled at her, then turned to her husband.

"Our thanks, Prince Odaenathus, Queen Zenobia, for this gift, but even more for this symbol of your loyalty to our sovereignty and to Rome. As I said, it's not always easy to forgo our own ambitions for the good of the empire. This gift pleases us well."

Under the cover of bowing to the emperor, Zenobia watched carefully for the reactions. Everyone seemed to toast to his thanks except Artabanes, who was swaying where he sat. He mumbled vaguely, then slurred loudly for all to hear.

"Well, it would please us if Odaenathus was proclaimed emperor of all Assyria, and Persia, too, after we finish conquering those buggers. He's earned it."

Aurelian stiffened, and his staff began to protest the insult.

Odaenathus slammed his fist on the table. "General Artabanes!"

Zenobia sprang to her feet, fury on her features. "General Artabanes, have you no shame for this drunken display? Your prince has just said that this land already has an emperor, and we remain loyal to him and to Rome. Lord Odaenathus is content to serve under the titles Rome grants him. Do you presume to gainsay both of these worthy leaders?"

The nurse, alarmed at the uproar, rapidly led Odaenathus' sons out of the room.

Artabanes goggled at the crowd, his eyes blinking and his mouth open. He stood up uncertainly. He looked down at Zabdas, who glared at him. That seemed to be the final blow to his pride. "I'm sorry." He raised his eyes and slowly turned, his mouth still working like a landed fish desperate to sort oxygen from the liquid. "I'm sorry." Then he stumbled from the room.

The happy mood was irrevocably broken, and there was much private muttering. Zenobia stole a look at Mucapor, who leaned back and hid a sly smile as he stroked his bald chin thoughtfully.

*　　　*　　　*

Within the royal bedroom, Odaenathus and Zenobia were making love. It was even more tepid than usual, but Zenobia could well understand that her husband was upset. Odaenathus suddenly rolled away.

"I'm sorry, my love. I'm too distracted."

"How could you not be upset?"

"Not upset, furious." He leaped out of bed and started pacing as though to prove his point. "I don't know which of them I'd like to castrate first."

"Both of them." Zenobia scowled. "Especially that Roman snake. At least Artabanes was drunk."

"That only releases a man's thought, it doesn't excuse them."

Zenobia watched silently as her husband paced. There was nothing to be said that could comfort him—or her, for that matter.

Odaenathus stopped pacing and stared into space. "I wonder what Aurelian's thinking now."

Zenobia shrugged. "I hope he's thinking about the little diversion I sent him. Anything to take his mind off of that debacle long enough for us to talk with him in private."

"Yes. I hope you're right."

*　　　*　　　*

Aurelian was pacing on the balcony of his sumptuous palace bedchamber. He wore the cloak he had just been given, as though that symbol of unity could somehow heal the breeches that had been made that night. There was a soft knocking on the door.

"Come." Irritated by the intrusion, he strode into the room to greet his visitor. He hoped it would be someone he longed for, but knew she would not have knocked.

A young woman entered timidly, her head down. A nearly diaphanous gown displayed most of her charms. She approached Aurelian, but stopped and knelt some ten feet away, the eyes still down and hands submissively flat to the floor.

"Well?" His eyes grew wider, but his voice remained severe.

"I…I'm one of the prince's concubines, Imperial Majesty." She spoke so softly he could barely hear. "The queen sent me to serve you in any way you wish."

He stared at her for a moment, a slight stir of desire throbbing in his loins.

"Come closer."

Still on her knees, the concubine shuffled to Aurelian's feet. He lifted her chin up and inspected her. She was very young and very beautiful, with startlingly green eyes and long, lustrous black hair. He gently stroked her cheek, and she gave a timid smile.

Then he made an impatient sound and whirled to face outside again.

"Do I not please you, your majesty?

"You're lovely." He did not look at her. "However, it seems there are...other thoughts on my mind right now. You may go."

He stalked back out onto the balcony. The girl stood and bowed, then quietly left the room.

Absently touching the symbol of loyalty on the cloak which Zenobia had stroked earlier, Aurelian continued staring into the night.

*   *   *

"Zenobia!"

It was early morning. Zenobia walked down a small hallway in the palace that led to the garden, where she loved to sit and ponder for a short while each morning. It was one of the few times she was alone, and she enjoyed her brief moments of tranquility and solitude.

Aurelian knew this, and had obviously waited for her in a nearly invisible alcove which held a small statue of Asherali, the Canaanite Goddess of the Moon and fertility. He stepped into the hallway as Zenobia approached, grabbed her almost roughly, and pulled her back in with him. He kissed and groped at her, which both shocked and inflamed her. She encouraged him for a moment, returning his mad passion. Suddenly she pushed him away.

"Aurelian!" She gasped in her shock. "We Palmyrenes are no prudes, but this is too public even for us."

Aurelian twisted away as though scalded with burning oil, then turned back with his fists clenched and his breathing ragged. His eyes were wild, his movements jerky. Zenobia was amazed, hardly believing this was the same man she had met in the courtyard only days before.

"Too...public, too...passionate." Aurelian thrust a fist against his forehead, turning away again. "Too mad to conceive, let alone do. Too intoxicating to resist. I can't seem to control myself." He whirled back and grabbed her by the shoulders. "What have you done to me, woman?"

"Perhaps I've made you a mere mortal, like the rest of us." She did not know if she meant the remark to be honest or cruel; she had responded without thought for her words. Her body was stiff from anger and fear, and her shoulders hurt. Emperor or not, how dare he do this within her own palace where anyone could see them?

Aurelian searched her face. His own face was pale, but he was back under control.

"Was that your intent?" He stood like the statue beside him: cold and stony.

Zenobia relented. "No." She stepped forward again and stroked his cheek lightly, then sighed. "When I first saw you, it was like meeting a god. Not just the power, which you already know I crave. When I blocked your blade, I saw the admiration in your eyes. And then you jested with your men! You were so certain, so secure in your control over them that you did not need to preen or show anger to lift yourself up. You were already there, high above us, able to laugh at yourself without fear of falling. I did not believe even an emperor could have such supreme confidence. And later that night when you first took me...ah! You allowed me to soar with you."

They stared at each other a moment longer, the desire in his eyes burning into the core of her being. They grappled together in a fierce kiss. This time Aurelian tore himself away.

"I must have you once again, this very night."

"But my husband's just returned home!" Zenobia held out an arm as though to push him away. "I must be with him. Why is your need so urgent it cannot wait another night?"

"A messenger arrived this morning with an imperial command from Gallienus," Irritation clouded his tones. "Northern Italia has been invaded by the Franks and Goths, the Greuthungi and Tervingi. He requires me to lead my entire army to repel them. I must march immediately, so I'll have no more time with you after tonight."

"Cannot Gallienus send his own legions against the barbarians?"

"Even when I left Rome, most of his army was fighting throughout the Balkans. Yet, as thinly as they're spread, he's busy putting down insurrections within Rome itself." Aurelian made a contorted face that frightened Zenobia. "They're led by my replacement, his cavalry officer, Aureolus. He can't spare a single trainee, much less a legion. I can't refuse his entreaty, let alone his command."

"You can't delay one more day?"

"No. It must be tonight, or it may be years before I see you again."

Zenobia sighed more heavily this time. "Very well. I'll send my husband a few concubines to placate him. He'll be upset, but I know he'll understand and forgive."

Aurelian took a deep breath. He exhaled as though he had been about to burst.

"Thank you."

Zenobia looked at him as though she were equally vexed, but then smiled slowly and shook her head slightly. "There's no need for thanks. How can I refuse an entreaty from my emperor, let alone his command?"

*   *   *

Odaenathus tickled her, and she laughed lightly. Pillowing with the lord Odaenathus was always very playful and very enjoyable, if not terribly exciting. The other concubine started licking their lord in his privates, and he became distracted from her. Her thoughts wandered for a moment.

She wondered what it would have been like to pillow with the emperor. He had looked strong and rough in some exotic manner, and very intriguing. But he had refused her, which confused her when she saw his excitement. But she had not been punished for her failure, and was obviously still one of her own lord's favorites.

Which reminded her that she had no business taking her mind off her duties. Wanting to make certain she bested her rival, she dove back into the frolic.

*   *   *

Their love-making was more tempestuous than before. Knowing it might be their last time ever, it bordered on desperate. When the passion of Aurelian and Zenobia was finally consummated, they lay quietly for a long while.

"Can you stay with me until morning?" Zenobia tried to keep the pleading out of her voice.

Aurelian sighed. "You know I cannot. An official summons even takes precedence over a summons of the heart. I must meet with my staff at first light."

She stroked him needfully. "But surely you can stay for a few more minutes, or even another hour...."

"Another hour!" Then he laughed softly. "I cannot resist you. Nor do I want to!" He wrapped her fiercely in his arms and rolled on top of her.

*   *   *

Zenobia slipped quietly back into the royal chambers when Aurelian finally left to rejoin his troops. Exhausted from little sleep and an emotional and physical toll, the queen nevertheless rose at the usual time and met her servants in her dressing room. Odaenathus and Zenobia now faced each other in the antechamber, both dressed in formal robes as they prepared to go about their duties. Servants were putting the finishing touches on both of them.

The first order of the day was to visit the camp of the emperor and make a formal inspection. They would wish him good fortune against the barbarians from the north, knowing the continued economic success of their city was tied to the existence of Rome. There would be no banquet that night, as the Roman army would spend the rest of the day making ready to march before the first light.

"Wonderful, Bella." Zenobia stood still as her servant straightened the folds on her robe. "You may go now."

Bella bowed and left the chamber. Odaenathus waved at his attendant, who followed Bella out.

"How was your evening, my lord?" Zenobia worked to sound cheerful.

"Not quite what I expected on my return."

They exchanged glances. Immediately Odaenathus pretended to adjust something on his robe, not wanting to make his look too accusing. They both knew the ship of state must sail in many directions if it wanted to reach port safely. Odaenathus gave a small toss of his head as though to shrug off any unpleasant thoughts.

"However, quite pleasant, I must admit."

"Then I shall reward them."

"Oh, yes, you must." Odaenathus fussed with his robe again. "And how was your evening, my queen?"

"It was…." She searched to find the words that would be honest, yet not too insulting to her husband. "Exciting, invigorating. It was also quite pleasant."

"Ah. So we've made some intimate connections with our new emperor, have we? And may we hope for as good a relationship with him as we had with Valerian?"

"Yes. We have nothing to fear from that quarter."

"I'm glad you found him pleasant." His face clouded for an instant, then cleared. "His reputation is of someone quite cold, brutally efficient on the battlefield." He gave a small toss of his head again. "I had feared he might be the same in more...private circumstances."

"Not at all. I must confess I really liked Aurelian. As you said, he's not at all what I had expected. I have hopes that our association will be long and successful."

Odaenathus chose only to see the positive in that remark. "Well then, my congratulations. I must also confess he quite surprised me. First the honors, and then that speech after that general of his was so condescending. He struck me as quite genuine."

"Yes. I'm sure he is."

Odaenathus clapped his hands together and rubbed them. "In that case, we have much to plan with our staff for a possible invasion of Persia. Who knows what honors might fall on us if we're successful with that?"

"Yes. It's time you started involving Hairan in those meetings. His thirteenth birthday is next week, as you recall."

Odaenathus smiled warmly. "I'm grateful it's you who battles over the running of our household goods and staff. Somehow, my challenges seem much less."

Zenobia returned his smile and kissed her husband on the cheek. Satisfied both with their costumes and their relationship, they exited the royal chambers to fulfill their obligations.

CHAPTER SIX

The day had gone well. In keeping with Zenobia's advice, Odaenathus invited Hairan to accompany them as they inspected the Roman troops. The boy knew what was expected of him—on this occasion and in the future—and behaved accordingly. He was very serious and quiet, although he asked a few intelligent questions to do with differing tactics and equipment. Aurelian and Decius had escorted them around, so they were not forced to speak with General Mucapor, only to observe him as he presented the Praetorian Guard.

Later that evening, Odaenathus walked with Hairan in the palace garden, which was like a small park. Odaenathus rarely had the time or inclination to visit the beautiful area, where a person might wander for hours without being disturbed. Because he wanted to have a discussion with his son that he did not want overheard, Odaenathus had decided this casual setting would do better than within the palace itself. He had ordered his guards to remain inside to insure complete privacy.

Odaenathus began by getting Hairan's impressions of his visit to the Roman army. He was pleasantly surprised at the boy's grasp of the differences and similarities between the legions and their own military; that Roman tutor of his must be doing a good job. But he himself must insure that Hairan knew what would be needed once he took his father's position. He decided to see what the boy knew about leadership—and what he thought of their new leader.

"Well, what did you think of our new emperor, Hairan?"

"He seemed nice." The boy twisted his mouth. "Not like that general of his."

Odaenathus made his face very serious, trying to hide a smile. He liked the fact that his son spoke directly. "Hmm. Well, I'm glad you liked him. I'm getting old, you know, and he's fairly young. Someday soon it may be your duty to work with him to maintain this part of the empire."

"Work with him?" Hairan's voice showed surprise. "But Mother said only last month that we're vassals to Rome. Don't vassals have to do as they're told?"

Odaenathus was slightly annoyed, but hid it well. "Your mother said that, did she?"

Hairan nodded. Rather than saying she might now change her tune, Odaenathus decided to change tacks.

"Well, do you think you and your brother are vassals to your mother and myself?"

"No, of course not. We're your children." His voice was slightly puzzled, but mostly indignant.

"Exactly so. And children must honor and obey their parents, mustn't they?"

"Certainly, Father. But you aren't the emperor's child."

"Hmm. Well, in a way I am. You know that I'm a Roman citizen, don't you?"

"I know that other emperors said you were and gave you some titles, but we've always lived in Palmyra. Aren't we Assyrian?"

"We're both. Including your mother." The odd look on his son's face made him regret the comment. He hurried on. "Think of Assyria— of all the Roman provinces—as children of Rome. You have your duties, which right now are mostly to study: your academics, how to do battle, and how to rule. My duties are to collect taxes and to protect this part of mother Rome's empire."

"But can't the emperor tell us to do exactly what he wants?"

Odaenathus nodded. "Just the same as parents tell their children what they should do. However, just like you and Vaballathus, we're given great freedom to do as we please as long as we're faithful to our duties. So we remain loyal to mother Rome, just as you boys do to us."

"So we're not vassals?"

"I don't think so. Not at all."

Hairan stroked his fuzzy chin. Odaenathus almost laughed to see this imitation of a wise old man.

"I see."

They walked on for a moment, Hairan deep in thought, and Odaenathus letting him figure things out. As they strolled, Odaenathus really looked at the garden for the first time. Unlike both of his wives, he rarely made the time to visit, although only those invited by the royal family were permitted to enjoy its beauty and tranquility. Installed when the palace was built, it was perhaps a quarter of a hectare. Most of the flora had been imported from the eastern Mediterranean forests, and was considered a great treasure by most visitors simply because of the extravagance of water spent upon it.

At the very center of the garden was the towering Juniperusdrupacea, which formed a cone tree nearly seventy-five feet tall, with a trunk perhaps six feet thick. Several marble benches offered rest beneath its shade. Odaenathus was aware that his wife relaxed in this spot often. The strong, aromatic smells of it nearly drowned the fragrances of the smaller flora. Scattered all around were lesser junipers, half a dozen pistachio trees native to the desert, and other evergreen shrubs such as holm oak, tree heath, strawberry tree, buckthorn, sage, spurge olive and myrtle, some of which grew up to fourteen feet high. Carob trees, usually cultivated for their legume beans, were used as an ornamental tree in the garden. The most common flowering plant was the poppy anemone, although other lovely flowers lined the walkways and hid in surprising spots: anemone coronaria, the exotic smelling anise, the Golden Marguerite and Yellow Chamomile, a type of sunflower, the starflower, the Sweet Sagewort, and others. Unlike the desert, where the pungent smell of sage wafted to his nostrils on rare occasions, the sweet, delicate scents of the flowers fought through the overpowering presence of the juniper to provide surprising delights. There were also tufts of orchard grass, although it had proven difficult to grow thickly without using excessive water. It was much more beautiful and interesting than he remembered.

He had just determined to visit it more often when three men wearing black cloaks over their armor sprang from behind a high hedge. Odaenathus could clearly tell they were Romans. He was shocked they were here, and it took a few seconds to register that their intent was evil. That was made evident as the two men closest to him drew their swords, while the third grabbed Hairan. As Odaenathus drew his sword, the third man pulled a knife from his belt and held it to

Hairan's throat. He was short but powerfully built, and he held the boy across the chest with no effort.

"Stop!" The man closest to him spoke in Latin.

Both Hairan and Odaenathus froze. Hairan seemed more shocked than frightened.

"No!" Odaenathus looked at the man with the knife, although the speaker was evidently their leader. "Don't hurt the boy."

"Then drop your sword." The leader raised his weapon menacingly.

The short man pressed his knife deeper into Hairan's throat. After a moment's hesitation, Odaenathus did as he was commanded. The leader immediately stabbed him through the gut. The man next to him also attacked.

"Guards!" Odaenathus shouted, but the blade in his stomach dulled the sound.

As he looked down at his sword, the second swordsman stabbed him in the chest. The blade punctured a lung, and Odaenathus found himself starved for oxygen. For one moment no one moved as Odaenathus stood spitted on the two swords. Then he fell slowly to the ground. He stared up at his son, his mouth moving, but unable to speak. He tried to reach a hand to touch his son for the last time, but his arm would not obey.

Hairan tried to break free, but could not. "Father!"

Odaenathus looked up helplessly, the pain blurring both his vision and hearing.

Keeping his knife to the boy's throat, the soldier put his other hand over Hairan's mouth. "What about the boy?"

"We were told 'and anyone with him'." The soldier pulled his sword from Odaenathus' chest.

"Yes." The leader's face showed no emotion. "His bad fortune."

As though killing a chicken for dinner, the short man pulled his blade across Hairan's throat. Hairan's eyes went wide with pain and shock. With a gurgling sound, they boy fell at his feet. "Right. That's life."

There were several shouts and noises that indicated their victim's cries for help had been heard. Their leader threw his sword down between the father and son. All three men ran off towards the door where they had entered the garden.

Slumped on his side, Odaenathus strove to reach for his son to touch him one last time. He wanted to weep, to express the agony that tore his heart the way the blades had torn his flesh. But he could do nothing, could barely even regret the time he had not spent with Hairan in such moments as their last. Then his eyes closed, and he thought no more.

*   *   *

It was getting late. After the Palmyrenes left, as much of the Roman camp that was not needed for sleeping had been broken down and packed away. That included the command tent. Aurelian, Mucapor, Domitianus, Decius and Procus crowded around a tiny table in Aurelian's personal tent looking down at a map of northern Italia. No one seemed happy.

"By the sword of Mars!" Domitianus grasped the hilt of his sword tightly. "Are we supposed to fight the Vandals, Juthungi, and Sarmatians without any aid from Gallienus?"

"Yes." Aurelian looked him straight in the eye. "We must take our entire army into northern Italia. Except for the garrisons in Egypt; there's not enough time to send word and have them join us."

Decius looked at the representations of the barbarian forces on the map, which had been brought by the messenger. Different colors of blocks indicated both tribes and an estimation of how many men and cavalry they possessed. "Even with them, Caesar, it wouldn't look like enough by half to me."

"And in the meanwhile we leave the entire Eastern Empire without protection." Mucapor waved a dismissive hand.

"Not without protection." Aurelian turned his gaze to his second-in-command. "You heard Septimius Odeinat last night. He'll defend our interests."

"Caesar, you trust him enough to still serve Rome?" Domitianus glanced quickly at Mucapor, then back to the emperor. "His generals seemed quite eager to resume local control, and his loyalty might be put to the test without any Roman forces around to keep him in the fold."

"I trust him to defend the power that he has. An intelligent man will always do what serves his best interests. I certainly believe Odaenathus is intelligent, that he still loves Rome, and that he knows where his best interests lie."

"I must agree with the emperor, Domitianus." Mucapor nodded sagely. "An intelligent man will always serve his best interests."

Aurelian saw Decius give the general a suspicious look. At that moment a guard stepped into the tent and saluted.

"Caesar, a messenger says he has urgent news from the palace."

"News from Septimius Odaenathus? What an odd coincidence."

A smile passed between the men. Was the consul sending some further proof of his loyalty?

"Send him in."

The guard stepped out, and a Roman messenger rushed in and saluted.

"Caesar." He looked around nervously. "Prince Odaenathus and his eldest son have been assassinated."

"What?" Aurelian could not have heard correctly.

"I'm afraid it's true, Caesar." The messenger made a slight bow of apology. "I checked with several sources at the palace before I brought you the news."

"Then that was well done." Aurelian spoke kindly, although he was clearly agitated. "You're dismissed."

The messenger saluted and exited. Aurelian looked at his officers. Decius and Domitianus both looked shocked; only Mucapor appeared to be unfazed by the news. Well, the man had not liked the consul, so it was no surprise his death was not a bother. But it somehow troubled Aurelian even more that there was no apparent sympathy for the death of the boy. Well, everyone reacted in their own way to such news. The emperor shrugged off that line of thought and got back to the business at hand.

"These are ill tidings, especially at this delicate time. Decius, tell my private guard that I will go to the palace."

"To what purpose, Caesar?"

Aurelian turned to Mucapor, his irritation at the man's insouciance turning to anger at being questioned in such a manner.

"What purpose? Why, to assure Queen Zenobia that no Roman had anything to do with the murder, but only wants for Palmyra to continue as good friends and partners."

Mucapor did not back down in the least. "Does the emperor of the Eastern Roman Empire feel such a burning need to reassure a small province queen that Rome would not get involved with their local politics?"

Aurelian allowed his anger to show. "What are you implying, general?"

"I certainly think his Imperial Majesty owes no apologies or explanations to the court of Palmyra. I've also heard that Zenobia harbored ambitions, both for herself and her own son, and she might have felt that now was a good time to advance those ambitions."

"Now a good time? Meaning?"

"Meaning once she had—" Mucapor paused briefly and looked at Domitianus. "Once she had gained the emperor's favor, she might well have had her husband killed so that her own son could rule the land rather than the first born."

Aurelian swallowed several times, then licked his lips. He controlled his voice so that it was softer than before. "Be very careful, Mucapor. You insult us both with this conjecture."

Mucapor's tone became positively oily. "I beg your pardon if I seem to insult you, Imperial Majesty. It's only that this woman, who has obvious ambitions, seems to think her position is quite secure now that she has bewitched you."

He could control it no longer. He smashed his fist down on the table, hearing a slight crack at the blow. Both Domitianus and Decius flinched.

"You go too far! Your position may not be as secure as you seem to believe."

Mucapor seemed unaffected by his anger. "We both owe our current positions to Emperor Gallienus." His tone was no longer oily; it was nearly sanctimonious. "He's called for us with an imperial decree. We should march to his aid at first light."

"You don't need to remind me how much I owe Gallienus!"

He glared at Mucapor, who glared back fiercely for a moment. Domitianus took a slight step forward and put his hand on his commander's elbow. Mucapor immediately dropped his head and softened his voice.

"Forgive me, Lucius Domitius Aurelianus. I was too zealous. I only meant to stress that our loyalty is to Rome, not to this woman."

Aurelian held his anger in his chest for a long beat. Then he exhaled in a long, ragged breath. He inhaled and exhaled several more times before he spoke.

"There's no need to forgive. The empire is facing terrible dangers, both within as well as without." He put his hand on Mucapor's shoulder, and Domitianus stepped back. "If ever Rome needed true zeal from its soldiers, Bicius, it is indeed now. But we need the help of our allies as well."

Mucapor bowed slightly. "You are too gracious, Imperial Majesty."

"Caesar, I must add my voice to that of General Mucapor." Domitianus took one step forward. "So early in your reign as emperor, to delay our march merely to pacify this woman would show great weakness."

Aurelian grunted. He looked at his cavalry commander as if judging which side of the sword his interest lay. He turned to his aide-de-camp. "Decius? You haven't yet spoken."

"I...." Decius looked around as the others awaited his words. He swallowed once and licked his lips. "I hesitate to give the emperor advice on such a delicate matter, one that may indeed be of...well, somewhat of a personal nature. However, it would seem clear where our duty lies, if not necessarily our...our desires." He was slightly panting from the exertion of speaking so frankly.

Mucapor jumped back in. "If I may add, Caesar, Zabdas may be a broken down old war horse, but I agree with what he said about women. We're supposed to be the stronger sex. We mustn't let any weakness for a woman cloud our judgment or our duty."

Aurelian blinked several times. For a moment, it was not clear he would respond. Then he whispered: "A weakness. Yes."

"Caesar?" Decius furrowed his brow in concern.

Aurelian mentally shook himself. "Nothing." He breathed through his mouth until he was composed again. "Very well, continue preparing the legions. We march at first light."

"Shall I have the messenger take word to the queen?"

Aurelian looked at Decius for a moment. Then he exhaled once again. "Yes. Tell the queen she has my deep condolences."

"Nothing else, majesty?"

Aurelian hesitated, but was determined to remain firm. "No. Nothing else."

Decius saluted and exited. The other officers did the same. Aurelian stood and stared into space for a long time.

*　　　*　　　*

It was still dark, and the departure of the Roman army could be heard more than seen. Nevertheless, it was clear what was happening.

Zenobia, General Zabdas and Cassius Longinus stood on the city walls wrapped in heavy cloaks as they watched the Roman army march away. They had stood thus for more than twenty minutes. When Zenobia broke the silence, it was more of a mutter, low in her throat.

"He goes like a dog slinking off now that he has stolen the bone."

Zabdas leaned forward as though he had not heard correctly. "My lady?"

This time she spoke clearly. "Aurelian flees because of his guilt. He does not want to confront me."

"Ah." Longinus drew his cloak more tightly around his thin frame. "Why do you say this, my lady?"

Zenobia lifted up the side of her cloak and drew out a sword. It was the weapon that had been found next to the body of Odaenathus. "Do you recognize this sword?"

Longinus took it as though afraid it would burn his hands, having never handled one in anger. He examined it carefully. "Yes." He pointed to the hilt. "Look, an Eagle's head instead of the standard round ball. The symbol of the Praetorian Guard."

"Which must mean Aurelian sent the assassins."

Zabdas held out his hand, and Longinus gratefully gave him the sword to inspect.

"This seems very strange to me." Zabdas continued to inspect the sword, his heavy eyebrows knitting together.

"And to me." Longinus raised both shoulders in an elaborate gesture. "But, I admit, I can think of no other explanation."

Zenobia's voice was filled with anguish. "Why? Would he murder my husband to gain me?"

Zabdas widened his eyes at this speculation.

Longinus kept his voice neutral and spoke slowly. "As desirable as you are, my lady, I think he would have to covet much more than that to have done such a deed."

"Then what?"

Longinus pinched his long nose between his thumb and index finger. He wrinkled his eyes as he stroked the side of his nose gently, his gray eyebrows pulling together. "Ah, well. I can only guess. Perhaps he feared Odaenathus was growing too powerful. With the defeat of the Persian army, his popularity in this region might lead the people to declare him emperor, equal to Aurelian himself. This was voiced by General Artabanes, was it not?" His question was directed toward Zabdas, who merely nodded. Longinus shifted his hand downward to stroke his beard. "In which case Palmyra, and much of Assyria with it, might become much less—shall we say, dependent on the imperial favor?"

"But he must know I also lead our army into battle. Does he understand so little of our culture?"

Longinus made a hacking sound in his throat. "Oh, Aurelian made it clear he is aware of the stories. But it's ridiculous for him to think that Diana could do battle with Mars."

Zenobia cocked her head to the side and lowered one eyebrow.

Longinus gave his elaborate shrug once more. "Ah, well. It's not our way. No Roman woman would go near the battlefield."

"Except as a whore for the troops." Her voice was bitter, filled with contempt.

Longinus bowed his head in acceptance. "Frankly, I myself doubted those stories until I saw you practicing with your soldiers." He lifted his eyes again. "Ah, what a strange and wonderful sight! But no Roman soldier, from the lowliest recruit to the emperor himself, would ever believe a woman could fight like a man."

"I have no doubt." Zenobia made a thin, twisted smile. "And indeed I shall not fight like a mere man. Perhaps the mighty Roman emperor will learn that an Assyrian warrior queen is no myth."

The trio stared down once again at the departing army, the dawn starting to show their movement more clearly. Not another word was spoken until the last man had disappeared in a cloud of dust.

* * *

Zenobia paced down the main street of Palmyra, dressed in a plain black robe with a hood covering her head. She was followed by two servants, one who held large lamps with burning oil in each hand to dispel the Stygian darkness, and another who led a ram by a rope. The avenue was flanked with a double row of columns, fifteen hundred in total, which cast eerie shadows as the small procession made its way slowly through the city. At short intervals in the colonnade were portals with arches leading to the palaces and houses of the nobles, a few with lights burning, but most dark and silent. Zenobia glanced neither to the right nor left. At last they passed under a splendidly carved triumphal arch to the entrance of the great temple.

The most striking building in Palmyra was the huge temple of Ba'al—Malak-bel, as the Palmyrenes preferred. It originated as a Hellenistic temple, but was altered when the Greeks departed. It was then that the central shrine was added, followed by a large double-colonnaded portico in Corinthian style. Then a portico and a grand main entrance were added on the western side. The final temple measured six-hundred-and-seventy-five feet wide and six-hundred-and-ninety feet long.

It was approaching midnight when Zenobia walked up the steps of the main entrance into the temple. In both her hands, still stained with his dried blood, was the sword that killed Odaenathus. With their footsteps echoing from the marble walls, the three humans and the ram processed through the towering columns, erratically illuminated by the flickering lamps, until they reached the altar of the central shrine.

When at last the trio reached their destination Zenobia knelt in front of the altar, still holding the sword in front of her as though offering it to the god. Her eyes were fixed on the cold, stern face before her. The servant with the lamps placed one on the altar between his queen and the statue of Malak-bel so that the face of both were visible. The servant with the ram offered the rope to Zenobia. Without letting go of the sword or looking at the man, she took the stout hemp cord. Both servants bowed, then made their way back out of the temple.

Zenobia knelt without moving until the last sound of their exit had long died away. She leaned her head back until the hood fell away. When she spoke, her voice was not loud, but it echoed off the stone walls and high ceiling of the building.

"Great Malak-bel, father of my people, accept my humble sacrifice and hear my words. By the blood of this ram, I renounce my feelings for the Roman emperor Aurelian and vow to avenge the murder of my husband, the lord Odaenathus, and his son, Hairan."

She rose so that she could take a firm grip on the rope around the neck of the animal with one hand while she clasped the sword in her other. With a swift, deft movement, she cut the throat of the ram. It did not react until the pain hit, and by then it was nearly too late to bleat even once as its blood poured freely from the gaping wound. It tried to escape, but Zenobia held it fast in her grip. Within a minute it sank to its knees, and Zenobia released the rope. The creature shuddered once, then again, before it fell dead to the floor. The queen bent down and dipped her free hand into the heavy flow. She looked back up at Malak-bel and smeared her face with the blood.

"By the life I sacrifice to you, by the blood I shed for you, I swear that Rome will pay for this outrage in the worst way it could suffer, by the loss of its eastern empire."

She held the sword aloft. Her words rang out loudly in the vast hall and came back to her.

"The blood of two innocents has dried upon this cursed sword. But the tears of red on my own sword shall never cease to fall. In your name, great Malak-bel, I swear that Roman blood will run like the life's essence of this sacrificial ram. In your name and in the name of Palmyra, I will conquer the lands of the east and pass the new empire on to my son, Vaballathus. I shall not stop until Rome is no more than a cursed word we once tasted like bile in our mouths, and Aurelian no more than a cur on the streets. Great Malak-bel, hear my words! On this I swear. To you I swear."

CHAPTER SEVEN

Longinus entered the throne room quietly. Zenobia sat on the dais in front of her throne. For the first time he could recall, the queen looked tired, although still beautiful. He did not know if she had slept, but he could tell from her hair that she had recently bathed and dressed.

After a moment, he bowed. "You sent for me, my lady."

He had meant to be respectful, not too intrusive. Evidently he had made it so respectful that there was no response. The queen remained deep in thought, and he did not have to be a savant to know the tenor of those thoughts. Finally, he cleared his throat.

Zenobia looked up. "Oh, Longinus. Yes. I want you as my prime minister."

Longinus blinked several times. His hand automatically went up to stroke his nose. As soon as he realized what he was doing, he pulled it back down to his side.

"Ah, well. You want...pardon me?"

"You heard me." She spoke more crisply. "Prime minister."

"But...but Nobonidus Zohan is the prime minister. It's my understanding that lord Odaenathus–"

"Was very satisfied with him. Yes, and that was fine for then. This is now."

Longinus reached up and rubbed a mole on his forehead. He screwed up his face, then did his best to stop all of his twitches. "Please pardon my stupidity, my lady, but I don't understand the distinction."

Zenobia spoke patiently. "My lord Odaenathus was the prince of Palmyra, and Zohan was the perfect prime minister for Palmyra. I no longer mean to limit myself to Palmyra. I intend to defy Rome."

"Defy Rome!"

There was a long pause as they stared at each other. Longinus could see that the queen was being patient with him, but it still took a long time to get himself back under control. "My ... my lady, you think too highly of me. I'm merely a wandering philosopher and poet, not a statesman. To be honest, I found I could make a much better living in the provinces than I could in Rome." He gave a weak smile. "No offense intended, my lady."

"And none taken."

Longinus gulped. "Ah, well. I thank you." He started to rub his nose again, but instantly dropped his hand. "However, I assure you that I'm not qualified for such an exalted post."

She simply stared at him.

He began to squirm. "I am not qualified, my lady." He tried to be insistent, but his voice sounded squeaky even to him.

"On the contrary. You have the best qualifications in the land at this time, because you are a Roman. As you say, you're advanced in years, and you know Roman politics and customs—at least, well enough to flee them. You have studied their manner of making war. You're the only person in my court who can intelligently advise me on how to deal with our masters."

Longinus turned away, cringing. He did not try to stop himself from rubbing and scratching until he finally felt somewhat composed. He knew the queen was much more determined than he was. Finally he exhaled deeply, stood up straight, and turned back to her.

"You are determined in this, my lady?"

"Yes. Have no fear of Zohan. I shall find another suitable post for him, and he shall be happy. So, what is your answer?"

He bowed stiffly. "Well. It shall be as my lady commands. I am honored for the chance to do my lady such a service."

"Excellent," she said. Her tone never changed. "You can begin now. Your first duty shall be to gather all of the Roman citizens within our walls. Have them in the palace courtyard tomorrow an hour after cock crow."

Longinus felt a surge of panic at such a task, but quickly controlled himself. Feeling his mind to be numb, he repeated himself.

"My lady, it shall be as you command."

"Thank you. You may go now." Zenobia remained seated, obviously falling back into deep thought.

Although he knew she had dismissed him from her mind, Longinus bowed before creeping from the throne room like a man condemned with the sentence of death.

*   *   *

Dozens of people huddled in the center of the courtyard, surrounded by guards. Longinus stood in front of his fellow Roman citizens. They were mostly traders, but some were minor dignitaries who represented various parts of the empire, many who had wives and children with them. There were also a number of adventurers who had come to Assyria to find some sort of success they had not found in the cities of the greater Empire—men such as Cassius Longinus himself. At the moment, he was wishing he had perhaps not been quite so successful in making himself useful to the royal family.

Exactly an hour after cock crow, Zenobia walked out of the palace. Every eye was on the queen as she stood on the edge of the portico, looking down on them. She was dressed in battle armor. The Roman sword dangled in one hand by her side. Longinus thought she looked both wonderful and terrible. Her eyes were obsidian; her mouth was a slash of a knife blade. Even Longinus was nervous by the time she spoke.

"I'm certain none of you are wondering why you're here. By now, you know that my husband, Prince Odaenathus, and our eldest son, Crown Prince Hairan, were assassinated. They were murdered with this sword."

She held the sword aloft. She turned slowly from side to side, allowing them to see the blood-crusted blade. Then she pivoted it so they could see the hilt. "For those of you who do not recognize it, this is the sword of a member of the Praetorian Guard."

There was a murmuring in the crowd. Zenobia allowed it to fade.

"Yes. It means that Emperor Aurelian had my husband and son murdered."

There was more murmuring, only louder, more concerned. Longinus became even more nervous as he sensed the mood of the crowd. He dreaded what the queen might do. As if she were reading his mind she spoke again, louder than before.

"How shall I repay the emperor for this gift?" She stabbed the sword at the sky. "Wives, should all of your husbands be killed in the way that my husband was killed? Should your sons have their throats cut as my son's was?"

She sliced the sword through the air and brought it to her side. A roar of voices answered her.

"Mercy!"

"Please, let us live!"

"Please, mighty queen!"

"Spare our sons!"

"Mercy?" Zenobia pointed at them with the sword. "You surprise me that Romans even know the word. What about honor? Do you know that word? What of the word 'revenge'?"

The Roman citizens continued their pleading. Many fell on their knees. Longinus looked at the weeping, frightened faces around him and trembled. Zenobia let them agonize. She glared at them until the noise reached a feverish pitch.

"Very well!"

Her voice cut through the courtyard. The crowd grew silent, hope visible in their faces.

"I will show all of you the mercy your leaders never showed." Her eyes stabbed at each one of them as she spoke. "Every Roman man, woman and child is henceforth expelled from all of Assyria. I will give you food and water for the journey to Ebla. From there, you must make your own way back to Rome."

The Roman citizens cried out once more.

"Thank you, great queen!"

"Blessings upon you!"

"May the gods bless you!"

The crowd wept again, this time with a relief that also washed over Longinus. They hugged each other as only those who have been spared from sudden death can do.

"Do not thank me!" Zenobia glared at them until they fell silent. "You are to bear a message."

The citizens looked up at her with trembling lips. Those who were on their knees took on an attitude of prayer.

"When you get back to Rome, tell your fellow citizens, tell your senate, tell your emperor, that Queen Zenobia of Palmyra repaid their treachery with kindness. But only this once. If any Roman dares to set foot on our soil again, they shall be met with the sword."

She held the sword aloft again, stabbing the sky.

"Tell them!"

*   *   *

The camel and goat-hair tents laid out across the Assyrian desert formed a virtual city. It was a rare sight. The bedu—people who preferred to live in the desert—were nomadic both by their independent nature and their manner of living, being forced to drive their flocks from place to place as the forage flourished or waned.

The huge encampment was rare because it represented two *Quabilah*: the Butainat and the Abadah. Both tribes were very wealthy because of their ownership of large flocks of sheep, although the hierarchy of wealth was horses, camels, sheep and goats. They had been contacted by a representative of Queen Zenobia and asked to meet with her in formal council. While the *mukhtar* of each *Aela*, or clan, took great authority from the *Aela'smajlis*—the council of the most respected men—no major decisions, especially those involving two or more *Aela*, could be made without consulting the shaykh of the entire *Quabilah*. Only an amir, the prince of the entire country, stood above the shaykhs.

While no longer living as a Beduin amir, the prince of Palmyra had for many decades still retained authority for resolving tribal disputes. Thus, when Zenobia sent word to Rasses, shaykh of the Butainat, and Sefer, shaykh of the Abadah, they had in turn asked their *mukhtars* within a week's ride to join them in this rare meeting. Deciding to make the queen's visit a festive occasion, many of the *Aela* had come in force to feast and enjoy competitions with their distant cousins.

As was the custom, several days of feasting and entertainment had passed before they got around to their true purpose. Zenobia and Longinus sat in private with Rasses and Sefer in the spacious, comfortable tent of Rasses. They had shared a meal, and now ate an occasional sweetmeat as the conversation became serious.

"As usual, your hospitality is magnificent," Zenobia praised their host. "This wine is superb!"

Rasses and Sefer both nodded graciously. They had been equally responsible for providing the food and wine for the queen and her entourage.

"We are always honored to have the queen of Palmyra as our guest. It is a pity that you come with such...tragic news, so that we can no longer serve our lord Odaenathus as well."

Rasses was in his early fifties, a large man who moved and spoke carefully. His flowing beard was shot through with white, although he could still ride and fight nearly as well as most of his young warriors.

"Thank you." Zenobia acknowledged his words with a gracious tilt of her head. "He always enjoyed speaking with you, as well as your overwhelming hospitality."

"He shall be greatly missed from our humble tents." Rasses moved his hand in a slight salaam. "But, if you will forgive my rudeness, please tell us why you honor us with this visit so...so soon after the tragedy."

"Amir Rasses, although we made our home in Palmyra, Odaenathus never lost his love for the desert or our people. This you know. He always strove to serve the Beduin as if he still lived in a tent. I believe all of the *Quabilah* returned his love and respect."

"I believe it is so." Rasses stroked his beard sagely.

Sefer also nodded in agreement. In his late twenties, he was still trying to learn the patience that went with his position. His beard was not yet long enough to give a good stroke.

"It is renowned how your *Quabilah* and several others swell our army with fierce riders when we must battle the Sassanids or other invaders. Your men are loyal to Palmyra, not Rome. Seeing this as a possible danger, the Romans grew wary of his growing power and murdered him in our own garden."

"Are you certain it was the emperor?"

Zenobia held her hands palm up toward Sefer to show sincerity. "I have shown you the sword." She included Rasses in her gaze as she put a little more tension in her voice. "I have told you how Aurelian cringed away early the next morning, no doubt fearing that his two legions might not be enough to protect him from my army."

"And you, Cassius Longinus?" Rasses had difficulty rolling the sounds around on his tongue. "You agree Aurelian's guard must have committed this foul deed?"

Longinus gave a quick glance at Zenobia. He addressed both of the shaykhs when he spoke. "Ah, well, as I've said, I can't think of any other explanation. The sword is clearly of the Praetorian Guard."

"You seem certain all of this shows some fear on the part of the emperor." It was evident from Sefer's tone he had great doubts on that point.

Zenobia allowed some excitement to show. "Can't you see how this shows their fear of us? Divided, only banding together when they call, we remain weak enough for them to rule us. United, we could send them all to hell. Yes, they did fear— they feared that my lord Odaenathus was growing powerful enough to unite us and drive them from our land."

"Drive them from our land!" Sefer had half-raised himself up from his divan, but sank back and let his eyebrows lower. "They're a very powerful military. They have weapons and tactics that outmatch ours."

Zenobia waved slightly towards Longinus. "Yes, but Prime Minister Longinus can help us match their weapons and understand their tactics. He studied the manner of war of both the Greeks and the Romans while living in Athens many years ago." She raised her eyebrows to imply that this was a significant advantage. "United, we would greatly outnumber them," Zenobia added.

"I am certain Minister Longinus is highly knowledgeable and clever." Rasses bent his head slightly toward Longinus, who returned the gesture. "However, even united, I have my doubts we could defeat the Roman legions. I've heard this new emperor is a great general."

Zenobia wanted to stand, but that would have been rude. She settled for an engaging smile. "Ah, but you haven't heard that Aurelian and his legions have been called back to Italia to protect their capital from invading barbarians. The nearest Roman legions are now in Egypt, and they are few in number."

"Only Egypt?" Sefer asked.

"And, of course, Palmyra…." Rasses added.

"Yes," Zenobia said. "Palmyra was indeed their overseer for the Assyrian territories. But our loyalty died with my husband. If you two join with me, we'll soon have all of the *Quabilah* with us, one way or the other. Then we'll present a mighty army to fight the Romans."

"But you know the *Quabilah* will never accept a woman as our main leader."

Rasses' voice was gentle, but Zenobia understood this was a personal comment as well as a general belief.

"That's why Vaballathus, son of Odaenathus, will become king." She saw their brows go up at the fact she had anticipated their objection and prepared for it. "That is, if the shaykhs of the two largest *Quabilah* are beneficent enough to swear their allegiance. If so, even such independent *Quabilah* as the Allegat and the Hamada will follow your lead."

"Forgive me, but your son is now, what, five years?"

"That is correct, Shaykh Sefer."

Rasses made a show of selecting a sweetmeat before speaking. "Therefore you, of course, would act as his regent."

Zenobia nodded. "True. But I shall be much more than that."

"And what more would that be, Queen Zenobia?" Rasses popped the delicacy into his mouth.

"I will be Our Lady of Victory."

"Our Lady of Victory?" Sefer looked from one to the other. "I've never heard of this."

Zenobia remained patient, although enthusiastic. "You know of Ishtar of Arbela, the goddess of war, called the 'Lady of the Battles'."

"I have heard this story."

The Beduin were rich in their oral traditions, and this was an old, respected story. Nevertheless, Zenobia repeated the details she wanted to emphasize.

"She used a hunting bow, and rode with breasts bared to show she had no fear of her enemies. The legendary King Assur-bani-pal claimed he had received his bow from her, and passed it on to his warrior queen, who rode in his chariot like Ishtar herself. Other warrior queens did the same to inspire their soldiers in battle."

Rasses waved his hand languidly. "That is a very old custom among our people, hardly more than a myth now."

Zenobia's eyes bored into his. "My lord Rasses, I am no myth. I promise you, if you two will join with us, I shall resurrect the warrior queen of Assyria. I shall become Our Lady of Victory."

The two shaykhs looked at each other thoughtfully. Sefer turned to her with the same direct stare.

"You would ride at the head of the army, dressed as the Lady of Victory, but your son would bear the title of king?"

"I swear. I shall serve as the inspiration only."

"That could be made to work." Rasses reached for another sweetmeat, but leaned back without taking one. "I must think about this."

"I urge you, do not think too long, Shaykh Rasses. Aurelian has taken his troops from our lands, but he will not be gone forever."

"I need no more time to think about it," Sefer declared. "As Queen Zenobia says, if we wish to free our necks from the yoke of the Roman invaders, the time to strike is now. As it is, we shed most of the blood to repel the Sassanids, yet they collect our taxes. In two years, perhaps three, they will return, and wish to put their heel on our necks once again."

"Exactly. If we unite now, we will never have to bow down to those dogs again."

"If we can unite all of the *Quabilah*," Rasses emphasized dubiously.

Sefer looked at Zenobia with shining eyes. "I believe our queen could make this happen."

Rasses grunted. "Our Lady of Victory."

Zenobia knew when to hold her peace. She restrained herself to making her mouth and eyes as appealing she could manage. Sefer also waited respectfully.

"Yes." Rasses took another sweetmeat and chewed it thoughtfully. "Yes, you are both right. Great Malak-bel has given us our chance. The time to unite is indeed now."

$$* \qquad * \qquad *$$

"But, Mother, I thought you said I was to be the king."

"You are the king, darling."

"Then shouldn't I lead the army?"

Zenobia smiled. "Someday you will lead the army…the largest Assyria has ever seen. But, for now, you need to stay here, continue your studies, and prepare for the time when you're old enough to command, both in war and in peace."

"Will Sius still be my teacher?"

"I'm afraid I'll need Cassius with me to advise me on the Romans. You know he has new duties now—just as we do."

Vaballathus sat quietly, a slight frown on his face. They sat in the shade of the garden, and the dappled light playing through the trees emphasized the rippling of features across the boy's face as he fought his emotions. Zenobia thought he might break down in tears, but she said nothing. The preparations had all been made, and the army was only a few days away from marching north. This was one of the lessons he had to learn in life, and it was just as well to start now.

"But you will go away with them. And I can't even come with you?"

Zenobia took one of his hands in hers and patted it gently. She did not remind him that they had been through all of this before. "It will be very dangerous, darling. And we might be gone for a long time."

His lower lip trembled and one eye began to sag a tiny bit, but then he wiped the weakness from his face. She was very proud of him.

"Besides, with me gone, you must look after Palmyra. You'll have advisors, just as I'll have Cassius along with me. But you are the king, and you'll be making a lot of very important decisions. Our people are now your responsibility. They'll depend on you to be very strong."

"Yes, Mother." The voice was almost a whisper, forced through a tight throat. Finally, his face sagged. "Is it…is it alright if I miss you?"

Zenobia pulled him into her arms, and his own small arms clamped around her with the desperation of the doomed. Her own throat tightened just for a moment as she remembered a time she had also clung desperately to her own mother.

"Yes, darling," she breathed gently into his ear. "Of course it's alright if you miss me."

CHAPTER EIGHT

Mucapor and Domitianus lounged on divans in Mucapor's tent as Procus entered. He saluted and stood at attention. For a moment longer they both ignored him as they sipped their wine. Then Mucapor made a gesture with his free hand.

"At ease, Commanding Centurion."

Procus relaxed, but remained standing. As commander of the first cohort he was under the direct authority of General Mucapor, but he had not felt comfortable with the young man since they met. Mucapor was zealous and had received good training, but Procus felt the man was much too callous with the lives of his men. He had been much happier when Aurelian had been his direct superior. Aurelian got results without recklessly endangering his men.

Mucapor seemed to ignore him as he sipped his wine. "What's the mood of the legion?"

Procus shrugged. The march from Assyria had been long and hard to reach the northern borders of the empire, where invading hordes were reported. The following year had offered little rest. At first, the campaign had been successful, but then disaster struck.

A huge host of Asding Vandals had seen the opening on the Pannonian frontier and crossed the river near Aquincum. Joined by thousands of Sarmatians, they were spreading chaos, looting and burning villages and terrifying the countryside. Although short on supplies from the journey north, Aurelian had marched over the Julian Alps to meet them. Near Siscia, Aurelian ordered his army to take what crops and food they could and to destroy the rest so the raiders would find nothing to eat as they advanced. Within two weeks, the Sarmatians decided to abandon the invasion. While he was busy starving and harassing the Vandals into submission, fighting running skirmishes rather than pitched battles, more Germanic tribes seized their opportunity. An even larger army of Alamanni, both Goths and Juthungi, crossed the Danube farther north and laid waste through

Raetia as far as Lake Constance. Then they turned south, crossing the Alps over the Splugen Pass to Milan, one of the few times barbarians had actually entered Italia itself.

To insure the withdrawal of the Vandals, Aurelian was forced to split his army. He left his elite forces to deal with the Vandals, and marched the bulk of his troops to meet the Goths and Juthungi. Exhausted from the forced march from the Balkans, hungry and not at full force, the Roman army sped toward Placentia, which the Alamanni had recently sacked. Knowing of their approach, the invaders hid in a large wood outside of Placentia.

The barbarians had swarmed out of the trees with screams and shouts, many with faces painted, wolf or bear skin coverings flapping, more like wild animals than humans. They had flung spears and *francisca*, their heavy throwing axes, at the startled Romans, while others had fired slings and short bows. Then they attacked all along the weary and disorganized line with battle axes, maces, huge curved swords, pikes, wooden clubs with spikes through them, and the *falx*, a ferocious double-handed weapon with a scythed blade on a stout wooden handle.

The bizarreness of the Alamanni, their strange and savage weapons, but mostly the ferocity of the unexpected attack, caused panic through much of legion. Many died. Many others fled. By the time they could escape from the fearsome warriors, Emperor Aurelian's forces had suffered a devastating and embarrassing defeat.

Satisfied with their victory, the barbarians continued to move south. Aurelian's scouts were still trying to round up their scattered soldiers.

Procus cleared his throat before responding, as though the bitter taste of defeat still stuck there. "Shocked. A little discouraged."

"Is that all?"

Procus shrugged again. What was there to say these men did not already know? "Many of them were new recruits before we went to Assyria, fresh from the auxiliaries. The Vandals were their first real action, and that was nothing to prepare them for this."

Domitianus leaned forward. "But they still love Aurelian?"

Procus frowned, then wiped the expression from his face. Were they expecting him to criticize the emperor? "Of course. The emperor can be, well, a little...."

"Unforgiving? A hard ass?" Domitianus prompted.

"General!"

"You have no fear of us repeating any private conversations, Procus," Mucapor interceded smoothly. "It's not disloyal to speak frankly between us, but if those of us a little closer to the common legionary misjudge their mood, we can't be of much help to the emperor, can we?"

"Yes, of course, General Mucapor. I just don't want to be disrespectful."

"Naturally, we all respect the emperor as much as ever." Domitianus leaned back and sipped more wine. "But we need to know how your men feel after that disaster at Placentia."

"The men all know that was an ambush." Procus kept the irritation out of his voice. "There was no way the emperor could have predicted that when even my scouts, some of the best in the entire empire, didn't see the signs."

"But the citizens of Rome will be quivering with fear at the advancing horde. They won't give a damn why he was defeated."

"Gently, Domitianus." Mucapor put his hand lightly on the other man's forearm. He turned back to Procus with a charming smile. "No one blames you any more than they blame Aurelian. But sometimes men's moods don't depend on logic as much as whether or not they think they'll survive the next battle."

"Yes, sir."

Domitianus would not relent. "So?"

Procus straightened his spine. "The men still love him, General. They still think of him as one of them. And, after all, this was the emperor's first major defeat—and who could have done any better?"

"Yes, yes, Procus."

There was a pause as the two generals drank more wine and Procus practiced his breathing, working hard to keep his temper in check.

"But now the Alamanni are swarming across the Po plain, sacking towns as they go, and heading for the river." Mucapor turned to

Domitianus. "What's the mood of the cavalry?"

"The same." Domitianus jerked his goblet, spilling a few drops of wine. "They're still loyal and motivated. After all, the infantry took the heavy casualties."

Procus bristled a little, but Mucapor ignored him.

"All right, then. We'll be heading for the Po as soon as we can regroup. That might take a while, as many of the men scattered like chickens from a fox."

"The men were stunned by the vicious, nearly mad tactics of the barbarians, General. I was very startled myself. Those who ran are terribly ashamed of themselves."

"Yes, perhaps they were. Well, let's hope things go better the next time, when we're prepared to meet the barbarians on our own terms. You're dismissed, centurion."

Procus came to attention and saluted. "Generals."

*   *   *

Mucapor sipped his wine as Procus left, the man's body stiff as a newly-made *scutum*. He stared at the retreating back, licking his lips in contemplation as much as from the lingering taste of the sweet wine.

"Do you think he can be swayed?"

"It's possible." Mucapor did not look at his companion, continuing to stare at the tent flap. "But we'll need to sow a lot more seeds in that ground before he becomes our flower."

"Or plant one if he is not."

Mucapor turned to him in surprise, then laughed. "You begin to grow on me, Domitianus."

Domitianus returned the laugh. "Speaking of growing, have you found someone to use who's close to Aurelian?"

Mucapor ran his finger gently over the rim of his goblet. "I've thought about that very carefully. I think Mnestheus will do perfectly."

Domitianus reared back and raised both eyebrows. "By Adonis—or perhaps I should say Venus—couldn't you find better than that as a lover?"

"Such as you, perhaps?"

There was a long pause as the men stared at each other. Then

Domitianus dropped his gaze. Mucapor continued in an even tone.

"For his appearance, certainly. But not for information." He sipped his wine, studying his companion. "Everyone has alluring qualities if only you know how to choose them and use them correctly."

Domitianus nodded slightly. Both men kept their own thoughts as they finished the flask of wine.

*   *   *

Zenobia looked back over her shoulder. "How stands our forces?"

The Palmyrene army was again on the march. Zenobia, shaykhs Rasses and Sefer, Cassius Longinus, and General Zabdas rode at the head. The small group was closely followed by the queen's personal guard, commanded by her lieutenant, Amar.

Immediately behind the leaders came their major force, the cavalry. Khalid, second in command to Artabanes, rode as commander of the Palmyrene cavalry. Because each shaykh really commanded the horsemen from his own *Quabilah*, Khalid had also been put in charge of the *Musarkisus*, a special corps tasked with keeping the army supplied with horses. Next marched a fairly small infantry led by Auzaina, formerly aide-de-camp to Odaenathus. Centuries before, the Assyrians had found cavalry to be much more effective for quick desert warfare than foot soldiers. There was consequently no heavy infantry, which had once boasted soldiers with a helmet, body armor, boots, and a particular Assyrian innovation, a backpack. Now the infantry consisted mostly of archers who carried short but very powerful bows, and shield bearers who protected them and carried a lance in case of close fighting. The infantry were followed by the chariot corps, which was led by General Artabanes. These were mostly comprised of light chariots, as the expensive-to-build heavy chariots had been abandoned as too cumbersome for modern warfare. At the rear of the column came the supply camels, which carried five times the load of donkeys or horses yet required less water.

In a column that stretched for miles, they were all slowly moving down the coast of the Mediterranean. It was a much more pleasant journey than their trek through the desert to unite the tribes and recruit soldiers for the army.

"Perhaps thirty thousand." Rasses quirked his mouth in a semblance of a smile. "Most of the other *Quabilah* have joined us, or been coerced into the fold."

Sefer scowled. "They're all looking for loot, no doubt."

Zenobia's voice was stern. "There must be none of that. We're trying to reunite the kingdom, not pillage it." She returned to Rasses. "But others resist joining us?"

"Some of the less aggressive chieftains have, shall we say, wandered away," he said. "The settled tribes have all sent some men, but only as a token. They're not certain if they want to give offense to Rome."

"Tell their chieftains that Rome gives offense to us!" Zenobia softened her tone. "Longinus, send word that, if they don't commit more men to our army, we'll have to assume they are enemies to Assyria. We must have total control."

"Yes, my lady."

Zabdas, who had not said much for several days, finally allowed his doubts to show. "And that's where I begin to lose sight of what we're doing, if you'll excuse an old soldier." Zenobia gave no sign of invitation, but he continued anyhow. "Ebla, Aleppo, Ugarit, and Latakia have been taken, and even Busra ash Sham has sent obeisance. Yet now we move south to Byblos."

"And?"

Zabdas was not cowed by her gruff manner. He was aware that, while she had led the army in a few battles, this sort of empire building was way beyond her experience. In fact, it was unproven ground for all of them, and he could well understand her defensive attitude. Still, if he was to give her the support she needed, he would have to fully comprehend, if not necessarily agree with her plans. Even if she could not admit this in front of the others, he knew she was aware.

"I beg your pardon, my queen, but why did we not continue just a little farther north to Antakya? It's a rich city, and would have given us a buttress in Thrace when Aurelian turns his attention back to the east."

"That would have been an excellent gambit." She clearly wanted to give him credit for his knowledge of campaigns. "However, we must totally unify our own territories before we invade others. We need seaports to control trade, so Byblos and then Berytus are only logical."

Longinus made a chopping motion. "And we just happen to be cutting off the Roman trade and supply routes for when they do return in force."

Zabdas nodded. Even if the old Roman knew nothing of military matters, he was clearly well-versed in questions of logistics. He had taught areas of trade and other aspects of commerce to the young princes, and his knowledge must be respected.

"Exactly." Zenobia was pleased with the cooperative attitude of her general. "From Berytus, we'll continue south, and by the time we reach Jerusalem, all of Assyria will once again be united."

Sefer placed his hand on the hilt of his sword. "I long for the day when we meet the Romans sword to sword and let them know who the masters of this land are!"

"Patience, my lord." Zenobia once more surveyed her army. "That day shall come. But we must make certain we can support the claim before the question is asked."

*   *   *

As Domitianus had predicted, the news of their defeat produced consternation in Rome. As the Alamanni continued to move towards the defenseless capital, which had grown far beyond its old walls, the comfortable country life of many wealthy citizens turned into a mad flight for the supposed safety of the city. The Sibylline Books were consulted, and religious ceremonies performed to call for the gods' help. When news of this reached Aurelian, he told his oldest battle comrades that the citizens would do better to spend their money on new swords and shields than on animal sacrifices, which would be much more useful if given to their troops to eat.

Since his defeat at Placentia, Aurelian had rallied his men and pursued the Alamanni. The Roman army caught up with the marauders just inland of Fano, at the confluence of the Trebbia and the Po, the major waterway of northern Italia. Aurelian thought that had been a major tactical error on their part—or perhaps more the result of arrogance—and he intended to make them pay dearly.

Less than a league from where the Alamanni had turned to make their stand, the Roman army stood in ranks as Aurelian surveyed his legions from horseback. His elite troops had rejoined them, but they were still outnumbered by more than two-to-one. Nevertheless, they had a duty to perform, and it was his task to make them ready to once again face the foe that had inflicted such physical and psychological damage on them.

"Soldiers of Rome, I salute you!" He saluted, and the army saluted back as one man. "You know that Rome has conquered many nations."

Many soldiers cheered at this reminder of past glories.

"But we have always offered the palm, bringing those nations into the empire, offering their citizens the chance to become one of us." He swept his pointed finger from one end of the ranks to the other. "Some of you who serve under me now were once a conquered foe."

Some of the soldiers nodded in agreement, and there were a few low comments. Aurelian's horse wanted to prance, but he held it in check.

"Now Rome is in turn invaded by barbarians. The Sarmatians and the Vandals have been turned away, but the Goths and Juthungi tribes have joined forces to conquer us." Now he let his horse pace along the ranks, wanting every man to hear his voice rather than just having his message passed on. The eyes of every man followed him as he moved slowly. "However, if they are victorious, they shall not offer the palm. They took Placentia, and leveled it to the ground. They crossed the Po plain, sacking every village they passed. These barbarians have no interest in empire, only killing, looting, raping and burning. Today, this huge horde seeks to cross the river to threaten Rome itself. Today, we few stand in their way. We will make our stand at Fano. If we fall, Rome falls."

He reined in his horse and swept his gaze over their grim faces. His voice was intense, but not a shout. "Do you wish for Rome to fall?"

"No!" his soldiers shouted in unison.

"Our enemies fight like savages. Make no mistake, they are fierce, they have courage, and they will cut us down to the last man if we cannot be just as fierce. Then they will march to Rome. They will loot your houses." Aurelian's voice became more strident. "Will you let them loot?"

"No!" the legions shouted.

"They will rape your wives and daughters. Will you let them rape?"

"NO!"

"They will dash the heads of your babies on the walls of your own homes. Will you let them slaughter?"

"NO!"

His voice became more ominous, even more demanding. "They will burn Rome to the ground. Will you let them burn?"

"NO!" thundered the soldiers of Rome.

Aurelian drew his sword. "Then we must not fail. We must fight to the death." He raised his sword and held it aloft. "Victory or death!"

The soldiers drew their swords and raised them.

"Victory or death!"

"Victory or death!" Aurelian thrust his sword into the air.

"Victory or death!" they chorused, mimicking his gesture.

"Then let us march to victory!"

"TO VICTORY!"

Aurelian hoped the invaders could hear that peal of thunder, which would make them tremble.

*   *   *

The Roman infantry advanced in its typical assault formation. The legionaries walked in a close, open-order formation behind the protection of their shields. Their archers followed behind the infantry; the cavalry would be almost useless in the battle until the enemy was well-engaged, as the rivers prevented them from circling around.

When the Alamanni began firing their bows and slings, the legionaries raised their *scuta* into an overlapping formation: the *testudo*, or tortoise. A rectangular, curved shield about two-and-a-half feet wide and four feet long, a *scutum* was made from two planks of wood glued together and secured by an iron boss in the center; the outside was canvas and leather, and the edges bound in iron. These strong shields formed a mutually-supportive roof and walls that could stop large boulders during a siege. The Roman archers returned fire as best they could. When they got within a hundred feet, the Alamanni once more flung their spears and *francisca*, but the *testudo* came up once again, and no casualties were suffered. As soon as the hail of weapons ceased, the soldiers lowered their shields and threw their javelins at the enemy. As the Alamanni protected themselves with their smaller shields from the javelins and arrows, the legionaries drew swords and charged at a dead run. The loose wedge battered into the horde with the boss of their shields and used their short swords to stab around the edges of the *scuta*, fighting from a protected posture.

This time it was the barbarians who were startled by the disciplined attack of the Romans. Stunned by the ruthless efficiency of an army they had easily defeated only a few months before, the front ranks of the Germanic line was forced to give way. As he saw the Alamanni milling in confusion and their rear ranks pinned against the river, Aurelian gave his signal corps a wave. A blast of trumpets warned the infantry that the *lituus* had been waved to signal the cavalry. The legionaries made way as their horses charged into the fray, again shocking and confusing the enemy. As those bearing the brunt of the charge tried to run, many of the Alamanni in the rear were forced back into the river and drowned. Within an hour, the battle became a rout.

Due to their sheer numbers, at least half of the Goths and Juthungi managed to escape. They fled towards Macedonia, but were harassed all along their route by the Roman cavalry. Now the Alamanni were the weary and starved army. The Roman legions methodically pursued and surrounded the survivors at Mount Haemus. After another bloody battle, some of the invaders escaped again. They were pursued until they either surrendered or died.

Emperor Aurelian sent word that the Alamanni had been soundly defeated. Having escaped disaster, all of Rome blessed his name, and great celebrations raged throughout the city.

CHAPTER NINE

Zenobia's eyes swept the terrain from the vantage point of her saddle. "What's the lay of the land here?" She glanced sideways at her new prime minister.

"We stand on the border of the Sinai, my queen." Longinus gestured as he spoke. "Arabia stands straight ahead. Egypt lies just to the southwest around the sea."

Zenobia nodded, pleased. She decided she'd had enough of the smell of salt in her nostrils. It had been a long campaign, and it was good to get back to the desert.

Her army had marched to Emesa, still a staunchly Roman city, where it had met strong resistance. However, the few Roman soldiers remaining after Aurelian had taken his army back to Italia were not enough to challenge her mighty multitudes. Leaving her own garrison behind, she had then marched north to Hamath, Ebla and Aleppo, and from there headed west to the sea to secure all of the seaports along the Mediterranean coast.

In the midst of a summer meant to fry men's soles, the trek back south had brought welcome relief. There had been long stretches of beaches invitingly offering soft, white sand and the clear blue sea and green mountains. These had been interspersed with low mountains covered with pine and oak trees, their slopes reaching down to touch the shore. From Antakya, Zenobia's forces had made their way through Ugarit, Tripolis, Byblos, Sidon, and finally to Tyre, where fabled Alexander had been forced to mount a terrible siege. But Tyre, as had all the Assyrian cities except Emesa, had welcomed Zenobia as their rightful queen. Taking a page out of the Roman handbook on empire, Zenobia had offered amnesty to all. She reminded the city elders that they were of Phoenice first and Rome a distant second. Whether they secretly disagreed with her or happily complied, they had quickly come back into the fold.

Then her growing ranks, swelled by many young men from the

cities seeking adventure and glory—along with possible riches—had turned slightly inland to Hasor and into the land of Canaan, finally reaching Jerusalem. Whereas Gaza had also defied Alexander, that city immediately sent word that it would be faithful to the new ruler of Assyria.

The scenery and the cooler weather had been a pleasant novelty for several months, but now the sea bored her. And, as even more long months dragged by since they had marched out of those welcome gates of home, the adventure had lost much of its charm. She missed the true desert, the long, flat expanses that seemed so barren to outsiders. She missed Palmyra, and the comfort of her own bed. But most of all she missed Vaballathus, whom she had left in the care of Nobonidus Zohan.

At the thought of her son, Zenobia compressed her mouth and swished her riding crop. Her horse's ears twitched at the sudden sound, which perhaps reminded him of the angry buzzing of a large fly, but he did not break his steady stride.

It had not been a mere sop to the man's ego: when she told Zohan that Longinus was to be her prime minister, Zenobia explained that the Roman must travel with the army to be able to give them his advice. Zohan was not only charged with the safety of his new king, but with the management of the city. In her absence, his new titles were Lord Protector of Palmyra and Governor of the King's Person. Zohan had been very pleased with his new position, and the fact that he could remain comfortably within the city walls while others went out to rebuild the Assyrian empire.

After Jerusalem, they had continued south. Zenobia knew they must be approaching the border of the old territories, before the Greeks and Romans had come in conquest. Riding slowly along in the vanguard of the army, she looked around.

Zenobia reined in her horse, the news abruptly sinking in. "Then that's it? Assyria is mine?"

When she stopped, so did her escort. Like an ox realizing he must bring his lumbering body to a halt, the army behind them gradually did the same.

Auzaina grinned broadly. "Yes, my queen. Even the cities we bypassed sent word they have joined us. Some sent men, as you know, but others sent vital supplies."

Zenobia sat mutely in acceptance of this information. Because an army was only as healthy as the food and water they carried, Auzaina had been greatly worried about the rapid growth of their forces. An army normally received supplies from the friendly cities it passed, or from the enemy cities it sacked. Not wanting to plunder so much as food, her entire command was grateful for all of the contributions. So far, it had been easy. Zenobia knew that it would become much more difficult once they crossed out of the Phoenician lands.

"Shall we continue south to Arabia?"

Zenobia could hear the anxiety in Auzaina's voice, worried he would have to struggle to find supplies in hostile territory. She quickly reassured him. "There's nothing in Arabia but desert, camels and the endlessly burning sun."

Rasses raised a warning hand. "And the Tanukh. They could pose a threat at our rear."

Normally fiercely independent, the nomad Arab tribes had formed a federation due to the threat of the Sassanid Persians and now the Palmyrene Empire. Fearing an invasion by her growing army, they might well launch an attack from the rear as she marched her forces into Egypt.

"That's true." Zenobia swept her hand outward, toward the east. "We'll leave ten thousand of our infantry to make a slow foray east to defend our rear. We'll go west with the remainder."

"But the Roman garrisons in Egypt?" Zabdas leaned forward in his saddle. "They're dangerous. Especially if we split our forces. Why not go back north to Byzantium in Thrace?"

"We already decided that's too close to Aurelian's legions fighting in northern Italia," Sefer reminded him.

"But if we invade Egypt, we'll be in open revolt from Rome. Why not Babylon and then into Persia, your natural enemy?"

Zenobia frowned. Longinus had subtly voiced his opinion before, but now that it had come to the point, his anxiety must be overriding his normally passive nature. Until that moment, everything had been focused on reuniting the Phoenician Empire, not about what would happen after that was accomplished.

"Yes." Rasses bent forward to pat the neck of his horse. "There's a lot more wealth to be found in Persia than what remains in Egypt. The Romans have already looted most of Cleopatra's ancient treasures, or they've been buried in those stone mausoleums."

"Shapur and his treasures are not going anywhere soon."

"I agree with you, my lady," Sefer said. "However, I'm worried about the Roman weapons and tactics, even though their force is small."

It seemed that, as they stood on the brink of the precipice, Longinus' anxiety was beginning to affect some of her other commanders. She must eliminate this indecision at once.

"Cassius Longinus, what do your native countrymen call the land of my ancestors?"

"You mean the Two Lands, my lady?"

She tried to curb her impatience. "Think food."

"Oh." Longinus made his elaborate shoulder shrug. "They call it the breadbasket, because so much of Rome's grain comes from the fertile lands bordering the Nile."

"Exactly. And if we are ever to have a chance of challenging the Empire, we must weaken it first in the best manner we can." Zenobia could see the light dawning in their faces, but she had to drive her point home. "General Zabdas, could we defeat those garrisons?"

Zabdas stroked his chin. "Yes, I suppose so. As Shaykh Sefer says, those damned tactics they use present a problem. We certainly have numbers on them. Not a full legion in either Memphis or Alexandria, so we're told. On the other hand...." He rubbed his chin again.

"Yes?"

Zabdas' voice became more decisive. "You're right about the grain. So, if you're determined to take on Rome, then you'd be better off getting rid of those garrisons right now. When Aurelian comes marching back to say hello, you don't want them nipping at your heels as you try to meet a full army from the front."

Artabanes bobbed his head. "An excellent point, Zabdas."

"Indeed, it is. And what of you, General Artabanes? Do you think your chariots and cavalry could be a match for the Romans?"

Artabanes cocked his head to the side. "Of course we could defeat them. We're four times as strong as we were a couple of years ago. However, I hate to think of the losses we'd suffer."

"Why is that?" Zenobia was genuinely curious. On the occasions she had led the Palmyrene army into battle, they had been skirmishes against fairly small bands of invaders. Odaenathus had always led the army against the might of Persia, being much more knowledgeable and experienced. Consequently, her forays had never been with a combined force, and she had never personally witnessed the strength of the Roman legions.

She turned in the direction of Longinus, the only person present who had studied the history and manner of Roman warfare, although he had never served in the military.

Longinus stroked his long, thin neck. He abruptly dismounted. "Most of the time, chariots can plow right through foot soldiers. But the Roman legions have long, wide, and very thick shields they use as a wall."

An excellent instructor in most subjects, Longinus used his hands and body effectively to pantomime his words. Shaykhs Rasses and Sefer, who had never witnessed Roman battle tactics, paid careful attention. The other officers had all been in battles with their Roman allies, but they had been too busy to actually watch the legions in action, and were happy to listen as well.

"If chariots are bearing down the *centuria*, or even an entire *cohort* of six *centuriae*, forms a wall." He spread his arms wide and high. "The second rank leans its shields forward, the front rank bends down and uses that as a reinforcement for their shields." Longinus crouched and leaned forward. "The chariots either bounce off or fly over the shields. It's a variation on their 'tortoise' formation. It crushes a few men, but the rest can then butcher the chariots. Either way, they're so disciplined that the ranks behind immediately step in if one of the front two is cut down, and they maintain a virtual wall against the enemy." He stood upright again and steepled his fingers, then split his hands apart. "Sometimes the cohort simply divides into *contubernium*, their 'tent units' of eight men, and let the chariots pass through individually. The *contubernium* closes in on the chariots that go in between and hack them down." With that, he gave a chop with his right hand.

"What about cavalry instead of chariots?" asked Sefer.

"Ah. Well, basically the same thing. They present their javelins as short spears through the shield wall, aiming for the legs of the horses."

"I've seen this tactic." Artabanes twisted his mouth at the remembrance. "It's incredibly effective. Rasses is right; we'd need some kind of miracle to defeat them before they could extract their toll."

"A miracle." Zenobia looked at each of her generals. "Such as some sort of new tactic?"

Auzaina raised his eyebrows. "A new tactic? Do you have something, Artabanes?"

Artabanes laughed shortly. "Not that I'm aware of."

Zabdas just stared at her.

"Then perhaps we'll have to think of something. Because, as far as I'm concerned, there's only one thing to do. We invade Egypt."

*   *   *

Zenobia's army approached Memphis, still several days' march away. In the distance, a cloud of dust announced another group moving toward them, although more of a mote when compared with the billowing dust raised by their own force.

Sefer looked at Zabdas. "Perhaps the legion comes out to meet us."

Zabdas grunted. "Probably think they have a better chance out in the open."

Zenobia considered what she had learned about the home of her ancestors. For centuries, Memphis had been the capital of Egypt. As the city began to lose importance, many of the great stones used in its buildings and surrounding wall were moved some fifteen miles up the Nile to the newly emerging city of Per-hapi-on. Consequently, neither city was well-protected by sturdy walls. Closer to the Mediterranean, Memphis was where the Romans collected most of their taxes in Egypt, as well as centering their grain storage in Memphis and nearby Al-Jizah. Well, they would soon find out.

As the two armies halted at a distance, a chariot with a standard bearer and an officer wearing fancy armor rode towards Zenobia's army. The chariot approached at a leisurely pace.

Zabdas turned toward Longinus with a quizzical expression. "That's not a Roman standard."

"No. I don't recognize it."

Zenobia scrutinized the standard as it came closer. "The markings are Egyptian."

"But with no imperial crest to mark the unit." Longinus stroked his neck. "Very strange."

Zenobia kicked the flanks of her horse lightly. Zabdas, Artabanes, Rasses, Sefer, and Longinus followed her to meet the approaching vehicle, accompanied by Auzaina and Zenobia's personal guard. Each side stopped when they were half a dozen paces apart. No salutes were given.

"Greetings." The man spoke in Egyptian, although he was wearing the armor of a Roman officer. "I have heard that Zenobia, widow to Odaenathus, brings an army against the city of Memphis."

Zenobia looked at him coldly. "I'm Zenobia. And you are?"

The man stepped down from the chariot, walked closer to them and bowed.

"I am Decurio Timagenes, appointed by the Roman prefect of Egypt, Tenagino Probus, as commander of the cavalry and liaison to the Egyptian people in Alexandria."

"That must be a singular honor, as I was not aware any Egyptians had been given such a rank by the tyrants who rule your land."

A hard look came over Timagenes' face, and he gave a slight bow. "You are quite correct, Queen Zenobia. I was singled out because Probus believed I was loyal to Rome and would do my best to help keep my people in their subjugation."

"I see." Zenobia looked at him coldly for several seconds. The man did not flinch under her scrutiny. "I presume you speak Latin, in such a case?"

"I do indeed, my lady." He spoke in formal Latin, not the vulgar form she had expected. He smiled. "I suspect you wish for your officers to understand our conversation?"

Zenobia was impressed by his discernment, but did not let that influence her attitude towards this unknown entity. She switched to the same language. "Have you and your—" Zenobia made a deprecatory wave of her hand toward his small force, not even a full legion, "your army been sent to stop us, Decurio Timagenes?"

"I have not, my lady."

Zabdas interrupted impatiently. "Then why are you here?"

Timagenes looked at Zabdas, then back toward Zenobia. He seemed to have dismissed Zabdas with that look.

"It is known that my lady Zenobia is of Egyptian birth. It is even rumored that she is descended from the great Cleopatra, may beneficent Ra light her path through the underworld for eternity."

Zenobia gave a slight nod. "That is true."

Timagenes drew his sword, knelt down, and offered it in both hands.

"Then, my lady, if you are indeed a daughter of Cleopatra, I have come to offer you my allegiance and my sword."

"That's a most generous offer." Zenobia made no move to take the sword. Her instincts told her the man sounded sincere, but she had been fooled by one man already. "Why would you betray your Roman masters, Timagenes?"

"For the same reason you would, my lady. Because they are not my masters." Timagenes leaned to the side and spat in the sand. "I chafe under the yoke of Roman slavery, as you must have done yourself. I would willingly spill my blood in this sand to drive them from our common land."

"And all of your men feel the same?"

"My personal guard is loyal to me. Many of the soldiers conscripted into the general army came to join us when they heard a liberator was on her way."

Zenobia felt torn, wanting to believe in the sincerity of this man who shared a common blood, but knowing she should remain cautious for the sake of those who depended on her good judgment. What if he had been sent to lead them into a trap?

Zenobia looked at Zabdas. He shrugged.

Zabdas switched to Assyrian. "He knows the lay of the land. And he could certainly help us know the defenses and the tactics of this Probus, my queen."

Zenobia felt her eyebrows lift. That was a pleasing thought—but not proof. She addressed Timagenes in Latin once more. "Tell us of this Probus."

"Admiral Probus was sent from Rome to clear the sea of pirates. When we received word of your approach, he began to gather a great force of Romans, Egyptians and Africans as well. That is when I decided to join you. By now, they will be marching toward Memphis. He is well trained in both sea and land warfare. It will be difficult to expel them from Egypt."

Zenobia lightly stroked the mane of her horse. "But you would tell us his strength and location, as well as help us with tactics to defeat him?"

"It would be a pleasure."

"And you will swear your loyalty toward myself and Palmyra, Timagenes?"

"To be truthful, I care nothing for Palmyra. But, so long as you seek to remove the Romans from our motherland, I swear my allegiance."

Above everything the man had said, this struck her as true. And to have an Egyptian in charge after they had left, and bound to her completely….

"And would you desire to take charge of an Egyptian army here after we had returned to Assyria, serving in my name?"

Timagenes looked directly into her eyes, with no hint of guile. "If that is your wish, majesty. What I desire is to have Egypt once more in the hands of the descendants of the great pharaohs."

She lifted her hand in the air as though to raise him up with the gesture. "Then rise…General Timagenes. We welcome your sword and the allegiance of your men."

Timagenes rose eagerly to his feet and turned to shout towards his men. "As promised when she took the asp to her bosom, Queen

Cleopatra has returned to cleanse our land from the scourge of the Romans!"

His men shouted and waved their swords. The two forces slowly came together to explore their new friendship.

"So, perhaps great Malak-bel heard my prayers and has granted us our miracle."

Zenobia spoke to no one in particular, but both Zabdas and Artabanes nodded at her words.

*   *   *

General Artabanes waited impatiently, eager to have the action begin and test out this new tactic. The signal pennant hung slack, with no breeze to expose the dragon and winged disk, the symbol of Ashur, foremost in the Assyrian pantheon and god of earth and war. It was carried by a rider who sat next to Zenobia as the Palmyrene army faced the Roman garrison on the plains outside of Memphis.

General Timagenes had predicted their foe would choose to meet them in the open where their formations could give them more protection than the incomplete city walls. Based on this, General Zabdas had planned a strategy that would minimize their own losses. As he surveyed the legionaires standing stolidly in their ranks, Artabanes grunted in satisfaction. It was going exactly as planned.

The Roman banners also hung limply, but there was no need to identify them. Timagenes had given a complete report. The legion was clearly short of its usual six thousand men and did not have the small cavalry that normally supported a legion, but they still presented a brave and formidable front to the much larger army.

Artabanes permitted himself a small smile as Zabdas lifted a hand. Led by General Timagenes, with Auzaina acting as his second-in-command, the Palmyrene infantry marched forward, but stopped well short of bow range. Zabdas gave another signal; this was the moment Artabanes had waited for. The herald gave a blast of his horn, and Artabanes lifted his arm into the air and thrust it forward, his finger pointing toward the city and its defenders. Up to full speed within moments, the heavy carriages raced in a single line down the left side of the infantry formation. The Roman legion immediately formed the variation of the tortoise that Longinus had described.

Instead of the usual charge toward the center to split the ranks, General Artabanes led the chariots toward the right flank of the Roman formation. The few Roman bowmen behind the lines loosed at them. Either confused by the unusual attack or hampered by the angle, most of their arrows missed.

The Romans shifted their formation under the assumption the chariots meant to circle them. Having waited for this moment, Artabanes shouted to his driver. The speeding chariot veered sharply to the right, followed in turn by all the others. The maneuver exposed a heavy sword that had been tightly strapped to a staff, which was in turn heavily lashed to the undercarriage of each chariot. Now running parallel to the formation, the highly-sharpened swords scythed into the *scuta*. The first few swords were blunted by the iron bands around the Roman shields. But the weight and speed of the heavy chariots, and the repeated blows from the sharpened swords, quickly began to take their toll. Legionaries flew sideways from the power of the violent attack, screaming in agony. Many of the blows cut through the protective wall and through the bodies of the Romans.

One chariot after the other crashed into the wall of men and shields, but the lines held. One defender after the other stepped up to take the place of their fallen comrades, but they were in turn cut down. When the last heavy chariot passed beyond the point of attack, two sharp blasts of the herald's horn sounded. The front ranks of the Palmyrene infantry stepped aside to expose archers, who fired into the staggering legionaries. These were well trained troops, and they quickly stepped around their dead and wounded comrades and reformed into a tortoise.

The archers were a diversion. The heavy chariots—minus two that had been toppled and another half dozen whose cutting blades had been snapped off—circled for another run. When they began their approach toward the Roman formation, the archers were given the signal to cease fire. Again the heavy chariots thundered down the ranks of the legionaries, their dulled blades not doing as much damage. But it was enough. After the second pass, nearly two-thirds of the *scuta* had been destroyed or badly damaged, and more than a hundred bodies writhed or lay inertly on the ground, mixing their blood with the thirsty sand. As the survivors tried to regroup, the arrows rained down on them once more.

Now the light chariots rushed at the Romans and attacked both flanks with bows and spears. Without their shields to provide covering, many of the helpless defenders were cut down. Another signal of the herald's horn brought the hail of arrows to a halt, and the light chariots withdrew. Before the Romans could regain their wits, the cavalry charged in using spears and swords to add to the slaughter. Only when the battle was obviously a rout was the infantry allowed to finish off any survivors, more to give them a hand in the victory than because they were needed. Timagenes did not partake in the butchery, preferring to rejoin the other commanders. When the infantry moved in, Artabanes' chariot broke away from his men and also rode back to the watching staff.

"A great victory, my queen!" Artabanes gave a salute to Timagenes. "A brilliant stratagem, General Timagenes."

Timagenes only nodded his head. He did not look pleased.

Longinus heaved a great sign. "Yes. But a pity so many brave Romans had to be slaughtered."

"Since Odaenathus died, I have no more pity for any Roman." At his stricken look, the queen softened her tone. "Except you, of course."

Longinus bowed his head. "Yes, my lady."

"Now are we ready to march back north?" Rasses did not sound very hopeful.

"We continue to Alexandria." Zenobia's blazing eyes defied any of her officers to contradict her. "Once we've taken that, we'll see about the rest of Rome's former Eastern Empire."

CHAPTER TEN

Mnestheus had no idea why he would be summoned to the tent of General Mucapor, and so late at night. How could he have offended? He gulped twice before he entered, and tried to be as silent as a mouse worried that the kitchen cat would notice. The general lounged on a divan, a cup of wine held carelessly in his hand. Mnestheus' eyes widened as he saw the general's beautiful, flowing robe—a pure white, with purple piping at the shoulders and gold edging on the sleeves and hem—which flattered the younger man's long, muscular body. He was shocked at this informality, but managed to keep any consternation from his voice.

"You sent for me, General?"

Mucapor waved his wine cup vaguely in the air. "Ah, Mnestheus. Welcome. I didn't send for you, I invited you to come visit me. Relax."

"Why, thank you!" Mnestheus had to keep himself from giggling in his nervousness. "I'm flattered. I didn't even know you would have noticed me, General."

"Please, call me Bicius. Some wine?" Mucapor motioned toward a flask of wine on a table.

"Wine?" Mnestheus goggled at his host. It was inconceivable that the general was actually offering to share wine with him.

"Yes. Why don't you pour some more for me, as well."

"Certainly. Um, thank you."

Mnestheus poured a small amount of wine in a goblet by the flask, then refilled Mucapor's goblet. They were probably silver; not wooden cups, as Aurelian carried in his traveling gear. Mucapor sat up and looked at the space beside him, a clear invitation to sit down. Mnestheus gave a tentative smile and sat on the very edge of the divan. They both sipped at their wine. Mnestheus noticed that his hand was shaking, and made an effort to make it stop.

"I've noticed you for quite a while, Mnestheus."

Mnestheus almost choked on his wine. He made certain his mouth was clear, so he would not spit any wine on the general's lovely robe, before he spoke. "Oh, well, certainly." He chuckled nervously. "You see me frequently in the emperor's tent."

"Ah, but he's gone off to Rome to receive even more great honors, hasn't he?"

"Yes. Well deserved honors."

Mucapor did not respond to that comment.

After their victory at Fano, the Roman army pursued the Alamanni through Lombardy. Aurelian closed the passes in the Alps, and at last encircled the invaders near Pavia. After several bloody battles, the Alamanni army was destroyed. On receiving his report, the senate sent word that Rome would hold a triumph at which Aurelian would receive the title *Germanicus Maximus*. Ordered to return immediately, Aurelian had ridden back to Rome with only one *centuria* of the Praetorian Guard. Mucapor was now tasked with marching the army back to the capital

"I thought now might be a good time for us to...well, spend time together."

Mnestheus realized that his lower his jaw was hanging down, and he quickly snapped it shut. He swallowed half his wine, barely managing not to cough. "But, I always thought—well, I'm a simple scribe, and you are so...powerful." In this setting, he could not help but dare to offer more. "And so handsome." Embarrassed, Mnestheus took another sip of wine.

"Nonsense!" Mucapor raised his hand in an uplifting gesture. "I don't think there's anything simple about you. But I want to learn so much more." He leaned toward his guest. "Please, tell me about yourself."

Mnestheus gulped down the rest of his wine. He gave Mucapor a tentative smile, who returned it like a satisfied cat.

* * *

"A long day, brother." Emperor Gallienus plopped his stocky body on a divan. He wore a beautiful *paludamentum*, but the excellent cut did little to hide his bulky figure. "I hope you enjoyed your triumph."

Aurelian gratefully sat down on a separate divan. He was surprised at how tired he was. It seemed much less taxing to battle while wearing full armor than to stand and smile and wave to the adoring throng. To honor Gallienus, Aurelian was dressed in the imperial robe he had been given by his benefactor. Each time he wore the garment, it reminded him of that first evening he had spent in Zenobia's company.

"Very impressive, Gallienus. I thank you and the senate for the honor, as well as the new title."

They were in the lounging chamber of Gallienus' palace in Rome. The furniture was sturdy and comfortable, the decorations few but tasteful. After the floods of people and constant din of the triumph, the room was quiet and calming. A servant entered and served them wine, then stood quietly in a corner.

"Don't thank me." Gallienus snorted. "The senate loves to come up with shit like that. Me, I'd reward you by raising taxes so you could have another legion to do their dirty work." He took a gulp of his wine. He flipped a hand in the air as though dismissing any thought of the loathed senate. "Anyhow, nothing more than you deserve."

Aurelian gave a small smile. "Then I shall thank each one of them tomorrow." He took a sip of his own wine, savoring the slightly sweet, full body of the liquid. He rarely enjoyed such luxuries out in the field.

"You'll have a hell of a time doing that." Gallienus slapped a meaty thigh. "I'll be frank with you, Rome was trembling. Until you stopped them at Fano, we were certain we'd be up to our arsses in barbarians. Half the senate was already in the country, and others were packing up right 'til we got word you'd finally routed them at Pavia. Not all have returned yet. Damned cowards."

"Don't be too harsh, Gallienus. Few of them were soldiers, after all."

"Soldiers!" Gallienus laughed loudly, reminding Aurelian of a warhorse neighing just before a battle. Then the older man drank down the rest of his wine. He held his cup out, and the servant moved silently to fill it. "Most of them are coddled, corpulent old men who complain when they have to exert themselves to beat their servants. They disgust me."

"But they keep us in power, brother, simply because we're willing to fight the wars that allow them to stay home safe and stout."

Gallienus laughed again. "Damn me, but you're right!" He raised his cup in a toast. "Here's to all the fat old buggerers who give us titles because we keep them safe."

Aurelian lifted his cup in the toast. There was silence as they drank. Then Aurelian sighed.

"Anyhow, I shall be glad to get back to my own part of the empire. I've heard...disturbing rumors of what Zenobia is doing in the east."

"Disturbing rumors!" Gallienus laughed again, but this time it was harsh, not his normal loud, equine sound. "Ah, you have been out in the field for too long, brother."

Having reclined onto his divan, Aurelian now sat up straight. "Then tell me."

"Zenobia's united all of Assyria and raised a rather large army. She's made expeditions into Anatolia as far as Ankara and Chalcedon, then she went south and conquered as far as Alexandria."

Aurelian leaped to his feet. Some of his wine sloshed to the floor, but he paid it no heed. "Alexandria! But what about Admiral Probus? He has his fleet and a good sized local army."

Gallienus scowled. "Probus was betrayed by Timagenes, an Egyptian officer he'd appointed to help control the locals in Alexandria. Combined, Zenobia's forces captured the city and beheaded Probus."

Aurelian paced like a lion without a tail to lash. "By all the gods...."

"There's more." Gallienus waited until Aurelian stood still and faced him. "Zenobia then proclaimed herself Queen of Egypt. Now she's threatening all our trade routes in the east. My reports say she's heading for Persia next." Gallienus made a sound of contempt at the back of his throat. "It seems she's left Timagenes behind with an army to hold her 'new territories'."

Aurelian swayed slightly, his breathing heavy and his fists clenched. "Damn the woman! And I thought...."

"Yes?"

"I thought...." Aurelian's face became more wary, and his fists unclenched. "I thought that Zenobia was loyal to Rome. I would have never thought her capable of this."

"A woman, I know. It's hard to believe." Gallienus shook his head. "It must be that old Roman she's got as an adviser who's pulling all the strings."

Aurelian looked at him with incredulity. "Cassius Longinus?" He was about to correct his fellow emperor, but Gallienus gave him no chance.

"Whomever." Gallienus waved his hand dismissively. "At any rate, all those reports have been confirmed."

Aurelian whirled and pointed at the servant. "My cloak!"

The servant immediately left the room.

"What's the hurry?"

Aurelian turned back to the older man. He couldn't tell if the sound in his brother emperor's voice was sarcasm or anger. The worst thing would be to be taken for a fool. "I must get back. There's not a moment to lose."

Gallienus shook his head. "I'm afraid not, brother. Not yet, at least."

Aurelian moved to stand in front of him. He looked down almost menacingly, but his taut voice remained low. "And why not?"

Gallienus frowned. "Come, sit, sit. This is not an argument. We emperors must stick together, brother."

Aurelian exhaled slowly. Then he turned back to the divan and sat rigidly, his hands on his knees. The servant returned carrying the cloak and a cloth. As he saw Aurelian sitting, he put the cloak over another divan, then poured them both more wine. Aurelian reluctantly took it and sipped. The servant used the cloth to mop up the spilled wine, then faded into the background They drank in silence for a moment.

Gallienus frowned into his cup. "I need you to fight the invaders from the west."

"From the west? But General Tetricus is charged with keeping the peace there."

"Humph. Unfortunately, that dog Tetricus is the problem. He's declared himself the 'Gallic Emperor', promising to free Britannica from our rule. He's landed an army on the continent and he's marching toward Paris."

Aurelian shook his head, bemused by the entire situation. "No offense, brother, but Rome and the west are your empire. I need to worry about mine."

"I think not," Gallienus said bluntly. "At least Zenobia seems to be sticking to her home territory. In fact, it might be a good thing if she can conquer all of those damn tribes that keep nipping at our heels like rats in a granary. That way, when you do get back to defeat her, you'll find your empire a lot easier to manage."

Aurelian strove to hide his irritation. "Gallienus, I know how much I owe you, but why can't you take your own legions against Tetricus?"

"Tetricus is actually the lesser of our worries. My spies tell me all he really wants is a cozy estate, a fancy title and a nice income, and he'll abandon his pretensions and his primitive 'Gallic Empire' quicker than you can dump a turd in a pot. We need to show that we're ready to fight him first. No, there are other slimy termites who are trying to eat our house right out from under us."

"Such as?"

Gallienus spoke slowly, enunciating each syllable of the name as though he were spitting. "Such as Marcus Claudius Tacitus."

Aurelian beetled his brows together. "Tacitus? But he's only a consul. Why would the senate even consider him?"

"Because he's one of them. Old family. Rich. Fat. And he'll lick their behinds like neither of us would ever think of. If you were to go marching off east and I went to bring Tetricus to heel, guess what would happen while we were both off playing soldier?"

"You're certain of this?"

"And more." Gallienus held up his goblet, and the servant refilled it. "Look, I can give you a couple of legions so you can make things easier, but I need most of my army to stay right here and keep the dogs at bay. For both our sakes, Aurelian."

Aurelian screwed his face up as though at a bitter taste, and then sighed again. "Yes. I see."

"Incidentally, the legions I had in mind are led by Marcus Aurelius Probus. A damn good general. He was also modestly born, and made a tribune by my father."

"Any relation?"

"Perhaps distantly; I did not know the family well."

"Well, if you recommend him, then I'm sure he's fine. I'll leave my men here to rest and take yours against Tetricus."

Gallienus stood and went to clap him on the shoulder.

"I knew I could count on you, brother!"

They clinked cups, Aurelian not nearly as enthusiastically as Gallienus. Obviously the cheerful sound he had heard in Gallienus' voice was more about the man's own situation than his. Aurelian was relieved to know Gallienus did not think less of him because of that damned woman. He drank and forced a smile to his face.

"Of course you can."

Gallienus nodded. "First we bring the damn hounds to heel." His voice became a growl. "Then you can go take care of the bitch."

*   *   *

Mindful of Gallienus' desire for haste, Aurelian rode out to meet his advancing army. As soon as he arrived, he began preparations for his campaign to Gaul. That evening, Aurelian stood in his tent dictating a letter to Mnestheus. He took a sip of wine, with a brief thought to the difference between the taste of the wine Gallienus had served. Then he resumed his instruction.

"The coin shall have the phrase 'harmony between the soldiers' inscribed on it around the eagle. On the other side it shall have the phrase 'emperor of all the east' encircling my likeness."

Aurelian's back was to the tent entrance when he heard Mucapor and Domitianus enter. Mnestheus looked up from his writing and cleared his throat as Aurelian turned to face his generals.

"You sent for us, Caesar?" Mucapor exchanged a look with Mnestheus, who blushed and looked back down at his parchment.

"What? Oh, yes." Aurelian held up a hand to indicate a pause. "One moment, Mnestheus. Generals, I have been given the honor by Emperor Gallienus to march west to subdue an uprising in the Gallic Empire."

"Shall I prepare the troops to march, Caesar?"

"No, Domitianus. They've had some tough campaigns over the last few years and deserve a rest. Gallienus has given me a couple of his legions, and that should be enough to handle that riff-raff. However, I'm leaving you in charge of our men. When you get back to Rome, give them leave as you see fit. Limit drilling to practice weapons exercises."

"Yes, Caesar." Domitianus saluted.

"Shall I be going with you, then?"

Aurelian gave a brief shake of his head. "No. I've got an assignment for you as well, Mucapor. First, I want you to go to the mint of Mediolanum. You're to have a bag of silver *antoniniani* minted. I'm giving Mnestheus instructions now on the details. And tell that bandit Felicissimus he'd better not debase these coins. I want actual silver, not something reduced to a scrap of silver-plated copper."

"Felicissimus!" Disgust dripped from the tongue of Domitianus.

Aurelian gave a wry smile. The financial minister of the state treasury had a bad reputation throughout the legions for providing their pay in coins that were alloyed far below their face value. He was universally hated by all legionaires, no matter their rank.

"I'll deliver that message with pleasure, Caesar." Mucapor sneered his contempt. "That man has far too great a sense of his own importance as the mint master. And what shall I do with the coins?"

"I want you to take the Praetorian Guard to Palmyra. No doubt you've heard of Zenobia's conquests in Assyria and Egypt. Remind her of her vows to Rome. Tell her this will be her last chance to be loyal to the empire." Aurelian hesitated for a moment, then added: "And to me."

"I shall be even more pleased to deliver that message, Caesar."

"Yes. As I recall from that banquet, I doubt you'll be intimidated by Zenobia."

"Not a chance."

Aurelian stared at his subordinate for a moment, wanting to wipe that smug look from Mucapor's face. He decided this was not the time to pursue the matter. "Very well, generals, you have your orders."

They both saluted. Mucapor once again exchanged a glance with Mnestheus before leaving the tent. Aurelian briefly wondered what that was all about, but had more important matters to finish before departing on his new mission.

"Now, Mnestheus, where were we?"

CHAPTER ELEVEN

It was a beautiful day in late spring, and the palace garden was in full bloom. A small group of people enjoyed the weather, the vibrant colors of the trees and flowers, the acidic and fragrant aromas that competed in the warm air, and the company of each other. They also enjoyed the mock battle being waged.

Zenobia and Vaballathus knocked wooden swords against one another. Nearly nine years old now, her son had grown tremendously. Zenobia smiled to see how seriously he took his practice. Several of the queen's guards, including their lieutenant, Amar, shouted instructions to the boy as they watched, their encouragement mixed with laughter.

Longinus entered from the palace and stood quietly off to the side. Zenobia tried to ignore her prime minister as she continued the mock duel, but the doleful expression took her back to the time when he had always had a slight smile on his pleasant features. Without any conscious intent, she let her gaze rest on the bemused face of Longinus.

Her attention returned to where it should have been just in time. Vaballathus was about to whack her across the ribs, not having realized his mother had stopped play-fighting and was looking elsewhere. He swung his weapon hard, and Zenobia managed to pivot away, partially blocking him. When his wooden sword glanced off her side, she gave a loud gasp and dropped her weapon. "You are too mighty for me!" Her son smiled at the compliment.

She looked back at Longinus. "You have something to tell me?"

"Majesty, another delegation has arrived to seek an alliance with you." Longinus gave an apologetic smile.

"Another one?" She laughed. "At this rate, Vaballathus may never get to use his fighting skills in a real battle!" She bent down and picked up her sword.

"I would have supposed that would be a pleasant thought, Your Majesty." His disapproval was clear.

Zenobia waggled the sword at him. "Oh, don't be such an old man, Longinus. You know I jest."

Longinus shrugged in his exaggerated fashion, then bowed. "I beg your pardon. I suppose it's just that, since Alexandria...well, I take my duties more seriously."

Zenobia moved to put her hand on his fragile arm; his white hair proved he had indeed aged much in the past five years. He had been a gentle person of learning, knowing war only in an academic manner, and she had forced him to witness sights in Egypt that had changed him profoundly. If Memphis had been traumatic for him, the beheadings in Alexandria of those who would not surrender had been far worse. She felt badly that she had been forced to use him in such a way, but his advice had proved very valuable. Since their return to Palmyra only a few months past, he had been more quiet and reserved than ever before. She wished there were some way she could restore his previous enthusiasm about everything.

"And you do a wonderful job, my friend. I could not wish for a more able adviser."

"You flatter me, my queen." Longinus looked wistful for a moment, but then smiled wryly. "But I do appreciate it."

"Not in the least, I assure you." Zenobia patted him on the arm with sincere affection, and he gave a wan smile in return. She turned to the lieutenant of her guard. "Amar, will you fill in for me a while?"

She tossed her sword to him. He caught it deftly.

"I dare not, Majesty! Prince Vaballathus is such a fierce swordsman, and my own pitiful skills are no match for yours."

Zenobia laughed. "Looking for another promotion, Amar? Lieutenant is not good enough for you this week?"

Amar bowed. "I shall do my best, Majesty."

"Come on, Amar!" Vaballathus held up his sword. "I'll best you this time."

"No doubt, Your Highness."

Amar began fencing with Vaballathus. Zenobia watched for a moment, then she and Longinus walked into the palace.

"Who is it this time?"

"A delegation from Arabia, Majesty." Longinus stroked his long, thin neck. "I think they become nervous at your growing empire and fear you may turn your attentions to their beautiful deserts."

"First Persia, then Armenia, and now Arabia." Zenobia shook her head. "It's hard to believe all of these highly independent, male-dominated kingdoms grow so frightened of a mere woman."

"Well, you did push the issue with Persia, as you recall. Your army was halfway to Persepolis before they sued for peace."

"Which is why I doubled the tribute they offered." Zenobia snorted in a very unladylike way. Longinus knew her far too well by now to expect any pretense to ladylike behavior amongst those she trusted, so she made none. "Well, let's see what these desert bandits have to offer. Not that I would have bothered with that god-forsaken, burning stretch of underworld anyway."

"But we shall not comfort them with that thought, shall we, my queen?"

"No. Comfort is the last thing I want to give those hawk-beaked brigands."

Zenobia suddenly stopped and glanced down, aware that she wore a light tunic and sandals and that her skin glowed from a sheen of perspiration. Longinus raised his heavy brows, no doubt wondering if she indeed intended to greet her visitors without changing her attire. She frowned at him and decided that these unexpected supplicants would just have to take her as she was.

They entered the throne room, which was bustling with courtiers and foreign visitors. Zenobia walked directly to sit on her throne, not even glancing at anyone in the room.

As soon as she was seated, a tall, handsome, young Arabian nobleman, elegantly dressed, approached her. Still aware of her sandals, she looked first at his feet. His *babush* were crusted with small jewels and curled at the toes. Above those were brightly colored pantaloons, loose-fitting pants that were tight around the ankles. The pantaloons were held up by a scarlet sash; tucked into one side was a jewel-encrusted dagger, and from the other side hung a *saif*, it's long, curved blade safely shielded inside an elaborately decorated scabbard.

A white linen undershirt was visible beneath a striped vest, open at the front. Flowing over his clothing was an indigo robe, no doubt made of fine silk from China, with gold threads forming intricate patterns on the material. Crowning everything was a brilliant white turban, which featured a massive emerald in a gold setting that held the material together.

Zenobia was so amused by the contrast in their respective appearances that she almost laughed. It was with great effort that she maintained her composure.

Showing proper respect, the man stopped half a dozen paces away. "May the rains be bountiful to you, Queen Zenobia." He salaamed deeply. "I am Shaykh Qalb Lozeh, humble emissary of the great Caliph of Damascus, Abd al-Malik. I bear greetings from the great caliph."

Zenobia was as amused by his obsequious manner as she was by his appearance. She pinched her leg hard with her right hand and gave a slight nod of her head. Her voice came out without a quaver. "You are most welcome, Sheikh Qalb Lozeh. I send greetings to your master on your safe return."

"You are most gracious, Queen Zenobia, as your fame and reputation, which have spread like a wind storm on the desert, have led us to understand."

"Oh?" Zenobia arched her brows. "And what does this little desert wind tell you of me, shaykh?"

"Great Queen, it is said that the steady administration of Zenobia is guided by the most judicious maxims of policy." His hand swept grandly through the air as he made each pronouncement, his robe flowing gracefully with the gesture. "If it is expedient to pardon, you calm any resentment; if it is necessary to punish, you impose silence on the voice of pity. Your dominions practice strict economy, yet on every proper occasion, such as in greeting my humble self, you are magnificent and liberal. It is wondered how you have blended the popular manners of Roman princes with the stately pomp of the courts of the east, and exacted from your subjects the same adoration that was paid to the successors of Cyrus. Perhaps that is because, as I have learned for myself, the brilliance of your mind is exceeded only by the exquisiteness of your grace and beauty, my lady." Qalb Lozeh salaamed again.

"Great Malak-bel, you've gained so much knowledge in such a short span of time?" The shaykh looked perplexed, and Zenobia decided to soften her mockery a bit. "Your tongue slices the air more keenly than the saif that hangs at your side, my lord."

Now Qalb Lozeh look relieved. "Ah, great queen, you flatter this poor messenger!"

"No, shaykh, it is you who flatter, but you do it so prettily that I shall forgive you."

Qalb Lozeh salaamed again.

"Now, what is it your master wishes you to say on his behalf?"

"Great queen, Caliph Adb al-Malik bids me to say that Damascus, and, indeed, most of the great cities of Arabia, seek only peace with the Palmyrene Empire. If it pleases your majesty, we would seek an alliance against any invaders, including those from Rome."

"And did your master send any tokens of his sincerity with you, shaykh?

"Ah, more evidence of her majesty's perspicacity! Indeed, he did."

Qalb Lozeh turned and clapped his hands. One of his servants, who had been stationed by a side door, opened it. Immediately other servants entered carrying large, ornately decorated chests. It was common knowledge that she now had a combined army of more than seventy-thousand strong, and Zenobia wondered how much it would be worth to the caliph to buy her friendship.

While the chests were being placed in front of the queen, she saw a palace servant sidle up to Longinus and whisper in his ear. After listening to the message, her prime minister leaned over and spoke quietly to Zenobia.

"Your majesty, there is another delegation that wishes an audience."

"Another one!" Zenobia laughed gaily. "Great Malak-bel, at this rate we'll have no time for any other business."

Longinus kept his voice quiet, and Zenobia stopped laughing as she heard the urgency in it.

"This one is rather different, my queen. It's General Mucapor and the Praetorian Guard, sent by Aurelian."

"Mucapor!" Zenobia's eyes went blank for a second, then she refocused on her adviser. "I must have time to consider. Tell him I'll grant him an audience in the morning."

Longinus bowed and exited. Zenobia rubbed her lips lightly with the fingertips of one hand, wondering how she would handle this moment now that it had arrived. A slight sound reminded her that Qalb Lozeh waited impatiently to show her the caliph's bribe.

"I beg your pardon, Shaykh Qalb Lozeh. Please continue with this show of sincerity from your caliph."

"With pleasure, Queen Zenobia."

The man continued talking and ostentatiously showing her the offerings of the caliph. As a luxurious robe caught her attention, Zenobia began to stroke her lips once again. She became vaguely aware that the man continued to drone on, but she could no longer focus on his words or gifts.

*　　　*　　　*

The next morning, Zenobia once more sat on her throne. This time she wore robes of state and a crown. Beside her, on the king's throne, Vaballathus also wore a crown and robes of state. Longinus stood by Zenobia's side, dressed in the formal robes of the prime minister.

At a signal from the queen, servants opened the main doors to the throne room. Mucapor entered, wearing the uniform of the Praetorian Guard. In his left hand, slightly forward of his body so it could not help but be noticed, was a small leather bag. He marched boldly up to the thrones where Zenobia and Vaballathus sat with their faces kept rigid. Mucapor came to an exaggerated halt and gave Zenobia a slight bow.

"My lady."

Zenobia did not allow her expression to change at the title, nor did she incline her head at all. "General Mucapor."

"And, of course, King Vaballathus." Mucapor stressed the title mockingly. He placed his hand over his heart and gave a much more exaggerated bow.

Warned by his mother not to be surprised by any rude treatment, Vaballathus did not react.

"You've grown quite a bit since I last saw you, Your Majesty."

Vaballathus was not prepared for the personal comment. He looked at his mother uncertainly, but she gave no sign. He nodded his head slightly to Mucapor.

"I'm told you come with a message from Aurelian, General." Zenobia's voice was as cold as her stare.

Mucapor looked surprised. "Does the king not speak for himself, my lady? Or does he in actuality not rule?"

"The king is young and still learning the ways of state." She cocked her head slightly. "It seems as though it takes some males many years to learn proper court etiquette." Mucapor stiffened, and Zenobia gave him a smile as thin as his courtesy. "Therefore, as his regent, I will assist him until he has better learned to deal with people...such as yourself."

"Oh, and I'm certain he could not wish for a better mentor in the ways of state...Queen Zenobia."

Mucapor twisted his face into a semblance of a smile as though to belie the intent of his words, but Zenobia maintained her composure.

"What is it your master instructed you to say, General?"

"The Emperor...." Again Mucapor emphasized a title, but this time with more feeling. "That is, Emperor Aurelian, instructed me to have new coinage minted for the province of Assyria."

Mucapor held out the bag in his hand. A servant stepped forward and took it from him and gave it to Zenobia. She extracted a coin from the bag and carefully inspected both sides. Without a word she handed it to Vaballathus, who also inspected it. She extracted another coin out and gave it to Longinus. None of them showed any reaction. Longinus had predicted that Aurelian would send some sign of his authority.

"And the message from your emperor?"

"Emperor Aurelian instructs me to say that this will be your last chance to be loyal to the empire...and to him."

Zenobia half rose from her throne. "Loyal to him?"

They glared at each other as she fought to bring her temper back under check. Exhaling heavily, she sat down.

"Return in three days. I will have my answer for you then. In the meantime, you and your men may enjoy the hospitality of Palmyra."

Mucapor gave a slight bow and strutted from the room. Zenobia turned to her prime minister.

"I have a small task for you to perform, Longinus."

*   *   *

Three days later, Zenobia and Vaballathus were again sitting on their thrones wearing formal robes and crowns. Longinus stood by Zenobia's side, holding the bag Mucapor had given to Zenobia. Although Mucapor did not swagger in this time, when he approached the throne he bowed his head only slightly. He ignored Vaballathus.

"Queen Zenobia."

"General Mucapor." Her nod was half as deep as Mucapor's had been.

Mucapor drew himself up haughtily. His voice was stern, like a pedant lecturing a school child.

"Are you prepared to serve your emperor, my lady?"

Zenobia kept her voice serene. "I already serve my emperor."

Mucapor frowned, clearly not understanding her meaning. Zenobia motioned to Longinus, who stepped forward and handed the bag to Mucapor.

"You're returning the coins to Emperor Aurelian?"

"Not quite." She waved her hand at the bag. "Have a look."

Mucapor looked at her quizzically, then reached into the bag and extracted a coin. As he looked at each side he was obviously startled. Then a smug, evil look came over his face. Zenobia was slightly disconcerted by his expression, but she did not allow her mask to slip. When he spoke, his voice was like the silk cord of an *hashsashin*.

"Are you certain this is the answer you wish for me to convey to the emperor?"

"It is."

Mucapor gave one more glance at each side of the coin, then turned on his heel and started to leave with no word or gesture. Zenobia kept her voice calm, but she could not keep her disdain totally in check.

"Oh, and one more thing."

Mucapor turned back, clearly with great reluctance.

"Tell your emperor that these are real silver, not like those thinly-plated nickel coins he sent me. Rome should be more careful of the value of its trinkets...not to mention its promises."

Mucapor's face flushed red as he strode heavily from the room.

CHAPTER TWELVE

Aurelian glared at the tall, thin man standing before him. The would-be emperor had intelligent eyes, but there was something about the narrow nose and weak chin that reminded Aurelian of a ferret, or some other shifty, sly animal.

It had been a long journey to France. Gallienus' legions were obedient, but not as well trained as his own. The weather was freezing and damp, the food not to his liking, and these barbarians drank mead instead of good wine. But the worst was being haunted by the thought of what disasters were occurring in Assyria while he pissed away his time bringing this excuse for a conqueror to heel. It was hard to focus on his task, let alone be patient with a traitor.

As Gallienus had indicated, Tetricus had come immediately to his summons. He had arrived in the darkness of night, wearing a heavy, plain gray robe with a hood, which he had thrown back as soon as he entered Aurelian's tent. Aurelian and Tetricus both stood, conducting their brief negotiations with no formality, no courtesies. The "negotiations" had mostly consisted of Aurelian laying down the terms for Tetricus' surrender to Rome.

"So, do we have an agreement, Tetricus?"

"Absolutely, Aurelian." Tetricus pulled his robe tighter. "I'll wait in your camp while you sort things out with my army, eh?"

Aurelian snorted in disgust. "Oh, no. You don't get off that easily. If you want what you've been promised, you ride out with me at Chalons-en-Champagne. If they see you against your own forces, the Gallic army will lose heart and be easily defeated."

"But—"

Aurelian cut him off. "But nothing, Tetricus. Your appearance will save the lives of many of my men. Frankly, I think this is a pretty small price to pay for your double treachery, first to Rome, and then your own army."

Tetricus drew himself up, trying to look proud. Aurelian thought he failed miserably.

"Very well, Emperor Aurelian. It shall be as you say."

Without any salutes, Tetricus left the tent. Aurelian poured himself a cup of wine and paced. There wasn't much of the good stuff left, but he drank more quickly than usual. As though drawn by some magnetic force, he went over to a chest and pulled out the cloak that Odaenathus had given him. He put the cup down and stroked the warm, thick material.

"What is it you're doing now?" His words were so soft his own ears could barely hear them. "Whose hands are allowed to caress that beautiful flesh now that I am gone and your husband dead?"

When he fully realized what he was doing, he hurled the cloak back into the chest. He picked up the cup of wine and gulped it down.

*　　　*　　　*

Aurelian, Decius and Domitianus were seated in the lounging chamber of Aurelian's palace in Rome, drinking wine and laughing as Aurelian recounted his meeting with Tetricus. Domitianus laughed more loudly than was warranted—as usual—but for once Aurelian did not mind.

As the laughter died down, Aurelian added, "So then he said, 'At least send a man into the camp to get my armor. I can't let my army see me dressed in this robe!'"

They laughed again. Decius slapped his knee in delight.

"And did you, Caesar?"

"Of course not. I wanted his men to see him for exactly what he was, not dressed like a warrior."

The battle—if he could call it that—had gone remarkably smoothly. As he thought, when Tetricus rode beside him with his hood thrown back, the spirit had gone out of the fierce Gallic fighters. Some had just turned and begun to walk away. Others, who perhaps hated the Romans more, had put up a brief fight. Before long, all of the enemy were on the run. Aurelian had not let his men chase, as he was certain the invaders would not be back. His casualties had been practically nil.

"He sounds more vain than a woman!" Domitianus crowed. "It's hard to believe such a man could ever lead legions into battle, let alone think of himself as an emperor."

A they drank again, Aurelian's faithful servant, Valen, entered the room. When Aurelian looked at him, the old man spoke.

"Caesar, General Bicius Nastrud Mucapor awaits your pleasure."

"Send him in." Aurelian gave a jovial wave of his bronze goblet. Like all of the rooms in his palace, the vessel was plain, but functional.

Valen retreated silently from the room.

"Well." Aurelian looked around at his officers with a smile. "It seems we shall be together again after all these long months."

Mucapor, followed closely by the servant, swaggered in and saluted. Aurelian waved his second-in-command to a seat.

"Valen, wine for the general. He's no doubt very thirsty after his long sojourn in the desert."

When Mucapor was settled on a divan, Valen served him wine. Satisfied that all of the goblets were full, Valen slipped out of the room.

"Thank you for seeing me so quickly, Caesar."

Mucapor raised his cup in a toast. They all raised their goblets and drank.

"I hear you did well on your recent campaign."

"Did well!" Domitianus' voice was fill with admiration. "Why, Bicius, Emperor Aurelian was just telling us how he humiliated our pretend 'Gallic Emperor' and then crushed his motley army. No doubt you've heard the senate gave him another triumph last week and proclaimed him *Restitutor Orbis*."

"Indeed, the streets are still full of the news. I've only been back one day and hear of little but the 'Restorer of the World'." Mucapor took a careful sip of his wine. "My congratulations, Emperor Aurelian."

"Thank you, Mucapor. It was even more insignificant than Domitianus describes it."

"Insignificant!" Decius leaped to his feet. "In five years, Emperor Aurelian has secured the frontiers of the empire and reunified it, giving Rome a totally new lease on life. This peace shall last for another thousand years!"

"Oh, at least." Aurelian furrowed his brow and pinched his mouth in a mock-serious expression. "Perhaps a million!"

The others all laughed. Decius looked a little embarrassed as he resume his seat.

"But enough of that." Aurelian relaxed his face and leaned back on the divan. "How went your mission, Mucapor?"

Mucapor toyed with his cup. "In that same five years, Zenobia has done as much to wreak havoc in the east. Now she spits upon the Roman Empire, Caesar." He took a long drink of his wine.

"What?"

"I fear it's true. Zenobia has destroyed Roman control in the entire Middle East and created her own empire."

Domitianus leaped to his feet. "The bitch!"

Aurelian felt slightly dizzy, and struggled to get himself back under control. "Tell me about this."

"No doubt you already know all about her conquests." When Aurelian nodded, Mucapor went on. "This will tell you the rest."

Mucapor reached into his tunic and pulled out the bag of coins. He handed the bag to Aurelian, who took out a coin and examined it. His jaw clenched, and he could feel his teeth grinding.

"This is her son's likeness?"

Mucapor nodded.

Aurelian read aloud from one side. "King of kings, corrector of all the world, and Prince of Palmyra."

He looked at the other men one at a time, then turned the coin over. "Zenobia! Not me, not the eagle. 'Zenobia Augusta.'" There was a long, angry pause. If the goblet in his hand had not been made of bronze, it may have bent from his grip. "She usurps the title Augustus, which is reserved for an emperor of Rome?"

Aurelian looked upwards, cracking his neck. Working his jaw, mouth open as though gasping for breath, he blinked at the heavens several times, breathing heavily. That was the only sound in the room. Slowly he lowered his eyes to survey his top staff members. Decius appeared frightened, perplexed, Domitianus confused, while Mucapor clearly tried to hide a smug, satisfied grin.

"So, she answers me coin for coin, does she? Well, I shall repay her in kind."

"I take it this signals a break with Rome, Caesar?" Mucapor raised an inquiring eyebrow and with the voice of innocence.

In reply, Aurelian drew his sword. He tossed the bag up in the air and sliced it viciously with his sword. Coins scattered across the marble floor.

"Damn you! Must your memory haunt me forever?"

He saw Mucapor and Domitianus exchange looks, but Aurelian did not care. Mucapor's words from years before over a man's weakness for a woman rang once again in his ears.

*   *   *

Mucapor was met in the entry garden to the house of Marcus Claudius Tacitus by the consul's wife. She was attractive enough, but Mucapor saw the same expression on her face he had witnessed from slaves who were frequently beaten. With the most timid of greetings, she ushered him into a large, ornate lounge where Tacitus was sitting. Although the man's legs barely reached the floor, Mucapor was certain the divan would buckle under his weight. He was perhaps fifteen years older, but Mucapor thought he looked at least double his own age.

"Leave us." Tacitus' voice was gruff, but he did not look at the woman.

Without a word, his wife fled the room. As soon as she had gone, a servant entered with wine. He poured the thick liquid into golden goblets heavily incrusted with precious jewels, then melted into the background. Not waiting for an invitation, Mucapor sat on a nearby divan.

Tacitus smiled at Mucapor. "We must keep women in their place, don't you agree, General?"

Mucapor raised one eyebrow. He had dressed in an expensive toga with no markings of office to be inconspicuous. But Tacitus had used his military title in spite of that. Interesting.

"With all my heart, Consul."

Tacitus raised his goblet, and Mucapor followed suit. Tacitus took a gulp.

"Splendid. Some men treat them too gently. I find that a great weakness in a man."

Mucapor give a non-committal "um" and sipped at his wine.

"Do you find my judgment of such men too harsh, General?" Tacitus thrust his chins forward in a challenge.

Mucapor kept a pleasant smile on his face, hiding his impatience. "Is that why you were so kind as to invite me to your lovely home, Consul Tacitus, to discuss the treatment of women?"

Tacitus laughed, a sharp, staccato sound, more like a bark. "Among other things. We can discuss whatever you'd like."

Mucapor let his smile slip a trifle. "With respect, Consul, why don't you tell me what you would prefer to discuss?"

"Oh, you generals!"

Tacitus slapped his meaty thigh, although Mucapor was certain there was not enough force to sting.

"Always wanting to get right to the point, no wasting of time, eh? Splendid."

"All professional soldiers find it aggravating to waste time, Consul. Time becomes much more precious when one's life can be ended suddenly. Of course, I suppose that's not much of a consideration for— well, politicians who have the luxury of being safely at home most nights."

"Hah! Shows how little you know of politics here in Rome, young man." Tacitus tried to look jovial, but there was a twist to his mouth that told Mucapor there was bitterness behind his words. He gulped down more of the liquid.

Not wanting to insult the man in spite of this silly game, Mucapor smiled slightly and tipped his cup in a gesture of acknowledgment. Evidently, Tacitus had also tired of the preliminary chatter.

"But, let that be as it may. By all means, let us talk of more important matters."

"So, not women," Mucapor said smoothly.

Tacitus barked again. "Perhaps of them also. I understand you serve a master who is, shall we say, having some difficulty dealing with one woman in particular."

Mucapor nodded sagely. "Ah, I see." He sipped at his wine again. "So I am here to discuss Emperor Aurelian."

"'Emperor' Aurelian."

Tacitus snorted, his heavy jowls quivering, then drank deeply once again. He looked into his cup as though surprised to find it empty. He held it up, and the servant moved quickly to refill it. The man looked at Mucapor, who shook his head.

"He was of humble birth, you know." Tacitus took a long pull at his wine.

"So I've heard, Consul."

"Splendid." Tacitus squinted at him, perhaps weighing his next words. "His father was a tenant of a senator named Aurelius who lived at Sirmium in Pannonia. Evidently, when he raised the family up, he gave the boy his name."

"I've heard something of this." Mucapor decided this conversation was much more to his taste. "I do know he was a minor tribune until he had a bit of success under Emperor Claudius."

"Yes." Tacitus sneered. "Rome loves mighty war heroes." He shook his head as though clearing it of such a stupid thought, then drank of his wine again. "The senate seems to think that valor and victories greatly equate with the ability to lead men in all endeavors, including politics." He leaned forward and waggled a fat finger at Mucapor. "But don't you think it's men who were born to nobility, trained to understand the proper machinations of power and wealth, who can best run the empire?"

Mucapor cocked his head. "Men such as...?"

"Such as you, Bicius Nastrud Mucapor...and me."

Mucapor toyed with his cup as he contemplated a response. This was even more interesting than he had anticipated. "You seem to flatter me, Consul, speaking so freely of your feelings towards the emperor."

"Oh, I don't know about flattery." Tacitus looked smug. "I understand you bear Aurelian little love, General Mucapor."

"Where have you heard such malicious gossip, Consul Tacitus?" Mucapor kept his voice calm. He continued to toy with the cup, looking at the other man through lidded eyes.

Tacitus tapped the side of his nose with his finger. "A good politician has eyes for everything that moves, and ears for all that is said. I have informants everywhere."

Mucapor looked at him directly and nodded. "I see."

Tacitus stared glumly down at his wine. "The senate granted Aurelian the title of emperor. Hah! Another one of the new 'Barracks Emperors'. Then they honored him with *Germanicus Maximus* and *Gothicus Maximus*. A week ago they added *Restitutor Orbis*. And now he builds a wall around Rome. No doubt they'll honor him for that, as well."

"No doubt they will."

Tacitus inhaled his wine. Mucapor sipped, remaining silent as they drank. He wanted Tacitus to continue to take the lead. At last, the older man could stand it no longer.

"Perhaps it's time that some honors and titles came your way, eh, Mucapor?"

Mucapor's face was impassive. Let the man play out his hand on his own. "I would welcome the opportunity to win such titles."

"Indeed." His voice was calculating now.

Mucapor sat up straighter, waiting for the offer.

"You know, I have great support within the senate, General."

"So it is said, Consul."

Now even Tacitus weighed his words. "As you said yourself, generals put themselves in danger nearly every day. There are many battles, even many accidents, that occur frequently out in the field."

"That's very true."

"I suppose there's always the possibility that Aurelian himself might meet with such an … untimely injury."

Mucapor frowned. "Naturally, there's always that possibility."

"And if such a tragedy were to occur, then the empire would find itself in need of a new emperor."

Mucapor nodded. "Certainly."

Tacitus looked directly at him. Mucapor returned the stare.

"And if some great harm were to come to Aurelian, then perhaps you and General Domitianus might convince your legions to support me as the new emperor for the eastern regions."

Satisfied, Mucapor leaned back and fiddled with his cup. He did not allow a smile to cross his lips.

"There's always that possibility as well. I'm certain you would make a…a splendid emperor, Marcus Claudius Tacitus."

Tacitus inclined his head. "I'd do my best. But, of course, I'd have to stay here to consolidate my position. Therefore, I'd need to appoint a new governor of Palmyra, not to mention some of the cities Zenobia managed to conquer."

Mucapor leaned forward intently. "Would you? I had once hoped Emperor Aurelian might appoint me to that position after it had been…vacated. Years ago."

"Of course I would. As you know the area so well, I would be wise to appoint you, would I not, Bicius Nastrud Mucapor?"

"Ah, yes." At last, Mucapor felt he could lean back and smile, and drink some of the fine wine Tacitus had provided. "Yes, I think that would be very wise."

*   *   *

Aurelian paced as Gallienus examined one of the coins. They were once again in the lounging chamber of Gallienus' palace, but neither was sitting, let alone lounging. It was not long before Gallienus looked up.

"A bad business, brother. I'm sorry I had to extend your stay away from the east so long."

Aurelian shrugged dismissively. "That's the past. I need your permission to leave immediately to see what I can salvage."

"Yes. Yes, of course." Gallienus clenched the coin tightly in his fist. "Now that you've got Tetricus back in the fold, you need to put that witch back in her place. Take those two legions with you; it seems things will be quiet on the western front for a while."

"Thank you, brother." Aurelian exhaled with true gratitude; he knew the situation in Rome was still far from resolved. "From the sounds of it, I'll need them."

"I'll also send a ship to Carthage. We'll see what troops the prefect can spare from Carthage, Algiers and Tripoli to send against Egypt."

"But we need the grain from the Africa province!" Realizing that might sound ungrateful, Aurelian thought he should clarify his concern.

"If we weaken our army along that section of the Mediterranean, this infection might spread throughout the entire bread basket of Rome."

"That's why we need to get control back in Egypt," Gallienus explained patiently. "We need their corn as much as the other grains. It sounds like Zenobia's got more toms following her than a cat in heat, and we'll need all of the military might we can scrape up in the region to defeat her."

Aurelian shook his head at his own stupidity. If he was going to become a true emperor, he would have to learn to see the entire picture, not just the part that directly concerned him. "Of course, you're absolutely right. We need to hit her with everything we've got now or all could be lost. I'll send Marcus Aurelius Probus on that ship to bring an army together."

"An excellent choice." Gallienus' voice became hard. "I count on you to bring the wench back in chains and drag her through the streets." He looked at the coin again, and his voice softened once more. "Although, if this is truly her likeness, I can think of other things I'd like to do to her first."

Aurelian cleared his throat. "It's a very good likeness."

They looked at each other, neither actually revealing his thoughts, but both making a pretty good guess.

"We'll march in three days."

Gallienus looked at the coin once more and nodded. "May the gods go with you and bring you luck."

It was Aurelian's turn to make his voice hard. "It's not luck I'll need. It's ruthlessness."

Not wanting to waste another moment, Aurelian took his leave and marched out of the palace.

CHAPTER THIRTEEN

Longinus was more aware of his senses than ever in his life; like a wild animal relying on the information absorbed by its body for its very survival. And yet he was outside of the action. It was similar to the way he had studied the art of war, observing from a distance, asking questions of the participants before and afterward to clarify details, analyzing the conflict with the dispassionate nature of a scholar. It was the way he lived his life: he watched, he listened, he learned. He rarely participated. That was the main reason he had been so reluctant to accept the role into which the queen—now empress—had forced him. From a distance, he watched her now, always eager to learn. For the empress, this could indeed be a matter of life or death.

Zenobia stood on the hot sand wearing a tough leather jerkin, a short skirt and sandals. She held a hunting spear and had a short sword strapped by her side. Her private guard stood on chariots in a wide semi-circle around her. Safely off to the side, Longinus observed on horseback along with Rasses, Sefer, Vaballathus, and some of the other high-ranking courtiers. Standing next to them on chariots were the head priest of the temple of Malak-bel and the royal physician. All waited anxiously for the lion to be released.

Longinus was bemused by the ancient Assyrian custom of lion hunting, a sport reserved for kings. He was told it dated back at least as far as King Ashurbanipal, who would often kill a lion for political and religious purposes. The hunts were symbolic of the ruling monarch's duty to protect and fight for his—or in this case, her—people. Evidently, the Assyrians thought that if their ruler was good at hunting, the gods would favor them. In some ways, Longinus thought it resembled the current Roman trend of elevating great generals to emperor.

After the lion was killed, the king would pour a libation over it and give a speech to their god in thanks, which also assured the lion's evil spirit wouldn't come back to haunt him. As Vaballathus was too young and untrained—and everyone knew the empress was the real ruler, anyway—it was Zenobia who waited to perform the ritual killing.

Lions were not native to Assyria, so two had been brought back from Africa. Both now sat in cages some half a league away. A servant would raise a door and release one, then start running for his life. The king would often chase and kill the lion from a chariot with his bow and arrow or spear, but it was considered more auspicious if the king killed it on foot with a spear and sword. On this day, dogs and beaters would chase the lion in Zenobia's direction. If the lion escaped the circle or had to be killed by one of her guards—who were under orders to herd the lion toward her, but not to attack unless absolutely necessary to save her life—then the other would be released. Longinus thought the concept was worthy, but unnecessarily dangerous. Still, he agreed that a ruler should do something courageous, whether leading their army in battle or killing a dangerous beast, to prove their worth.

Zenobia lifted her spear, signaling that she was ready. The servant, who had stood next to the cage with his legs shaking for far too long, pulled the rope that dropped the cage door. He ran in the opposite direction as fast as his quivering limbs could take him. Several beaters, armed with shields and long sticks, whacked on the back of the cage to get the animal moving. A dozen large, solidly-built Tibetan mastiffs trained for hunting long before being imported into Greece and Mesopotamia, lunged against the leads of their handlers. The great cat stood up and looked around, snarling at the sudden noise. Suspicious of this supposed freedom, but alarmed by the violent noise and movement to its rear, the beast took one tremendous leap from the cage. It paused momentarily, but the Molosser were now barking and growling viciously, frantic to attack, and a dozen other beaters banged their sticks against their shields to add to the cacophony. The lion hesitated no longer, bounding away from the men and dogs with flowing strides.

As the frightened creature passed the tips of the semi-circle, the guards wheeled their chariots to close in and follow. The lion made directly for the single human who was not moving. It was at that moment that a Palmyrene messenger, who rode swiftly towards the group of watchers, pulled up next to Longinus.

"I bear urgent news." The messenger was breathing as heavily as his horse. "I must speak with the empress."

"When she has finished." Longinus gave him a quick, sidelong glance before looking back at the scene in front of them. "Unless you want to feel her wrath with the point of that spear instead of the lion."

The messenger followed the gaze of the prime minister to where Zenobia stood, stoically watching the approach of the loping lion. Wisely, Longinus thought, the messenger waited with the others to witness the action.

It was not clear if the lion saw her as prey or merely wished to clear the easiest obstacle from his path as he made his dash for safety. He doubled his speed as he made straight for the lone figure. Longinus recalled there were two basic maneuvers Zenobia could perform in this situation. The first was to throw her spear at a distance, hoping to hit the animal solidly enough that she could then handle it with her sword. The second was to stand her ground, place the butt of the spear in the ground and aim the point towards the lion, and hope it sprang normally so she could guide the point into its chest. She would then stab it with the sword if that did not finish the job. If she had been alone, the first would have been far riskier. The throw had to be perfect: if she missed or barely wounded the huge cat, she would have to fight an enraged hunter with only a short sword. In that case, her guards would swoop in to aid her. The second option was more dangerous because, if she did not hold the spear firm and true, the beast would be on top of her. Wounded or not, that heavy body might crush her and the claws, lightening quick and as sharp as any blade, would tear at her flesh. It would be nearly impossible to dodge to the side and thrust with her sword.

As tall as most men, she stood unflinchingly while the lion approached. Once more, Longinus gazed admiringly at her stunning physique and that proud profile, the dusky skin glowing with a light sheen of perspiration in the blazing sunlight. While he felt the lust of both a man and a courtier as he beheld his queen, his hopes were that she would make the wise choice and come out of this encounter unscathed.

As Longinus had guessed, Zenobia chose the second path. With the lion nearly upon her, she knelt low to the ground, pushed the butt of the spear between her feet, and tilted the point towards its breast. Unfortunately, the lion did not spring in the manner it would when hunting prey. Instead, it hurtled straight forward, swiping with its massive paw to knock this obstacle out of its way in order to continue towards the break in the line of chariots. Longinus gasped with alarm, but Zenobia obviously realized its intent before he did. She ducked even farther forward, crouching low to the left side of the beast as it raised its right paw. The point of the spear made contact with the chest of the heavy cat, but the swinging paw caught Zenobia on her upper left arm. The thick, heavy leather parted like cloth, and the claws dug deeply into her flesh. She screamed at the pain, but continued to drive the spear upwards into the cat's body as she rolled to the ground away from the attack.

The lion also roared in pain, the force of its charge having driven the spear deep into its body. Spouting blood from its chest and coughing it from the mouth, the beast desperately clawed at the wooden rod that had already created its doom. Unable to breathe properly, it grew weaker by the second.

Springing up several paces to the side of the wounded creature, Zenobia drew her sword and raised it into an attack position. Seeing the plight of the lion, she must know it would soon prove no further threat. Now it was important to finish the ceremony, putting the poor animal out of its misery. She circled warily, looking for a chance to drive her sword into the lion's heart, but not at further risk to herself. Her arm was bleeding freely, and she looked so weak Longinus feared her arm muscles may have been torn. She moved around the dying creature for several moments, and he could tell she was conscious of the protruding spear that might trip her, as well as the flailing paws of the lion. At last there was an opening, and she darted in like a cobra, striking to plunge the sword into the heart. Her aim was true, her right arm still strong, and the blade pierced through the heavy musculature and found its target. The lion groaned and twitched several times, then rolled onto its side, motionless.

Zenobia heaved a sigh of relief obvious to all. There was some excited chatter, although this was too solemn an occasion for cheering. Longinus gave a sideways glance to Vaballathus, who had been trained to remain impassive during the ceremony. The boy breathed deeply, and a smile creased his handsome face.

The head priest motioned to the driver, who brought his chariot close to the empress and her victim. Dressed in his ceremonial robes, the priest stepped down and handed a vial of holy ointment to Zenobia. She took the vial and touched it to her forehead and her chest, then poured the contents over the head and chest of the lion as the priest chanted sacred words. When the vial was empty, the priest raised his staff to the heavens and asked great Malak-bel to bless the nation in its upcoming war, and to bless their courageous leader. As soon as he finished, the physician took his place next to the empress, tending to her wounds.

Finally, her guards felt they could celebrate the kill. They closed to a small circle, offering congratulations and words of respect. Some moved the body of the lion onto a litter. The horses that would pull the carcass whinnied in fear, the smell of the beast and its blood assailing their nostrils. The prize would be displayed in the great temple of Malak-bel for all citizens to admire and see proof of the courage and prowess of their empress.

Longinus trotted forward a short distance on his horse and called out to her. "Empress Zenobia, there is a messenger with urgent news."

Zenobia grimaced. Longinus presumed her arm was starting to throb.

"Make certain this noble creature is treated with dignity," she ordered a guard.

The man salaamed, and Zenobia walked over to join her courtiers. She was handed a flask of wine and drank thirstily. The wine might fortify her after the ordeal, but Longinus guessed it did not dull the pain much. Because she was standing, the messenger dismounted as he waited for her to speak. Finally she turned to the man.

"Well?"

The messenger bowed. "Majesty."

"Yes, what is it?" Her pain must be making her impatient.

"Emperor Aurelian—I mean, the Roman Emperor Aurelian, has crossed Thrace with at least six legions."

"So, he finally comes!" Sefer exclaimed, his voice bubbling with excitement.

Zenobia gave him a brief nod. "Where is he heading?"

"Smyrna, Your Majesty."

Zenobia shifted her arm. "I see."

Longinus raised his brows. She seemed more interested in finding a less painful position to hold her arm than in this ominous message. "Forgive me, but this news doesn't seem to bother you too much."

Zenobia forced a crooked smile. "Oh, it bothers me. But it was expected, after all. And it's not nearly as important as the news I received this morning from Egypt."

"What news, Majesty?"

"I had a message from Firmus, Shaykh Rasses. Together with General Timagenes, they've started a revolt in Alexandria with the grain traders."

Sefer frowned heavily. "Who is this Firmus?"

"Firmus is an old friend of ours. A merchant from Seleukeia."

Longinus elaborated for the benefit of the two shaykhs. "He's very rich because of his business connections, which stretch as far as India. He controls most of the corn shipments that come out of Egypt."

Rasses' face brightened. "Ah! And I suppose this revolt has something to do with interrupting the corn supply for Rome?"

"Exactly." Zenobia made a chopping motion with her good arm, but winced as the pain travelled to the injured limb. "Firmus cuts off the grain shipments to Rome, we limit the supply of meats and other goods to what Aurelian can get from conquering cities, and eventually his supply lines will be stretched too far for his army to continue."

Rasses smiled. "And, while they battle their way across Thrace, your well-fed army rests and trains only to defeat him here at home."

"That's certainly what we hope."

"Then, along with this great omen of today, we indeed have reason to smile." Rasses suited his expression to his words. "A most excellent strategy, Your Majesty!"

"Thank you. Well, let's see what other little surprises we can cook up for this hungry Roman army, eh?"

*   *   *

The city of Tyana stood near the middle of the Central Anatolian Plateau. It was an ancient city built more for beauty than defense, with one towering wall pierced by magnificent arches all along its length. It had been a long, hard march to reach this point. Aurelian would have preferred to just sail into Nicomedia from the Propontis to begin with, but Zenobia had cleverly secured all of the ports, so he was forced to go the hard route through Anatolia if he wanted to face her.

The campaign started when he crossed the Danube from Illyricum into Thrace, which had pledged its loyalty to Zenobia. As they marched through Thrace, tribes of Goths harassed his flanks and occasionally fought set battles. Many of the small towns and villages he passed possessed a *mansiones*, which had storerooms for supplies and some quarters for soldiers as an emergency measure. The *mansios*, a standard feature of all Roman provinces, were provisioned by the locals. The people found this far more burdensome than monetary taxes but, regardless of the cost, they made the sacrifice as the lesser of two evils. During their slow progress, the Roman army took whatever supplies were available and destroyed most of the rest. While Rome was generous to communities that recognized its sovereignty, it had long ago learned the best deterrent to resistance was to obliterate any town or city that resisted, often literally leveling them.

The first major city Aurelian sacked was Byzantium, on the western side of the Bosporus, the strait which connected the Propontus to the Euxine Pontus. Chalcedon was directly across from Byzantium, and the crossing took a full week for the army to be marshaled together again. Rather than be destroyed, Chalcedon quickly went over to Aurelian after he entered the Balkan area. Bithynia, Smyrna, and Gordion in Phrygia were the next major cities to be destroyed. Wishing to gain his favor, other communities sent supplies to the army from regions that they never passed through.

The column of soldiers stretched for several miles as it approached the magnificent walls of Tyana, with Aurelian riding at the head. He was tired of the march, tired of fighting battles that had little to do with his main objective. After a cold, grueling trek over the Taurus Mountains, Aleppo would be the first significant city they reached in Assyria. He was tempted to bypass Tyana, get that damn climb over the mountains behind him, and just push straight on towards Palmyra. But that would be a very bad strategy indeed, leaving too many enemies behind and not setting enough of an example for those in front.

Half a league from the gates he saw an old man, supported by a much younger man, walk out slowly to meet him. Not wanting to halt the march, Aurelian rode forward from his guard. The two men stopped and waited for him. As he pulled to a halt, Aurelian stared at them. The old man was dressed in a simple white robe. His white hair fell far down his back, and his thin, leathery arms held a stout staff. The young man wore a gray robe. His black hair also hung long and loose, but he carried no staff in order to offer his arm to the older man.

"Who are you, old man? Are you the prince of this city?"

"I, a prince?" The old man raised his staff as if it were a talisman. "No, I am far more than that, and yet far less." He lowered his staff slowly, as though its weight was too much for him to bear for long. "I am Philostratus, a philosopher, a writer of words, a simple old man who says nothing, and yet tries to mean everything."

Aurelian frowned. "Well, that tells me a lot. Why have you come to meet us?"

"It is you who have come to meet us, as we have gone nowhere."

Aurelian leaned back in his saddle and laughed. "Yes, you are most correct, Philostratus. And what nothing do you have to say to me that will mean everything?"

As the younger man held onto his left arm, Philostratus lifted his staff with his right arm and slowly moved it from one side to the other. "Great emperor, like an irresistible gale from the Black Sea, your legions have swept across our land and sacked every city that has resisted you, including Ankara, and even magnificent Byzantium. Now you have come here, to the walls of frightened, insignificant Tyana, to wreak your havoc."

Aurelian looked at him with a face as implacable as marble. "I come to reclaim what once was mine, and shall be again."

"Well said, well said." Philostratus nodded in what might have been approval. Once again, his staff sank into the dust. "But I have also heard it said that you have some reverence for the words of Apollonius of Tyana, our great philosopher of some centuries past."

Aurelian leaned forward and regarded the old man gravely. "I've read the words of Apollonius. I have great respect for them."

"Then I beg you, hear my humble words, great emperor."

"Speak, Philostratus. I shall listen."

"I am a disciple of Apollonius. At the last full moon, I had a vision of him." His voice grew firmer, filled with the strength of his vision. "The master came to me in a dream. As though I stood in your place, he implored me, stating: 'Aurelian, if you desire to rule, abstain from the blood of the innocent! Aurelian, if you will conquer, be merciful!'"

Aurelian leaned forward almost menacingly. "Tyana has sworn allegiance to my usurper. Why should I offer mercy?"

"If you offer mercy, the city will surrender to you with no resistance."

Aurelian made a thoughtful 'humph' in the back of his throat. He leaned back once again. "That will save much bloodshed. However, I suspect there won't be much resistance no matter what."

Philostratus waved his staff in a dismissive manner. "Tyana is not important. Apollonius said more."

"If Tyana is not important, why have you come out here, risking your life to save it?"

"Because I am old and have seen too much senseless death and destruction. I must do what I can to protect the young."

"Humph. Possibly." Aurelian waved his hand. "Go on."

"Apollonius said: 'If you spare my city, I shall bless your campaign. Other cities will follow this example. In the last, your mercy shall be blessed.'"

Aurelian cocked his head. "'In the last.' What did the wise Apollonius mean by this, old man?"

"I know not, great emperor." Philostratus shrugged his frail shoulders. "I only know that your mercy will be rewarded."

Aurelian sat easily in his saddle and thought for a moment. Then he pointed to the city. "Go back to your prince, Philostratus. Tell him that his soldiers have until sundown to come out of the city and lay down their arms. If even one resists, I shall slaughter every creature in the city to the last dog. If indeed there is no resistance, then not one person shall be harmed."

Philostratus bowed his head. "I offer my thanks and joyful blessings, great emperor. It shall be as you command."

*   *   *

Inside the Palmyrene palace, one of the great halls had been converted into a war room. Many large tables were covered with maps, dispatches, requisitions and accounts, and other documents, and many officers and officials moved and talked incessantly, apparently with no order. Amid the hustle and bustle, Zenobia was speaking with her primary advisers when a messenger rushed in.

The messenger bowed quickly. "Majesty."

"Yes, what is it?" Administrative minutiae bored her, set her skin crawling with impatience. She would rather be out in the desert fighting, facing a lion, or just riding. She had not considered the amount of paperwork she would be subjected to as the supreme ruler. She wished she could delegate all of it to Longinus.

"Word of the Roman army. Aurelian has taken Tyana."

"Well, we had to expect that."

Zenobia nodded at the words of Rasses. In keeping with his reputation, Aurelian was being methodical and ruthless. "After Smyrna and Ephesus, has he destroyed Tyana as well?"

"No, Your Majesty." The messenger shifted from one foot to another. "He did not topple one stone or harm any living soul."

"What?" Sefer sounded shocked.

"No, my lord. The city has been left intact." The messenger made a slight shrug, as though to imply that it wasn't his fault.

"For what reason?" Zenobia was baffled. Had the leopard changed its spots?

"My lord, it is said the sage Philostratus, a disciple of the great philosopher Apollonius, had a vision of Apollonius, which he did relate to Aurelian."

"And?"

"And the Roman army did not sack the city, but spared it according to the vision."

"Which was?" Rasses could not mask the wonder in his voice.

"That good fortune would fall upon the emperor for this act of mercy."

Sefer muttered as though to himself. "An act of mercy...." He turned away from the others, hands clasped behind his back, and stared upwards.

"Great Malak-bel! The man continues to amaze me."

Zenobia glared at Longinus. "Meaning?" Even if he was a Roman, she did not want her closest advisors openly admiring her greatest enemy.

Longinus looked embarrassed, but he was compelled to explain. "Meaning that the fall of Tyana will now lend itself to legend."

"A vision of Apollonius, one of the great Assyrian philosophers." Zenobia blinked twice as she looked at her prime minister. "An agreement to spare the city of any destruction if they surrendered completely."

"Exactly, my empress." Longinus was obviously relieved that she understood him. "Which probably means that many more cities will follow suit after seeing that Aurelian will not exact revenge if they submit completely."

"Yes. A very clever stratagem." Zenobia gave a disdainful look. "But a mere sop to the people. It doesn't change the balance of power."

Longinus stroked his nose. "Forgive me, but I think this news must alter your current plan."

Zenobia blinked. "Why? You think we can't wait for him to come to us any longer?"

"Exactly. If more cities follow the example of Tyana, he'll march through very quickly. Your clever plan of denying them supplies will also be foiled as cities become eager to beg his mercy. Even cities in Assyria may reconsider their allegiances."

"I agree, Majesty." Rasses raised his head with determination. "It will take some time to gather our fighters back together from their tribes. And some of our recent 'allies' may also think twice about standing against Rome, especially if Aurelian gathered recruits from Thrace and Anatolia."

Zenobia slapped her thigh. She turned to Zabdas. "General Zabdas?"

"We must take the fight to them." The old general raised a finger to the heavens. "Our allies support us now, at our peak. Our army has the advantage of numbers and knowing the terrain. We should march soon."

"General Artabanes?"

"My men are eager for a fight. We fortified our heavy chariots exactly as you commanded, and my men look forward to cutting the Romans to ribbons as we did in Egypt."

Zenobia contemplated the situation for a moment. She should have known Aurelian would find a way to lame the horse she intended to ride. "I agree. Generals, have your troops prepared to march in three weeks. Whatever horsemen from the tribes who cannot join us here must meet us along the way. We will meet Aurelian before he enters our borders."

"And I, Your Majesty?" Longinus' voice was faint, with a slight quaver in it.

Zenobia was about to snap that she needed his advice in the upcoming confrontation with Aurelian. She looked into his eyes to lend the glare of command to her voice, but she suddenly saw him as he was: an old man, timid and weak, who had been bent to the limits of his abilities like an ancient tree caught by a strong gale. She stilled her voice, composed herself, and spoke sweetly before she forced him to break.

"I would wish you to stay here, Longinus, and look after our kingdom." Longinus closed his eyes, and Zenobia could sense his deep sigh of relief more than she could hear it. "You have, I believe, given us all you can in the way of advice on Rome. Zohan shall remain Lord Protector of the King's Person, but you shall be governor of Palmyra."

Longinus bowed as deeply as his old bones would allow. "As you wish, my empress."

He made himself sound as resigned as possible, but it was all Zenobia could do to hide her amusement at the way he submitted himself to her will. For her part, she was certain she would miss his company on the long campaign she was about to begin.

CHAPTER FOURTEEN

Aurelian stared down at the map and struggled to suppress either a smile or a sigh of relief. It had been an arduous and dangerous crossing over the Taurus Mountains, but he wanted his staff to know it was just another day in their journey, another step on the way to victory. He ignored his grumbling stomach and aching lower back. Whatever he and his staff had suffered over the mountain passes, it had been much worse for his troops. Even down in the foothills, the constant wind blew the deadly chill through the gaps in the tents.

Other than a few wild goats, there had been precious little game for the foraging parties. The army had to rely on the supplies they packed on mules. The marching columns, which would normally stretch for miles, became ragged *contubernium*, tent units of eight legionaries and their sergeant, traveling together to make sure their tent and supplies were available at night. There was no such thing as a camp, as the tail end of the long train could not catch up by the end of the day. Due to the combination of a few treacherous passes, the freezing temperatures at the highest elevations, and the fraying tempers of thousands of aggressive men living in close proximity for many months, deaths were inevitable.

In addition to his own three legions and the two from Gallienus, one of the Celtic legions of Noricum and Rhaetia had joined him after Tetricus had abandoned his men. Along the way, Aurelian's forces had been augmented by Moesians, Pannonians, Tyaneans, Mesopotamians, Phoenicians, Palestinians, and a troop of both Dalmatian and Mauritanian cavalry. There had been some inevitable friction between the disparate groups, especially amongst the mercenaries who were still angry at not being allowed to loot Tyana. However, the excellent training and high morale of the legionaries, plus the stern discipline administered by the emperor, minimized how many were lost by the time they descended the last of the foothills.

By tradition, the army marched for six days and rested for one.

Because Aurelian wanted to get through the mountains as quickly as possible, he had allowed no rest days. Since Byzantium, they had traveled through Bithynia and Phrygia, including the cities of Ancyra, Galatia, Cappadocia, and Cilicia. The entire march had taken the better part of a year. Although he wanted to push on into Assyria immediately, he ordered a week of rest for the troops. It took three days for the stragglers to arrive, and he wanted to take a count and reorganize while the men recuperated.

On the sixth day, an impatient Aurelian found himself staring hard at his map once more. "We're at Aleppo, here." Aurelian rapped his wind-scoured knuckles on the curling parchment. He raised his voice to be heard; the tent walls constantly protested the buffeting they had to endure. "We'll go east to the Euphrates and follow it to Emar and Tattul, where we'll stock up on food and water. Then we'll march south to Palmyra."

For once, Decius questioned his commander. "But what about the port cities? You were concerned with lack of access, so I thought we'd go there first."

Aurelian shook his head. "The time and effort it would require to take those cities first, then march across a long stretch of desert to Palmyra without being resupplied, is not nearly as efficient. There's water between Aleppo and the Euphrates just past As Sifirah." He pointed out the route he described. "After the much shorter desert crossing, we should be better supplied for a long siege."

Decius nodded in agreement as he studied the map. "If she's smart, she'll stay behind those high walls. I know I would."

Mucapor folded his arms across his chest. "It will be difficult to take that city."

Aurelian smiled, although there was no mirth in his thoughts. "True. But, once we've cut off the head, the rest of the cities will fall back in line. I'm sure of it."

Domitianus nodded in agreement. "No doubt."

At that moment, a guard entered the command tent and saluted. The wind blowing through the flap carried the stench of animal excrement and sweaty men. Candles flickered, and two went out. Mnestheus hurried to relight them.

"Caesar, a messenger from Emperor Gallienus."

"Send him in."

The guard stepped out, and a messenger took his place. His face was chafed red, and his teeth chattered in spite of the heavy cloak wrapped around him.

"Emperor Aurelian, the Emperor Gallienus sends you greetings and tidings of Egypt."

"Yes, I understand the Africa province reinforcements are now camped at Banghazi. General Probus sends word they stand ready to support me when we arrive in Egypt. Is there something else?"

"Yes, Caesar." The messenger's tone implied there was bad news on the way. "An Egyptian officer, Timagenes, and a grain merchant started a revolt in Alexandria. This merchant, Firmus, has cut off the grain shipments to Rome. Emperor Gallienus regrets he can send you no more grain supplies until they are defeated."

"Damn these meddling merchants!" Mucapor smacked his fist into his palm. "Does the fool not know which side of his bread receives the butter?"

Domitianus leaned forward eagerly. "Do we change our plans, Caesar?"

Aurelian stared at the messenger for a long moment, although his thoughts bounced from Egypt to Rome to Palmyra before settling on that portion of Assyria that most concerned him.

"Yes."

Aurelian bent to inspect the map closely. No one said anything as the minutes passed. He straightened up, blinked several times, then focused on his general of the cavalry.

"Domitianus, have your swiftest courier ride to Banghazi and tell General Probus that you'll meet his African forces at Al-Jizah. Then take your chariots at top speed to support him. What few we have will be useless against Zenobia's huge fleet, and you can get there in about the same time it will take him to march four legions that distance. Before you leave Al-Jizah, make certain you've secured the crops. Then retake Memphis and see how many of our previous conscripts you can reclaim. Offer them total amnesty. After that, tell Probus I want him to march on Alexandria."

Domitianus saluted. "Yes, Caesar."

Aurelian turned to the messenger. "Return to Emperor Gallienus and tell him of these plans."

Without a word, the messenger saluted and exited the tent.

"You're going to offer those deserters total amnesty?"

It was clear from Mucapor's tone he disapproved. Aurelian once more kept his irritation in check. "Yes. We need their support more than we need revenge."

"And my cavalry, Caesar?" Domitianus asked.

"They'll stay with us. Procus, you'll take charge of the cavalry."

"Yes, Caesar."

"Forgive me, Aurelian." Mucapor spoke firmly, far from his usual supercilious tones. "Splitting our forces is exactly what they want."

"I'm aware of that," Aurelian snapped. It seemed the man deliberately set out to make him look an idiot sometimes. He sighed and rubbed his eyes. The march had been too long; the strain was beginning to wear on him. He wanted too badly to confront Zenobia immediately, but was not going to tell his staff that. Instead, he thought he should be a good emperor and explain the larger issues to them—especially Mucapor. "Because of this grain situation, Rome itself is in danger. We can't let the Palmyrenes grow too strong before we stop them."

Domitianus echoed the demanding tones of his general. "But this makes Zenobia's army far larger than ours! Her chariots alone outnumber all of my cavalry, even with those Dalmatians and Mauritanians. And those ragtag mercenaries, especially those Palestinians with their clubs and staves, aren't trained to face that sort of attack."

Aurelian looked at the both of them with his most steely glare. The moment of challenge had finally come. "Do not scorn any of our men." In fact, he had been quite pleased with the addition of the mercenaries. The reports on the size of Zenobia's army and the alliances she had made with several of the surrounding kingdoms had him more worried than he would admit. "Just remember the ferocity of the Alamanni, and hope these men fight half as valiantly."

"But what if she just waits behind the walls of Palmyra, as Decius said?" Mucapor did not back down in the least. "We don't have any siege engines, and she's undoubtedly much better supplied than we are."

Aurelian was perplexed. Why all this negativity from his primary generals? Other than the one defeat at Placentia—where they had been ambushed—their legions had only known victory. Was Mucapor angling for command of his own legions, and Domitianus supporting him out of friendship or equal ambition? They had yet to prove to him that they were capable of independent command—perhaps this campaign would resolve that issue. He shrugged off his irritation; it could only cloud his judgment at this critical time.

"Both of you are correct. But, from what we heard of her campaign in Egypt, she relies far too much on her heavy chariots. She can't use them if she's hiding behind city walls."

"So you believe she will come out against us, Caesar?" Decius spoke in his most reasonable terms, not looking at the two generals.

Aurelian blinked. He had assumed she would continue to gather her forces, allowing them to be well-rested while his own army marched, fought and hunted for food. Based on this new information, he considered the situation from Zenobia's standpoint.

"If we can't be supplied from behind, she may want to cut us off from reaching her major cities. We'll have to send scouts to find out."

Mucapor remained unrelenting. "What if she dispatches her chariot forces and cavalry, but remains in Palmyra with her infantry? Our army would be reduced, and she'd have a stronger position to defend."

Aurelian shook his head. "Zenobia won't let them fight without leading them in battle herself. As you suggested, she won't want to split her forces. If we can counter her tactics with the chariots, it will break her strength and perhaps offset her advantage in numbers."

"And how could we possibly do that?" Mucapor's scorn was barely concealed.

Aurelian stared hard at the general of his Praetorian Guard before he answered. "I don't know. But maybe it's time to find out how much my mercy in Tyana is really going to be blessed."

*   *   *

Across the plains of Assyria, a huge cloud of dust moved like a storm. It was created by more than seventy-thousand men, plus their animals and wagons, crossing the desert floor. The column wound for many miles. Empress Zenobia glanced back at the column and smiled: her army was on the march. As usual, the empress and her staff, minus those who rode at the head of their individual commands, led the procession.

In the great distance, a tiny plume of dust announced a rider rapidly approaching from the opposite direction. Half an hour later, a Palmyrene scout reached Zenobia and her staff. Reining his mount in, the scout turned to pace them.

"Your Majesty."

"What news of the Romans?"

"They've split their forces." The scout pointed south. "The chariots have all gone south. Emperor Aurelian is about the same distance from Antakya as we are, with less than seven legions and several troops of cavalry."

Rasses thumped his chest with delight. "Excellent! Then we outnumber Aurelian's army by more than two to one."

"And we have a full force of heavy chariots to crush their vaunted formations!" Artabanes' voice sounded greedy at the thought.

"Yes, that all bodes very well." Zenobia raised a corner of her mouth. "Still, we won't take him lightly. He's defeated armies larger than ours, and I'm sure he's got something up his tunic that he thinks he can use to win or he wouldn't face us head on."

Sefer leaned forward with a strange intensity. "Do you believe so, Majesty?"

"Of course."

"Aurelian's no fool." Zabdas patted the neck of his horse. "Still, our situation is very promising."

Sefer did not blink as he looked at the general. "Promising is not the same as certain,"

Zenobia gave him a searching look. "Nothing is certain in this life, Shaykh Sefer."

"No, nothing is certain, Empress Zenobia." Sefer gave her a slight salaam. "And so we must all act as we believe our fate decrees, is that not so?"

"Yes, that is exactly so. And within a few days I hope our fate is to meet Aurelian and his legions, and to defeat him decisively."

*   *   *

Aurelian stood in his tent, dictating a letter to Mnestheus. His scouts had confirmed his suspicions: Zenobia was marching her entire army across the plains of Assyria to meet him. He wanted to meet her in the hills outside of Antakya, which would to some extent diminish the effectiveness of her chariots—especially if he could get there first. He ordered a forced march, which so far had taken four days. By the next time Sol Invictis took his rest, Aurelian wanted to be camped on the high ground.

It would be a very difficult battle. In case he did not survive, Aurelian wanted to put his affairs in order back in Rome. Trusting that Mnestheus would be allowed to live and return to Rome regardless of the battle's outcome, Aurelian was in the middle of settling his affairs: "...and so, should the gods decree my death, I hereby bequeath all of my lands to...."

Decius entered his tent without being announced, a puzzled look on his face. "Caesar, there's an Assyrian outside who wishes an audience."

Aurelian held up a hand to Mnestheus, not bothered at his aide-de-camp's interruption. "An Assyrian? Is he begging food from us or trying to sell it?"

"Neither, Caesar. He claims he has news of Zenobia's army."

"Oh. Tell him we're already aware of the situation."

"I did, but he claims to know Zenobia's tactics in defeating our legions in Egypt."

"What!" He cocked his head and lowered an eyebrow. Decius shrugged. Aurelian scratched his head. "There's only one way he could possibly know that. Where is he now?"

"Still with the guards at the entrance to the camp."

Aurelian thought for a moment longer. "Very well. Send him in."

Decius saluted and left the tent. Although he knew Decius would make certain the man was unarmed, Aurelian reached for his short sword. It would do no harm to let the man know he was suspicious. His scribe looked at him quizzically, and Aurelian remembered what he had been doing.

"Mnestheus, we'll continue this later."

Without a word, Mnestheus bowed and exited.

Aurelian stroked his chin gently with the point of his sword. "So! Perhaps that old philosopher helped bring me some luck after all. Or at least one traitor."

*   *   *

It was late, but Aurelian knew the news could not wait. Mucapor, Decius and Procus had been told to join him in his tent, and they had just finished discussing strategy. Aurelian tapped the map to emphasize his orders.

"So, you all understand clearly what you must do, correct?"

Procus wrinkled his nose. "Yes, Caesar, but it's very risky. What if Zenobia sends her cavalry after us instead of the chariots?"

"According to my informant, she's committed nearly all of her horses because she believes so thoroughly in them." Aurelian gave Procus a reassuring smile. "What cavalry is left won't be a match for ours. They wear heavy armor, and they aren't trained to fight as a unit. They rely too much on the type of individual combat they practice amongst themselves."

"Forgive me, Caesar, but I must repeat that splitting our forces could be exactly what she wants." Decius glanced at the front of the tent, as though looking through it to see the face of their mysterious visitor. "This may not be the way Zenobia fights at all. What makes you believe you can trust this traitor?"

"Nothing." Aurelian made a slight frown, then shrugged. "He claims he wants us to spare his tribe, as we did with Tyana. I've promised him that, and more."

"Hah!" Mucapor scoffed in a low tone.

Aurelian ignored him. "In return, he's promised to have a little surprise for Zenobia during the battle." His eyes swept those of his staff. "It's clear we have to take great risks. Anyhow, I'll have him right next to me in case he lied."

Mucapor folded his arms across his chest. "And if he's willing to sacrifice himself in order to trick us?"

Aurelian allowed his disdain to show in the curl of his lip. "Then, General Mucapor, I will probably be dead. But, if you succeed in your part of this plan, you'll be in charge of the legions. If so, wait until Domitianus returns from Egypt with the rest of our forces before you face her."

Mucapor nodded. "As you command. The plan is bold, but perhaps we'll both be successful."

"I'm certain you'll make a sacrifice to the gods for the victory of us all, General."

*　　　　*　　　　*

Aurelian stood on the edge of his camp and stared across the plains of Assyria. It was late at night. Although the moon was on the wane, the bright stars illuminated the huge camp of the Palmyrenes below. Aided by the light provided by thousands of campfires, he could see Zenobia's large tent in the middle, better lit than the others. He pulled his cloak more tightly around him, unable to curb thoughts of what Zenobia was doing at that very moment. His face contorted, although he was not certain whether in a smile or a grimace; it was strange to think of himself as an emperor of the Roman Empire in love with a beautiful queen of an exotic land. His experiences as a young man had never prepared him to deal with such a circumstance.

There was a taste in his mouth like the blade of a knife. He still cared very deeply for Zenobia, and he was certain that, in some way, she also cared for him. And yet they were about to go to war, to spill blood to see which of them would rule this desert instead of happily exploring how they might share it. It was a thought too bitter to bear. Then another strange thought struck him. Suddenly, he wheeled and headed for his own tent.

*　　　　*　　　　*

Zenobia knelt in her tent before a small statue of Malak-bel. Four candles burned, two on either side of the statue, steady flames to light the features of the god. Otherwise, the walls of her tent were bare. Her sword lay in front of the shrine like an offering to the god, or a symbol of what she prayed for. In spite of their superior numbers and the confidence in her army and her generals, she wanted all the advantages she could get.

"Great Malak-bel, grant my army victory in your honor. Grant me revenge over the Roman emperor, who betrayed me and my family. Grant me—"

Suddenly a ripping sound to her right caused her to jerk, and a sword slashed through the rear of her tent. A figure entered, cloaked and hooded. With the speed of a striking adder, Zenobia leaped to her feet and grabbed her sword. The intruder made no move to get closer to her as he entered the tent. Then the man threw back the hood on his cloak, which she unconsciously recognized as that of a commanding Palmyrene general.

"Aurelian!"

Aurelian stood motionless for a moment, perhaps to give her time to absorb his incredible entry. Her mouth worked to speak, but disbelief made her mute.

"Aren't you going to invite me in?"

Finally, her brain functioned once more. "You're already in." Although he kept his sword down, she did not lower hers. "Why are you here?"

While his body did not move, his mouth tightened and his cheek twitched. "I wanted to see you, to talk with you. Perhaps to stop this slaughter. To come to some sort of agreement."

"You could have sent a delegation." Zenobia did not bother to hide the anger in her voice. "It would have been safer for you."

"I didn't want a delegation. I wanted it to be me…and you."

Zenobia finally lowered her sword, although not the amount of anger in her voice. "I see you wore my husband's cloak to carry you through my guards. Are you so unfeeling that your treachery to him does not haunt you?"

Aurelian cocked his head slightly to the side; his brows furrowed and his mouth parted slightly. "My treachery to Odaenathus? I don't understand."

Zenobia sneered. "Did you think I would not discover you had him murdered?"

Aurelian lifted his free hand in protest. "I didn't order the murder of Odaenathus. I admired and honored your husband as a true subject of Rome."

"Then what of this?" Still holding her sword, Zenobia went to a chest and withdrew the Roman sword, crusted over with the blood of the dead.

"This was the weapon that murdered Odaenathus?"

Zenobia looked at him searchingly. Either he had the skill to perform in a tragedy at the amphitheater in Palmyra, or he was genuinely unaware of the assassination. Her voice faltered.

"Truly, you did not know?"

Aurelian reached for the sword. After a brief hesitation, she handed it to him. He inspected it carefully. His cheek muscle lifted, a wry smile that denoted he perceived a painful irony. His voice was also sad. "I see, I see. So, I have a snake within my cradle."

"You're saying you have a conspirator, and he had Odaenathus killed to make it look like you had it done?"

Aurelian nodded slowly. "It would seem so. I'm not sure who…but I have a suspicion."

There was a long pause as each stood lost in thought.

The sword—so obvious a device. Perhaps too obvious, in retrospect. Had she wanted to believe the message it sent? Had her true motives been hidden even from her? Her impetuous, girlish liaison with Emperor Valerian. Her immediate acceptance the offer of Odaenathus to wed shortly after they had met. Her strong attraction to the new emperor, excused by the expediencies of many royal houses. Was it the men in power, or the power itself? She was lost in the maelstrom of her own feelings, her own mind.

Zenobia broke into an anguished cry.

"Oh, why? Why did you come here, Aurelian?"

Aurelian straightened his shoulders. Whatever distressing thought had crossed his features was now gone like water evaporated by the sun.

"Because I had to see you again. I wanted to talk with you."

"I see. To talk."

Emotions crossed his face, but they moved so rapidly she could not follow. She recognized the last: distress. The offending sword fell from his hand. She stiffened her resolve not to show him any pity.

"Perhaps even…to touch you once again. To hold you."

"Oh. To hold me."

"Yes." Ignoring the sword still in her hand, Aurelian stepped forward and put his hands on her shoulders. "I've finally succumbed to a weakness: my love for you. I can't sleep without waking from dreams of you. I can't concentrate on my duties because my mind wanders to thoughts of you. You're ruining me!"

Zenobia lifted her chin, and her voice carried her disdain. "Ah, I see. You've found your weakness. And you're ashamed of it, aren't you?"

"Ashamed?" Aurelian's brow creased once again. She could see he was truly searching out his feelings. "No. I'm…baffled. Confused. Amazed. But not ashamed." His face became calm once more. "When we first met, you were right. I was cold, repressed, totally wrapped up in my logical, unemotional approach to battle." He puffed out a breath of air. "It's what sustained me."

He half-turned, taking his hands away from her. For just a fraction of a second, Zenobia felt a loss.

"Perhaps if you knew something more about me…as you told me about yourself."

"Perhaps." She gave a small smile of encouragement. She could imagine how difficult this was for him.

He returned her wan smile. "I was born near Sirmium in Moesia to an obscure provincial family. My father was poor, a tenant farmer to a senator named Aurelius." Aurelian shrugged. "Aurelius gave his name to the family, as great men sometimes do when they're pleased by the services of their retainers."

A slight breeze from the rent Aurelian had made caused the candles to flicker. As much as the tent would allow, he paced, his boots scuffing softly on the carpets that covered the sand.

"When I was eighteen, I was married to a woman named Ulpia Severina. She was several years older, and everyone knew she had been the mistress of Aurelius." Aurelian made a slight face, but did not stop his monologue. "She brought a nice dowry along with a small, private house on the estate of Aurelius. Five months after our marriage, she bore a healthy son. I named him Commodus. Although Ulpia was a great beauty, I could not bear to touch her any longer."

Zenobia nodded her understanding, encouraging him to go on.

"Two years after the marriage, I asked our patron for permission to join the army. Using his influence with Emperor Claudius, Aurelius procured me a position as tribune in one of Claudius' crack legions. It turned out to be a propitious event for both myself and Claudius, I think, and insured that I would never have to see my wife or son—and our new daughter—ever again."

The flickering candles played softly across his rough, chiseled features. Zenobia was tempted to reach out and touch them, but she let him talk about his past, perhaps for the first time ever.

"Over the next few years, I managed to distinguish myself somewhat as a junior officer, especially with the cavalry." The memory illuminated his face. "I loved it; going to war on the back of a horse was what I had been born for. I was promoted rapidly, and given command of the elite Dalmatian cavalry. There seemed no end of battles to be fought."

Zenobia thought of sitting, but she didn't want to break the mood. "And you never missed them—I mean, your parents. Your…family."

Aurelian stopped pacing and looked at her directly. "The men and horses became my family, Claudius my surrogate father. I never returned to Moesia." Aurelian cleared his throat and lifted one shoulder in a shrug. "One day word came of large-scale attacks from the Heruli, Goths, Gepids, and the Bastarnae in the Balkans. Claudius immediately dispatched me with my one troop of cavalry to contain the invasion as best I could until he arrived with the main army. The Goths were besieging Thessalonica; we harassed their rear until they were forced to abandon the siege. Next came the Heruli. My splendid Dalmatian cavalry rode tirelessly from one invader to another, inflicting great damage in a series of minor skirmishes. When the main army finally arrived, we helped Claudius gain a victory over the Goths at the Battle of Naissus. In recognition of my personal contributions, Claudius honored me with a villa in Tibur. I was promoted to overall commander of the cavalry—the emperor's position before his own elevation."

"But then Claudius died."

Aurelian nodded. "Yes. It was a very sad time for me."

"But then…?"

"Due to my reputation as a cavalry officer, Emperor Gallienus made me a member of his general staff. After more years of proving myself as a commander of more than just the horse, Gallienus made me emperor—as you know."

"And gave you a reason to visit the city of Palmyra."

"And to meet a beautiful woman named Zenobia."

They stared at one another with no words. Zenobia gripped her sword tightly in her hands, her knuckles tense. Aurelian stood as though limp from the effort of telling his story. The only sound was that of their breathing; the only movement the dancing of the candle light. Zenobia felt she had to break the spell.

"So, you're married."

"Hah!" Aurelian scoffed, waving the thought away with his hand. "Since joining the army, I'd barely given consideration to any woman."

"Oh yes, the army was your love." She said it mockingly, but knew it was true.

"It's what I'd done since I was a boy." Aurelian scrunched up his face and shrugged one shoulder. He moved restlessly, shifting his feet as though they wanted to march off, but had been somehow rooted to the spot. Then he calmed himself and half lifted a hand toward her. "In some ways, I was never really alive. But the moment my sword clashed with yours, and I looked into your eyes and saw such fire, such determination…it was as if my own spirit had risen from a crypt where it had been buried for centuries. That one moment fulfilled a part of me I had never known was missing." The hand rose higher, now a fist. "This...this passion that I feel makes my blood race, my mind churn with possibilities, my hands yearn to touch what once I would have been ashamed to desire so much."

He looked directly into her eyes. She knew the truth, and she was amazed.

"You truly desire me?"

The passion in his voice made her knees tremble.

"Oh, deeply! I'll make you my consort if only you will surrender, both to Rome and to our passion. Surrender to me, my love!"

Their eyes locked for another moment, then they wildly moved together as one, meeting in a passionate kiss. Her sword fell to the carpet. Aurelian's hands roamed her body greedily. Her lips felt crushed, her loins burned, and her head spun. Losing their balance, they fell to the bed, thrashing about in their passion. Aurelian lifted the hem of her robe. Abruptly she pushed him away and rolled off the bed. In one fluid movement she grabbed her sword, which she held out towards his throat. Breathing heavily, they stared at each other with huge eyes. Anger, desire, frustration, all flowed through her in waves, breaking themselves on the impenetrable barrier of her heart.

"No!"

"No?" he repeated stupidly.

"No." A small sob escaped her throat. "I cannot."

The anguish returned to his voice. "But why?"

Zenobia opened her mouth, exhaling rapidly. But the answer came to her slowly. Her breathing returned to normal.

"I might have, years ago. But now I've known the taste of power." She lowered the sword slowly, looking into the distance as much as at him. "Even when I was with Odaenathus, I knew I wasn't satisfied, not fulfilled. I wanted more. These past few years have been all I dreamed of, all I wanted. I have been supreme, making the hard choices, in command of both my armies and my people. My empire grows because of my decisions, because of what I do, not due to any man." She drew herself up regally. "Today I'm not your vassal, nor your consort, Aurelian. I'm your equal. As your consort, we could never be equals. I will never go back to the servitude of a submissive woman."

Aurelian searched her face. Then he nodded. "Yes. Yes, I see." He turned away, his forehead bowed in sorrow in his hands.

Zenobia reached her hand towards him, but did not touch. "Can't you understand, Aurelian?"

Aurelian turned back to her and squared his shoulders. He cleared his throat, and his voice was once again firm. "I understand completely. You're a general and an empress. Did you think for a moment I would not understand?"

Zenobia attempted to smile in gratitude, but her cheeks seemed set in cold granite. "No. I knew you would."

"Then we must settle this on the battlefield."

"Yes. On the battlefield."

CHAPTER FIFTEEN

Mounted at the front of the army, Zenobia and Zabdas went over the upcoming battle for at least the tenth time. Artabanes stood in the lead chariot a few yards away, flicking his whip idly as he waited for a signal. Sargon, the shield bearer of Artabanes' chariot, diced with Asu, the spear thrower.

Finding no more to say about strategy, Zenobia looked around at the multitude that surrounded her. While no one actually lounged around, men picked up pebbles and threw them, idly fingered their weapons, or just stood in small clusters and talked in low tones. At long last, Rasses trotted slowly towards her from their encampment, his mount pawing nervously at the sand as though reflecting the evident agitation of its master.

Seeing his expression, Zenobia frowned. As he rode alone, there could be only one explanation for this delay. "Shaykh Rasses, where is Shaykh Sefer?"

"I received a message only a few moments ago," Rasses cleared his throat, then licked his lips. "He is gravely ill, and still within his tent."

Zabdas grunted. "Roman legion fever, no doubt."

"Sefer may be young, but he is no coward, General." Rasses' voice was mild, but he was clearly irritated at the insult to his fellow shaykh.

Zenobia cut them off. "Enough. We must stay together."

She looked at them to make certain they were in accord, and smiled when they both nodded. Then she turned and waved to her troops.

As far as the eye could see, the Palmyrene military spread across the desert. The various units were formed up in ranks, the heavy chariots first, then the light ones, followed by a corps of archers. Finally came the foot soldiers, like cacti springing from the sand. Some horses had been conscripted to pull chariots, but the remaining cavalry of the two shaykhs were to each side of the foot soldiers. This had been one of the few bones of contention between Zenobia and her main lieutenants. However, the success of the heavy chariots against the Roman formations, and especially of the "blade chariots" that had been equipped after General Timagenes' advice, had won the day for the dedication of more horses to heavy chariots.

"Warriors of Assyria!" Zenobia's strong voice rang with confidence. "Citizens of the Palmyrene Empire! We have united in brotherhood, we have won great battles against our enemies, and convinced many to become our allies. Together, we have done great things."

Those who could hear cheered her words, and they passed the message on to those in the rear.

Zenobia waited for their cheers to die down. "But today, today we will do something which no other nation can claim, something that will be remembered throughout history. We defeated the Roman garrisons at Memphis, and again at Alexandria. But today we march against a Roman army, led by one of the Roman emperors. Today we will defeat the invaders from Italia. Today we will free our homeland from the yoke of the tyrants. Are you ready to be free?"

"YES!" they shouted.

"Are you ready to do battle?"

"YES!"

"Are you ready to follow me to victory?"

"YES!"

Zenobia looked over her army. Inspired by their enthusiasm, she dramatically reached up to her breastplate. She pulled it aside to show one bare breast. Her soldiers cheered wildly.

"Our Lady of Victory! Our Lady of Victory!"

Despite their vigor, the shouting died down much more quickly than she had expected. She followed the eyes of her soldiers to the hill above them, as did her commanders. The Roman cavalry trotted down the hill, moving to a position to the north. Zenobia refastened her breastplate.

"Where's Aurelian?" Zabdas gave an impatient flick of his reins. "Where are his legions?"

Artabanes pointed up the hill to the Roman encampment. "The camp looks deserted. This is very strange."

The others in the group looked at the camp. No one stood guard there, and only a few pennants fluttered in the mild breeze.

"By the gods, it does," Rasses waved to one of his lieutenants, who immediately rode up to him.

"Arum, ride up to the Roman camp—cautiously. Go in as far as you can safely. Bring us word."

"My lord."

With a glance toward the unmoving Roman cavalry, Arum spurred his horse up the hill. Zenobia squinted against the sun, watching him, and Artabanes moved his chariot closer to the other leaders.

Arum slowed his horse to a walk at the edge of the camp. Zenobia realized that his careful path kept him in sight of his own army. She nodded with approval as he swiveled in his saddle several times, darting his head around from one place to another as though he expected to catch a sudden, threatening movement. Finally, with an elaborate shrug of his shoulders visible across the distance, Arum turned back toward his shaykh and held out one hand, as though unsure of what to do.

Zenobia released the breath she hadn't realized she'd been holding.

Rasses beckoned him to return, which the man hastened to obey. He pulled his horse to a halt by the group of commanders. "The camp is deserted, my lord." Arum's heavy breathing betrayed the nervousness his face concealed.

Zenobia was puzzled. "The Romans have gone and left their tents?"

"It would seem so, Empress." Arum made a stiff bow, perhaps in apology.

"Has he fled and left his cavalry to cover his retreat?" Artabanes wondered.

"Don't tell me the man's a coward!"

Zenobia shook her head. "I doubt that, General Zabdas, but I can't understand this. I can only imagine it's some elaborate strategy he's conceived."

"Thank you, Arum. Return to your men."

Arum saluted his shaykh and trotted back to his position.

Zenobia waved at the mass of warriors behind her. "Well, if he won't come to us, then we'll take the battle to him. Our men are spoiling for a fight. General Artabanes, the Romans can't be more than a few hours ahead. Take your chariots and run them down. We'll follow at a quick march."

Artabanes bobbed his head. "Yes, Empress." He had his driver wheel the chariot back to the head of his command. "Light chariots, move out!" he called out. "Heavy chariots, follow behind."

   *   *   *

Procus watched with a mixture of interest and anxiety. He had been given both the Dalmatian and Mauritanian troops, and how he completed his assignment might make the difference between victory or defeat. He breathed evenly as he sat on his horse, forced his fingers to relax on the reins, and did his best to curl his lips upward in a smile or a sneer. It would be much worse to disgrace himself as a Roman officer than to die in battle. Above all, he wanted the emperor to be proud of him.

His spirits lifted a little as he watched the confusion of the Palmyrenes, then the amusing scene as they timidly explored the deserted camp. He became much more focused when their female leader loosed the might of her forces in his direction. As the chariots came into range, he gave his first independent command.

"Ready!"

Having waited long, tense minutes for this, each man nocked an arrow to his bow and pulled back on the string.

"Fire!"

As one they fired a volley of arrows. Most of the arrows were stopped by the shield bearers. There was time for one more volley before their next maneuver. While few arrows reached a man, a number of them scored a hit on the flesh of a horse. Those wounds would cause pain and bleeding, eventually having an effect. When the chariots got up to a full gallop, it was time to go.

"Retreat!"

The Roman cavalry whirled and fled. The chariots began the chase.

   *   *   *

Zenobia watched the initial encounter with exasperation. "Well, this isn't exactly the battle I imagined, but we'd better get marching or we may miss the action."

"Fear not, Empress." Rasses touched the hilt of his sword. "I suspect you will get your battle."

Zabdas glowered at him. "Wherever they overtake the legions, we'd better be close to support Artabanes." He turned to the empress. "Shall I give the order, Majesty?"

Watching her full complement of chariots chase the small band of horse riders, Zenobia sighed. Why couldn't Aurelian just have had his army face her man-to-man? Her eyes remained focused on the horses thundering off into the distance.

"Yes. Let's march."

Zabdas raised his sword and turned to the men behind him. "Forward!"

Ponderously, the mass of foot soldiers lurched into action. The troops of mounted tribesmen paced them on either side.

*   *   *

When the Palmyrene army had marched past the Roman camp, a single Roman soldier emerged from a tent to watch. He made certain they were well on their way and had not sent any scouts to once again inspect the camp. Then the soldier ran to the far side of the hill. He waved his arms slowly above his head.

*   *   *

At the bottom of the hill, General Mucapor sat mounted on his horse in front of two legions. At the signal, he turned to his men.

"March!"

In their normal quick, easy stride, the legions began marching over the hill, following the Palmyrene army. They made certain to not exceed the pace of their quarry.

CHAPTER SIXTEEN

Sargon wiped the sweat from his brow; the heavy helmet felt like a small oven. The sun beat down on the Assyrian desert with the wrath of Ishum, hurling his fires from the heavens, and the heat radiated back up from the sand like the breaths of the Rephaim, the angry gods of the underworld. After long hours of an eager, enthusiastic chase, the Palmyrene chariots had slowed to a walk. The men either stared grimly ahead or muttered curses. The horses plodded wearily, their tongues hanging and their tails whisking irritably at the insects that stung their flanks, with nothing they could do about those pests that buzzed around their eyes.

The Roman cavalry rode tantalizingly out of range. For the most part they stayed in front of their pursuers, but some riders occasionally dared to race to the sides of the chariot corps and fire arrows, which were having more effect as the horses slowed and the shield bearers tired. Because the general's chariot was still in the lead, Sargon was forced to block more arrows than most. Not nearly as maneuverable as a horse and rider, the chariots tried to keep in close formation for protection. This meant they ate more of each other's dust, and sometimes bumped into each other, further inflaming their bad tempers. At least being in front meant he didn't have to put up with that.

As he fended off yet another arrow, the shield bearer thought the weight of the shield must have doubled since the beginning of the day. He dared not lower it to snap off the embedded arrows for fear of exposing General Artabanes. He had been personally selected by the general for the strength of his arm, his courage under fire, and his dedication. But being used to his burdens did not keep him from voicing his complaints.

"General, they're picking us to pieces." Sargon had served the general for a dozen years and felt confident in their relationship. "Should we break off the pursuit and wait for the army?"

"No. The empress gave us the order to pursue them. It can't be long now 'til we find their army."

"Much more of this, General, and we may not want to find their army."

General Artabanes limited his response to a grunt. Sargon frowned, but there was nothing more he dared to say.

*   *   *

Zenobia glanced at the sun high on the horizon. The army had been marching for several hours, but they had seen no sign of anyone else, friend or foe. "It's mid-morning. We must be approaching Immae."

"No doubt we'll be there by midday," Zabdas wiped the heavy sweat from his forehead. "It's hot as the palace kitchen during bread-baking day. I hate to think how Artabanes' chariots are doing."

"I just wish I knew where Aurelian was," Zenobia tried to keep the irritation from her voice, but failed.

Rasses had a sour look on his face. "I hope that, when we do learn, we are pleased with the news."

*   *   *

The sun was past its zenith, and the heat was building. The chariots barely raised dust in their wake now. The men and horses drooped, too exhausted to show any irritation. Many of the men had been tempted to remove their hot, heavy armor, but the sporadic attack of Roman cavalrymen made that impossible. Fortunately for them the Romans, with their nimble horses and lighter armor, also suffered from the heat, and their quick forays had decreased.

Keeping his eyes roving to both sides, where the Romans were most likely to attack, Sargon saw some unusual movement. "What's their cavalry doing now, General?"

Artabanes' head moved from side to side as he studied the situation. "They're splitting, forming a row on either side of us. That must mean—" Artabanes shielded his eyes and squinted. He jabbed a finger toward a small hill in the distance. "Yes! There. Up on that hill."

Sargon looked at where his commander pointed. His eyes widened. "The Roman legions." He didn't know whether to feel nervous or sigh with relief.

The legions were in formation on the slope of a hill some distance away. The hill was not high, but it sloped towards the advancing Palmyrenes in a semi-circular shape, thus making it difficult to go around and attack from the rear. In addition, the Roman cavalry had divided into two groups, each in a line slightly up the slope of the descending ends of the hill, forming a "U" in front of the chariots.

Sargon was not a tactician, but he thought the spot had been well chosen. That supposition was quickly borne out by the general.

"No doubt they expect us to make a direct assault while their cavalry rains down arrows from each flank." He half turned and held his hand up in the air. "Halt!"

It did not take long for the chariots corps, already moving slowly, to rumble to a complete stop. Khalid pulled up his chariot next to that of Artabanes.

"What are your orders, General?"

"They're waiting for us to enter their little box." Artabanes scanned the situation once more before he continued. "Let them wait. Give the men half an hour rest and water all the horses. After we regroup, find out what our losses were."

"Yes, General." Khalid gave a small salaam and moved off to follow orders.

Sargon licked his lips. "Water sounds like a great idea."

"Yes. But the horses first."

"Yes, General," Sargon said grumpily.

*   *   *

The Palmyrene army was spread out across the plains of Assyria. Used to layers of light clothing that trapped perspiration and cooled the skin during the heat of the day, the soldiers wilted within their heavy armor. The neat formations were now ragged lines of individuals, with stragglers limping along far behind. Only the riders, who had kept their mounts to a walk to keep pace with the foot soldiers, could keep upright.

Rasses glanced over his shoulder, an action he had performed several times in the past half hour. "Your soldiers look exhausted, Empress."

Zabdas agreed immediately. "Yes. If Aurelian is waiting for us, his men marched in the coolness of the night and then rested. Our men must rest as well."

"Our chariots are up ahead somewhere, no doubt also exhausted." Zenobia flicked her riding crop. "If Aurelian has met them, they'll count on us for support. We march on."

Rasses nodded. "Yes, Empress. But five minutes for water."

Zenobia looked at him angrily, then relented. Even sitting on a horse, her eyes burned and her mouth was dry. How must her soldiers feel? "Five minutes."

*   *   *

Artabanes was almost dozing as he stood in his chariot. Sargon was sitting, his shoulder leaning against the inner wall of the chariot, his feet dangling from the open end. Artabanes gazed down at his shield bearer, wishing he could do the same. The soft wicker of a horse caused him to look up; Khalid was approaching once more. He blinked several times and snapped his mind to full attention.

"What were our losses, Khalid?"

"Less than one in ten, General."

Artabanes' felt his mouth make a thin line. "More than I would have thought. But we still have a significant advantage, both in number and in armor. We'll attack."

"My men are ready." Khalid did his best to appear eager.

"I'm certain." Artabanes pointed at the Romans. "Take your chariots against their cavalry. Engage them as much as possible. Our blade chariots will perform the same maneuver we did in Egypt. I'll take the heavy chariots straight at the Romans. "

Khalid made a small salaam. "Yes, General."

While Khalid divided his chariots, Artabanes aligned the blade chariots on the left side of his formation. The rest of the heavy chariots would follow at a slight distance, ready to charge the enemy lines as soon as the blade chariots created an opening.

"Light chariots!" Artabanes called out.

Khalid raised his sword. "Charge!"

The chariots raced towards the lines of cavalry. Artabanes waited until the Roman horsemen had no choice but to engage his first wave.

Then he raised his arm and gave the command, "Blade chariots, forward."

The heavy chariots started slowly, gradually picking up speed. When he was certain the Romans were fully engaged, darting and shooting amongst the light chariots, Artabanes gave the order for the remaining chariots to advance. Behind the Roman lines, archers started firing at the heavy chariots as they came closer. Unless they hit a horse squarely, they would cause little damage to the drivers and men behind their shields. Half way to the Roman lines, they were now hurtling at full speed.

Suddenly, one of the heavy chariots to Artabane's left dipped strangely. It only dropped a foot or so, but that was enough to send the chariot swerving thanks to its heavy load at high speed. Still wondering if a wheel might have come off its axle, Artabanes caught a similar movement on his far right. As the two crippled vehicles began to weave, totally out of control, those behind tried to swerve, with a few crashing. Then the chariot next to his did the same. This time it was one of the horses; the poor creature went down, and even over the thunder of the charge Artabanes could hear the sickening snap of its leg. Dragging the other horses down with it for just a fraction, the speeding carriage rolled right over them all, and the men within the carriage flew into the air.

Then he understood what was happening. The Romans had dug trenches in the sand and covered them with palm leaves. With a little sand sprinkled over the top, the hazards became nearly invisible to the drivers, who had their eyes focused on small hummocks or plants that could have the same effect. Other chariots encountered the same traps, causing chaos for those behind. Now many of the vehicles were destroying themselves, and the Roman archers had more targets.

"Damn those Roman dogs to the underworld!" Artabanes looked ahead to his far left and saw that most of the blade chariots were getting through. The Romans must have counted on him to charge closer to the center of their line, the traditional type of attack. "Hah!" He snarled, certain that their new tactic would win the day. "We'll still cut them to ribbons."

As the blade chariots approached the Roman lines, they turned right in the manner that had worked well in Egypt. The archers and spear throwers were already firing their weapons over the top of the shield bearers, hoping to find exposed targets in the back ranks. The lines of soldiers stood firm, although they did not adopt the "turtle" formation Artabanes had expected. When the first chariot was almost on top of the legionaries, the row directly in the path of the hurtling vehicles suddenly moved their shields back, exposing several sets of metal framework four or five feet high. Artabanes could not be certain at that distance, but it looked like chariot axles, bands from shields, and other miscellaneous metal objects had been joined together into a wicked looking contraption that made him gasp. Several soldiers crouched on the base of each one, anchoring them to the ground.

Artabanes watched in horror as the first blade chariot driver saw the danger. For several seconds he seemed puzzled, failing to react. Within a few paces of the metal monstrosity, he pulled hard on the reins, striving desperately to swerve away. The blade, its hilt firmly fastened to the underside of the carriage, caught the framework. The chariot careened wildly, flipping upwards and sideways. The driver screamed as he flew into the air. The archer and spear thrower, both about to fire once again as the chariot straightened out, tumbled out of the side and onto the ground, where they were quickly stabbed by the legionaries. The shield bearer, who had performed his duty to the end, gave a long shout of surprise as he pitched head-first over the line of Romans, and was also dispatched. The framework shuddered, but the legionaries hung on tightly to ensure it did not topple.

As the drivers directly behind witnessed what happened, they reacted immediately. Those in front still plowed into the frameworks, but others veered sharply—one too sharply, and his chariot also toppled. Because the terrain did not allow for a sharp turn to the left, three others rode into their fallen comrades or managed to avoid them, only to carry on into the next framework. A few even farther behind managed to steer clear of the wreckage and attempted to cut into the Roman lines, but it was difficult to get around the metal frames and then dodge back into a position where they could threaten the defending soldiers with their blades. Because they had to slow down to attempt that maneuver, some of the Romans were able to jab metal stakes through the spokes of their wheels.

Within minutes, most of the blade chariots had crashed, were blocked by their companions, or had veered off from the attack. The few that got through to the Roman lines did some damage, but even a couple of those were toppled. The main force of heavy chariots that managed to evade the traps, the hazards of their fallen friends and the arrows of the Roman archers, also enjoyed very little success because the blade chariots had failed to put much of a dent in the Roman lines.

General Artabanes knew a disaster when he saw it. It was time to cut his losses. He turned to Asu, who doubled as his trumpeter to pass on his commands. "Sound retreat."

As the driver worked to turn the chariot, Asu picked up his horn and blew a piercing note. The noise attracted the attention of more than their own men, for as he began to repeat the order, an arrow found its way past Sargon's shield and caught Asu in the side of the head. The horn fell from his lifeless fingers and his body tumbled off the speeding chariot. Sargon immediately bent to pick up the horn to sound the command, but an arrow caught him in the chest and he slumped against the side of the chariot. With a pang of anguish over the loss of his friend, Artabanes grabbed the shield from the dead man's hand and attempted to protect his driver from the hail of arrows as they led the retreat.

* * *

On the hillside above, Aurelian and Decius sat on horses on either side of Sefer, who was also mounted. While Decius was clearly pleased by the events transpiring below them, Aurelian and Sefer showed no expression. Even from that great distance, their noses were assailed by the acrid odor of blood, the pungent stench of sliced flesh, and the reek of urine and excrement that flowed from men and animals as they vacated their bowels in both fear and death. The Palmyrenes were routed.

"Your information was very good, Shaykh Sefer. This is going much better than I could have hoped."

Out of the corner of his eye Aurelian saw Sefer's face turn bitter, but the other man said nothing. There was a blast of a horn from one of the chariots below.

"Look!" Decius pointed at the chariot from which the sound came. "Archers, there! That chariot, the man with the crest on his helmet."

Several archers fired immediately, and one arrow caught the trumpeter in the head. Within an instant, another caught the shield bearer in the chest. The man with the fancy helmet, clearly the general of the chariot corps, grabbed the shield and tried to swing it to the side to protect his driver as they turned. Not used to the task, he held the shield forward, which left his back exposed. Within seconds, another arrow found a weakness in his armor and felled him as well. Now totally exposed, the driver was riddled by arrows.

Aurelian turned to look directly at Sefer. The younger man's face remained a carved stone.

Those chariots close enough to hear the sound of the horn turned and fled. As others saw the heavy chariots retreating, they also tried to disengage from the Roman cavalry who wove amongst them, firing arrows whenever possible.

Aurelian decided to save the remainder of his cavalry for the next battle, which might come at any moment. He turned to his own signalers and waved; a blast of trumpets ended the rain of arrows that had followed the chariots as they fled, and the *lituus* waved. Seeing the pennant fluttering in the air, the cavalry broke off the attack and rejoined the legions.

Smiling broadly, Procus rode up to Aurelian and saluted. His breathing was heavy, and one arm was bleeding from where an arrow had nicked him. Yet it was clear he made a strong effort to curb the enthusiasm in his voice. "Caesar, I think we got about half their light chariots."

"You did a fine job, Procus. My commendations."

"Thank you, Caesar."

Aurelian looked at the remaining horsemen and frowned. "And what of your cavalry?"

The joy of victory as a commander, and the relief at still being alive, fled from Procus' face and voice. "Not quite half, I think. Still, heavy losses."

"Yes," Aurelian knew that the deaths of good men always weighed on the mind of a conscientious leader. But whether a man lived or died was up to the gods; a commander could only strive to gain victory to make the deaths meaningful. "Yet you did very well against such odds."

Procus nodded his thanks, but his depressed expression—no doubt as much due to the easing of tension after the battle as to the losses—did not leave him. Aurelian turned to praise his other officer. "And you, Decius. Those were wonderful traps. And those contraptions you designed did marvelously well. Great work in such a short time."

"Thanks to the shaykh's information. Otherwise, I can't imagine how we would have countered those blades." Decius smiled at Sefer, but the other man refused to look at him. Decius shrugged, as if to imply the attitude of the man was of no concern to him.

Aurelian nodded. "Unfortunately, Decius, no time to rest on your laurels—which you will receive when we return to Rome. Now we must press them, give them no time to regroup." He leaned forward in his saddle and patted Decius on the shoulder. "Have your men re-arm while your horses have a drink. Then do the same thing: harass them from both flanks. Don't get close enough for their spears."

"Caesar!" Decius saluted and trotted off to carry out his orders.

Aurelian turned to the captain of his Praetorian Guard. "Procus, I want you to lead half of your men on a forced march half a league from our right flank. You'll escort the archers. Eventually, Zenobia's army will catch up to us. By the time they do, I want the archers in a position to come at their flank. That will give you only two hundred men, so you'll have to decide how long you stand once the battle begins."

"We won't wait here for them to come, Caesar?"

"No. The first time they were over-confident and fell into our trap. If we stayed here and I were them, I'd bottle off our escape to the front and send half their infantry—which still out-numbers us greatly—around these little hills to attack from the rear." Aurelian swept his hand across the ridge to make his point. "Then they'd have the high ground, and we're too weak to fight on both fronts. Much better to take the fight to them and wait for General Mucapor to take them by surprise from the rear."

Procus saluted. "Yes, Caesar."

"They should all be well-rested. Move them out as soon as you can. I'm going to march the rest of the legions to meet Zenobia."

"Good luck, Aurelian."

Aurelian's eyebrows went up. Since he had been proclaimed emperor, it was one of the few times Procus had used his name rather than his title. He smiled broadly.

"And to you, Procus. Let's see if we can end this upstart empire today."

Procus grinned back at his leader. He saluted once more and turned his horse to join the Praetorian Guard.

CHAPTER SEVENTEEN

Zenobia inspected the empty desert sprawled for miles in all directions. She both admired Aurelian's strategy and hated him for it. Rather than the glorious battle she had envisioned—pummeling his legions into the sand with her huge army and massive chariot corps—he had created this endless, enervating chase. It was sapping the energy and the morale of her soldiers. She held her horse to a steady walk and maintained a neutral facade.

General Zabdas, who had kept his gaze fixed ahead like a hunting dog on point, leaned forward in his saddle and shielded his eyes. "Look, dust on the horizon."

"Are those our chariots?" Zenobia squinted at the shimmering dust cloud moving toward them.

After a few more seconds, Zabdas answered. "Yes, by Malak-bel. And they're on the run!"

Zenobia snapped her mouth shut, aware that she was gaping. She had expected to see them engaged with the Romans, or at least bringing news of where the infantry could go to finish off the legions. She had never even considered they might be fleeing back to the safety of numbers.

"Rasses, take all of our horsemen and give them aid. Perhaps the Roman cavalry is chasing them."

"Majesty." Rasses raised in his stirrups and waved to his horsemen. "Arum! Follow."

Rasses took off at a gallop toward the chariots; the other riders instantly followed.

Zabdas shook his head. "This bodes ill."

Zenobia knew it would be foolish to increase the pace the army was marching simply to meet up with the chariots a few minutes sooner. To her consternation, she saw that, once they had spotted the army, the chariots had actually slowed down. It would not look good if she galloped off, leaving her infantry behind to trudge wearily on. Grinding her teeth, then breathing through her mouth to force herself to relax, Zenobia waited to learn the news.

At last Khalid's chariot approached her. He tried to salaam, but toppled against the side of his chariot. Zenobia saw that he had part of an arrow in his side, broken off to stop it from jabbing against the inner wall of the chariot.

"Get him attention!"

Men rushed to lift Khalid from the chariot and lay him down in the sand. Zenobia's personal physician dismounted from his horse to examine him. The expression on the healer's face was not promising.

Zenobia gentled her voice and expression. "Where is General Artabanes?"

He tried to lift his head, but fell back into the sand. "Dead, Empress." His choked voice failed, and he gasped several times. "My general has fallen," he repeated, as though it had somehow been his fault. "Our chariots…our men…so many lost."

She blinked at the few intact chariots, her mouth slightly open and her eyes. "Then these are all that remain?"

Khalid choked back unmanly tears. "It is, Empress."

Zenobia's eyes travelled one-by-one over what remained of her once proud fleet of chariots. Many were damaged, with wounded men groaning as they lay in the carriages or sprawled on the ground. The smells of men who had been in battle assaulted her nostrils. General Artabanes was dead, and Khalid was perhaps not far behind joining him in the next life. While it was not good to regret the passing from this life to the next, the loss of so many of her soldiers—and the danger that created in the upcoming battle—left her senses reeling.

"How could they have done this?" She whispered, more to herself than Khalid. She could see he gathered his strength to respond.

"They dug pits covered with palm leaves and sand. Many of our heavy chariots wrecked. They thwarted our blade chariots with some sort of barrier." His voice became weaker, and he paused. "We took heavy arrow fire from their cavalry, so I could not see those clearly."

Even though he had explained it, the reality still seemed incredible. Memories of days in armor swinging a sword, throwing a spear from horseback, sitting in on the meetings Odaenathus had held with his general to discuss strategy and tactics, reading scrolls of ancient conflicts and studying maps where they had taken place. Zenobia had worked hard. She had led a few border skirmishes, as her husband had said, and thought she was becoming a real warrior queen. Then she assumed real command and encountered a professional general, a man trained from boyhood, who had led real legions in countless real wars. She felt like a child playing at toy soldiers.

"Almost no heavy chariots left. Less than one in ten of the lights." Her voice was almost as faint as that of her captain.

Khalid's head sagged once again. "I beg your forgiveness, Empress Zenobia."

His words snapped her back to reality, and to the obligations of her station. She must not let him think he had failed her; in truth, the opposite was the case. Some stray hair had fallen in front of her eyes, and she swiped it back into place. "There's no cause for forgiveness, Khalid. You did your best, as did all of my warriors. Aurelian is a more experienced general; he had a better strategy."

"Majesty!" Zabdas deep voice was close to a squeal. "You should never admit a deficiency in front of the soldiers."

Zenobia turned to her general and squared her shoulders. "Why not? Should we pretend to be infallible, a god on earth, as do many of these Roman emperors?" She shook her head slowly. "No, Zabdas. I'm an empress, but I'm also human. I'm the same as any of my people, but I have the duty and privilege to lead them as though I were infallible. I must learn to do better for them."

"Empress Zenobia!" Rasses spoke with clear admiration in his voice. "I pray to all the gods that you have the opportunity to learn these great lessons."

Zenobia gave a fleeting smile. "Thank you, Shaykh Rasses. But at this moment, Aurelian is marching his legions to meet us. We must not fail this time."

*   *   *

Aurelian looked across the desert shimmering with the wrath of Sol Invictus, still at least two hours away from riding his fiery chariot over the horizon. Aurelian surveyed what was left of his Roman and mercenary forces. Would they be sufficient to ensure this would be the day the sun god set on the Palmyrene Empire, dooming Malak-bel to an eternity in the underworld? It seemed more likely he himself would become another shade in Hades. Either way, Aurelian had waited for too long to know the ending to this bizarre saga.

The remaining Palmyrene chariots were massed facing them; on both sides pranced the Assyrian horsemen, eager to be unleashed. Aurelian knew that on one side sat the men of Shaykh Sefer, and on the other those of Shaykh Rasses. Behind the horse corps, the Palmyrene infantry stretched in lines twice the depth of his own foot soldiers. Mounted at the front was a figure in burnished armor: Zenobia.

While the armies moved into position, Aurelian saw what he had looked for: the tip of a pennant raised very briefly over the top of a sand dune. Faithful Procus had managed to march the archers into position without being seen, and now waited for the sound of the charge to begin firing. Aurelian allowed himself a grim smile. If Mucapor did his job as well, the Palmyrenes would soon be caught on three sides. Outnumbered or not, they might just be able to win the day, Mars willing.

*　　　*　　　*

Zenobia sat on a beautiful, dark stallion. It was tall for an Arabian, above fourteen hands high, and pranced restlessly next to the slightly larger horse of Shaykh Rasses. One of the gifts from the Caliph of Damascus, it was the only thing she still valued from the visit of Shaykh Qalb. Most of those and other gifts and tributes had been sent to the secret treasure rooms at Emesa, inside a small but very well guarded palace. Once the thought of enriching her treasury had brought her great pride as well as pleasure, but in light of the death and destruction of this day—and more to come—a fleet horse to ride in battle satisfied all her desires. The musky smell of the horse comforted her.

Aurelian stood in front of his legions, clearly prepared to fight amongst them. As much as she ached to, she understood that she could not lead the initial attack. If Aurelian fell, the Romans would fight on to the death. If she were to die, she feared the confidence of her men, not long in her service, would be sapped. Unlike the battle-hardened, professional soldiers of Rome, they might then falter in their dedication. For the sake of her son and his future empire, she must safeguard herself as much as possible. She would stay with the reserves and lead them when the time seemed right.

"You must lead the attack, Shaykh Rasses."

Zenobia saw that the shaykh's face was set with determination. He did not bother to look around him, as they were well aware of the condition of the chariot forces. He gave a small salaam.

"We will do what we can, Empress." His voice was resolute, perhaps determined to make up for the disgrace of his fellow shaykh's desertion.

Zenobia smiled. "I know you will. May Malak-bel safeguard you and bring you success."

Rasses twitched his mouth, attempting to return her smile. "May Malak-bel safeguard you and bless this battle, Our Lady of Victory." Rasses waved for the chariots to ride. "Forward!"

His own horsemen rode alongside him. Sefer's men were to the right of the chariots. The empress sighed as they moved away. Without many heavy chariots, it would be difficult to break the ranks of the legionaries enough for the infantry to pour through their middle. Zenobia was certain they would indeed do what they could.

*   *   *

Shaykh Sefer watched the Palmyrene cavalry riding at an easy canter, conserving energy. When they were halfway to the Roman lines, Rasses gave the signal for the charge. Thundering across the scorching sand, both chariots and horsemen concentrated on the ground flying beneath them.

At the sight, Sefer moved forward from where he stood beside Procus, the emperor's adjutant, who kept an eye on him in spite of his earlier cooperation. Sefer looked at Aurelian, who gave a slight nod. The shaykh hesitated for as long as it took a man to sigh, then raised his standard high into the air. Within seconds, Sefer's men turned in their saddles and began firing arrows at the chariots. At the same moment, the archers under Procus sprang up from behind the dune where they had lain in wait and fired from the other side. The air suddenly darkened with arrows, taking the Palmyrene soldiers completely by surprise. A bitter taste flooded Sefer's mouth, and his stomach lurched.

Expecting the archers to be behind the front ranks of the legionaires, most of the shield bearers had not yet lifted their heavy burdens. The Roman archers used short bows that did not pack a lot of power, but made it easy to nock another arrow and fire within seconds. They angled their bows upward so that the missiles descended in a vertical torrent, accelerating into the mass of humanity and animals below.

While the men wore heavy armor, the poor horses did not. Above the pounding of hooves, Sefer heard the cries of those unlucky enough to stop an arrow from reaching the sand. Whether killed or wounded, many horses crumpled to the ground under the first rain of death, taking their riders out of the fight and fouling the charging chariots behind them. A full third of the attackers never reached their intended goal. Real or imagined, the stench of blood and offal filled his nostrils. Sefer forced himself to witness the carnage he had helped to create, and prayed he had made the best decision for his tribesmen.

*   *   *

"Damn the man."

Zenobia instantly knew that Zabdas meant Shaykh Sefer. Although Zabdas' tone was mild, she could hear the scorn in his voice. They could no longer see Sefer through the dust of the chariots, but they could clearly see his men firing on their own forces. It was a depressing sight.

"Yes. As you said, a definite case of Roman legion fever. Obviously he believes Aurelian will protect his tribe better than I would."

Zabdas grunted.

*   *   *

"Shaykh Rasses! There, on that rise!"

Rasses followed the pointing finger of his lieutenant. Arrows began to fall from the sky, launched by Roman archers standing on a long sand dune off to his left. Rasses knew the carnage and confusion would begin within moments. He raised his sword to signal his men.

"To the left! To the left!" He swung his sword to emphasize the direction.

His experienced fighters turned their horses in a flowing wave toward the new threat. Halfway to the dune, Rasses saw their targets were protected by Aurelian's guard, although perhaps only a couple hundred. The elite of Rome's well-trained soldiers, it would still be difficult to get by them. However, the archers would have to be eliminated before their chariots could safely reach the ranks of legionaires.

Shouting and waving his sword, Rasses led a charge up the slight, sandy slope where the Praetorians stood in stoic ranks, their shields braced and their spears pointing outwards. He could only hope the speed of their charge and heavy armor would allow them to crush the enemy before the more nimble guardsmen could duck under the horses and cut their legs out from under them. If the fall did not kill a cavalryman, his heavy armor would be a huge disadvantage in hand-to-hand combat. Falling was more dangerous than the arrows of the Romans. In spite of their own losses, they still outnumbered the Roman guard by nearly six-to-one. He briefly wished the empress had taken fewer of their horses to be used for chariots, but quickly put the thought aside to focus on the task at hand. However many men were left to him, they must be enough.

Despite the maddening impediments of slope and sand, the first line of cavalry hit the line of Praetorians hard. Through many battles, Rasses had developed his own special tactic: he and Arum looked for the leader of the enemy force and devoted their attention to him. Unlike many bandit tribes and barbarians, such as the Palestinians, the Roman army clearly identified their officers. Both men saw him and guided their mounts toward him.

Arum galloped ahead of him, and went in on the shield side. The idea was for the first attack to get the man to raise the shield high, perhaps even stab at the rider, which would leave the sword side of the man on the ground totally exposed. The second man in—in this case, Rasses—would stab with his lance before the enemy could see the real danger. Whether dead or wounded, the loss of their leader would at least discourage the soldiers, and sometimes leave them totally disorganized.

As Arum swept in to bang his lance off of the Roman's shield, the officer lunged upward with his sword. Whether by luck or incredible skill, Rasses saw that the point went into the gap between Arum's body armor and the plate above his upper leg. Simultaneously, Arum cried out and fell from his horse, and Rasses drove his lance into the unprotected side of the officer. The man fell heavily, pulling the lance out of Rasses' hand. Jerking his horse to a quick halt, Rasses drew his sword to finish the job. Looking down at the man sprawled in the sand, he could see that would not be necessary.

Rasses looked over to where Arum also lay in the sand. Blood gushed heavily from the wound on his upper thigh. Rasses did not know many of the intricacies of the body, but he had seen enough wounds to know that this would be fatal. Sadly, there was no time to give his lieutenant any comfort. Waving his sword in the air, he signaled for another charge.

Rasses lost count of how many times he regrouped his cavalry and clashed swords with the enemy. Even without their officer, the elite Roman troops fought valiantly and well. Only because they were heavily outnumbered, and because the Palmyrene armor protected them better than the light Roman covering, did they gradually give way.

Once the Praetorian Guard had been demolished, the real slaughter began.

*   *   *

Astride their horses, Zenobia and Zabdas had a good view of the action. The Romans had not been able to bring their metal contraptions along, but that was more than balanced by the paltry few heavy chariots left. The initial wave of the remaining "blade chariots" did some damage to the front rank, but the element of surprise had long vanished. The legionaires moved back quickly as the vehicles passed by, and a second rank of soldiers stepped forward with long poles, which they thrust into the wheels of the speeding vehicles. The screaming of horses and men, the violent thrusts and counter-thrusts, the clashing of swords on shields, and the blood spurting into the air and soaking quickly into the desert sand, all came clearly to their eyes and ears. Outwardly impassive, Zenobia and Zabdas watched as the chariots were inevitably demolished by the usual tactics of the Roman soldiers.

By contrast, they could see that Rasses had overrun the Praetorian Guard and now rampaged among the remaining archers. It was time for the main battle to be engaged.

Zenobia turned her horse around to face her army. With a dramatic gesture, she pulled her breast plate aside and bared her breast. "Men of Assyria! Let us march against cowards and Roman dogs!"

"Our Lady of Victory!" the army thundered back.

As the army started forward. Zenobia refastened her armor. Pacing her Arabian alongside General Zabdas' stallion, she led the advance.

*   *   *

The two armies came together in a clash of steel on steel. Aurelian fought alongside of Decius and a few trusted guards, not surrounded by the usual Praetorians. He hoped they would be of much more value protecting the archers, although it was hard to tell how much damage they had done to the Palmyrene infantry.

The stink of men pouring out their fear and adrenaline soon was mingled with the metallic tang of blood, and the foul odor of offal let loose by the dead and dying. The legionaires sought to counter the sheer numbers of Assyrians with their close-quarter tactics, but the Palmyrenes swarmed around both flanks, making it difficult for the outlanders to maintain their formations. The chinks between *scuta* became gaps, swords or spears thrust at one man were blocked by another, and men fell like the sands from an hour glass on both sides of the line.

Knowing the Palmyrenes would flank his troops as soon as the battle began, Aurelian had kept the wild Palestinians in reserve at the rear of his army. With the enemy focused on the action directly in front of their eyes, Aurelian sensed from the sudden change in flow of the fighting that the Palestinians had circled around both of the flanking arms to attack the natives from their rear. The Palmyrenes screamed and cursed in confusion, too bewildered to defend themselves at close quarters against the clubs and quarter-staves and blood-curdling screams of the maniacal savages. Aurelian smiled grimly, knowing that feeling all too well.

Unaccustomed to such weapons and naked barbaric ferocity, the defenders began to falter before the mixed forces of the Roman emperor. Then, above the tremendous din of the battle, Aurelian heard the sound of trumpets somewhere in front of him. It could only mean that the two legions under Mucapor had finally arrived to attack from the rear.

"Mucapor comes!" Aurelian stabbed his sword into the sky. "Now, my faithful men, now!"

He charged ahead, and those within the sound of his voice followed. Whether they heard the trumpets or followed their imperator, the other legionaries charged as well. The Palmyrenes held for long minutes, then broke beneath the fierce onslaught.

*   *   *

"Look to the rear, look to the rear!" From the added height his horse afforded, Zabdas scanned the faces near him. He spotted Amar through the swirl of bodies and the raging of weapons of all sorts, but the empress was nowhere to be seen. "Amar!"

Still mounted, Amar slashed at a legionary, his sword slicing through the man's upper body. He spurred his horse toward the general. "General."

"We're being attacked from the rear. Alert the men. We must regroup and organize a counter-attack."

"But the empress—"

"Will be without her army if we don't act now!"

Amar looked at his superior, uncertain if he should obey or seek out his primary duty, protecting the empress. A second later a look of shock came over the older man's face, and Amar saw the tip of a sword thrust out of his arm, blood spurting from the wound. Before the legionary could pull his gladius out for a killing blow, Amar sliced the man's throat with his own sword.

The decision had been made. Amar shouted for two soldiers to get the general away and get him treatment. He looked frantically around for the empress, who had been beside him only minutes before. She was nowhere to be seen. Then he gave his attention to the entire army.

"Regroup, regroup!" Zabdas was right: the best thing he could do for Zenobia now was to rally the troops and mount a counter-attack. They still outnumbered the enemy, but needed to counteract the element of surprise quickly. With great reluctance, Amar turned his mind from his empress and set about rallying the men.

*   *   *

Zenobia slapped her thigh hard, over and over. How could she be so stupid? She should have known Aurelian would have planned some strategy, some clever trick intended to offset her greater numbers. The fact that Zabdas had not reminded her of a possible attack from the rear was unimportant. The person at the very top was always responsible; she should have foreseen such a possibility. Now, only one way remained to try to create victory from a looming defeat.

In the middle of the battlefield, Zenobia found what she had been searching for: Aurelian stood back-to-back with one of his officers, a ring of dead or dying Palmyrenes at their feet. Both men glistened with blood and sweat. Spurring her horse through the mass swirling around her, hacking with her sword at any Roman uniform within in her reach, Zenobia made her way toward the tired pair. They turned in surprise when she jumped to the ground half a dozen paces away.

"Zenobia!"

Hearing her name on the lips of his emperor, the officer backed off. All of the men nearby ceased their fighting and did the same. Within seconds, a large circle had formed around the two leaders.

Aurelian panted heavily, his face such a spattered mess she could not say if he looked at her with love or hate. He lowered his sword. "I don't want to kill you."

"If I don't kill you, my empire dies." She raised her sword. "And all my hopes for my son."

Aurelian closed his weary eyes and sighed. Then his intense blue orbs snapped back open and his sword leaped to the ready position, as though suspecting she would strike at him while his guard was down. Regret flitted through her mind that this distrust had sprung from once intimate passions, but she immediately dismissed the weak notion and crouched into a fighting stance.

They circled each other as though the hot earth would burn their heels. To stumble over a body or in a bloody patch of ground might spell death. The carnage had been so heavy even the thirst of the desert sand had been slaked. This time when their swords clashed, there would be no playful posturing or witty repartee—and no quarter. Understanding the situation, nearby Roman and Palmyrene soldiers alike formed a ring of silence around them, no doubt enthralled at the unique spectacle about to unfold.

Zenobia struck first, as swift and deadly as a cobra. Her sword flashed in the waning sunlight, glints of red flying from the burnished steel as it flew through the air to be met by the blade of Aurelian. Thrusts and parries explored the skills of the other, with each as careful about their footing as they were of their opponent. She knew he was stronger, but tired from a long day of fighting. Minute after minute passed with neither able to find an advantage, an opening they could exploit. Aurelian flicked his head, clearing the heavy sweat that flowed into his eyes. Seizing the opening, Zenobia sent of flurry of blows aimed at Aurelian's low guard. She was rewarded when her blade bit into his hip, drawing blood. Aurelian bellowed with rage at the shallow cut, then rained down heavy swings using his slight height advantage. The ferocity of his attack drove Zenobia backwards. Her fears were realized when her foot slipped on something slick. She fell back, her sword jarred from her hand when she hit the ground.

Aurelian was on her in a flash, the point of his sword only an inch from her throat. "Surrender!"

Furious, Zenobia tasted the bitterness of defeat; she had given Aurelian no choice but to kill her if she did not concede. Before she could say the hated words, mail and flesh ripped above her. Aurelian spun away, an arrow protruding from his left arm. He fell to his knees, but did not lose the grip on his sword. Zenobia snatched up her sword and leaped to her feet. Without conscious thought, she raised the blade high and aimed for his exposed neck.

As the blade began to descend, a man jumped in between and parried the blow. Zenobia was more shocked by the intruder than by the intervention: it was Sefer. The two stared at each other, Sefer with his blade held high as though about to strike her, she in disbelief as this treachery. The spell broke when Rasses raced up, his bow still in his hand, the string still quivering. With his other hand he led a spare horse, and he threw her the reins as his own mount pawed the ground nervously.

"Traitorous dog!"

Sefer flinched, but made no move to stop Zenobia as she mounted. The air suddenly filled with shouts and the sounds of blows, and hands reached to pull at the reins of the horses. Striking right and left with their swords, Zenobia and Rasses raced off into the desert. The remaining Palmyrenes, seeing their leaders flee, also broke and ran, leaving their dead and dying behind.

*   *   *

Aurelian mutely surveyed the familiar sights at the end of a battle: mutilated corpses spilling their life's essence into the ground, wounded men screaming or groaning, most begging for water, with the mercenaries in his army already searching for anything of value they could put in their purses. And, as with most of the battles his army had fought, the backs of the remaining enemy as they ran for their lives. Unlike ever before, the thought of what had transpired with Zenobia left him cold, devoid of any emotion but regret.

He noticed Sefer standing by his side, sword still in hand. "My thanks for saving my life," he said automatically, not at all certain he wanted to be happy about it.

Sefer looked at him coldly. "Do not thank me for my betrayal. I need you alive to honor your end of our bargain." He pointed with a motion of his chin. "I certainly don't trust that general of yours to keep your promises."

Aurelian turned as Mucapor strode up to them.

"Shall we give chase?"

Aurelian shook his head. "No. Our men need tending. We know where they've gone." Aurelian took in several deep breaths, more weary than ever before in his life. "We'll march to Antakya and offer an amnesty before proceeding to Emesa. I shall visit the Temple of El-

Gabal, as Sol Invictus is called in this land, and give thanks for this great victory." Aurelian touched his fingertips to his forehead as a minor tribute to the sun god for having used his name. "When we're ready, we'll march to Palmyra and lay siege. Then we'll wait for Domitianus to return from Egypt." He gazed off into the distance, in the direction Zenobia had ridden. "When we're at full strength, we'll attack Palmyra."

CHAPTER EIGHTTEEN

"What's the matter, Roman? You let one little city defy you? Aren't you man enough to make us bend the knee to the power of the great Roman Empire?"

Astride his horse, Aurelian looked up at the main wall around Palmyra. No longer held in a sling, his left shoulder still ached from where the barbed arrow head had been cut out of it. He had developed a habit of rubbing it when irritated by something, and rubbed it now. Aurelian was frustrated at not being able to bring this conflict with Zenobia to a head, angry with Mucapor for constantly urging a suicidal full-scale attack on the city, and weary with the long, fruitless siege. And now a Palmyrene soldier chaffed him personally from the walls, taunting him with his inability to take the capitol. He was sick to death of all of it.

After a very brief visit to Antakya, where the city officials had been amazed to be offered the chance for a peaceful surrender, Aurelian had quickly marched to Emesa. That had given Zenobia time to regroup her forces, but he did not regret eliminating the possible threat of having an army from Antakya at his back. Mucapor had asked for permission to replace Procus with Lucresus Cimber as captain of the cavalry. Aurelian was aware Cimber was much more loyal to the general than to himself, but he could think of no legitimate objection. The man was a good officer.

The day after their arrival, Roman and Palmyrene forces clashed in the plain in front of the city, with the natives still outnumbering the invaders. As at Immae, the Palmyrene heavy cavalry was run ragged the more mobile Roman horsemen. The infantry were also massacred by the superior tactics of the Roman legions and their fierce Palestinian mercenaries.

This time, in spite of his lingering wound, General Zabdas commanded the entire army of the usurper, while Zenobia stayed in the rear guard. Inspired by the death of Captain Procus, Aurelian ordered a new tactic. Led by Captain Lucresus Cimber, a hand-picked unit of Dalmatians targeted the opposing general. They paid a heavy price, but the gambit was rewarded when Zabdas fought valiantly but fell from his horse, mortally wounded. In the madness that had been their retreat, his men had somehow managed to load him onto one of the undamaged chariots and helped him to escape.

While his men rested or enjoyed some of the hospitality of Emesa—a city eager to show the Roman emperor they had only changed their loyalty at the point of a sword—Aurelian visited the Temple of El-Gabal. As promised, he made a sacrifice to the sun god for his great victory. After paying tribute, Aurelian followed the Assyrians to Palmyra.

It was clear that Zenobia would not face him again, so he had been forced to mount a siege. Aurelian's engineers had managed to construct a few ballista, which could fire large arrows or small boulders, but those could not even dent the stone walls some forty feet high and at least a dozen thick. They resorted to shooting over the walls, hoping to hit the odd building or kill a few people by sheer luck; it was at best an annoyance to the defenders. And using those was itself problematic because they had to keep the ballista moving or face the greater firepower of Palmyra in return.

On top of their walls, the Palmyrenes had both springalds, larger catapults with amazing accuracy at fairly short distances, and several onagers. The Onagers truly kicked like the wild asses for which the Greeks had named them; the bowl-shaped missile container could hurl huge boulders up to five hundred paces. Aurelian had been forced to set up a perimeter half a league away from the city, which stretched his forces—decimated from the terrible slaughter near Antakya and then Emesa—terribly thin.

The Moesians, Pannonians and Palestinians melted away when he refused to let them loot Antakya or Emesa. A corps of Armenian mercenaries had offered their services a month after the siege began. Aurelian, suspicious of soldiers from a sworn ally of Palmyra, said he would not pay them until Palmyra fell. In truth, he was short of funds, but was damned if he'd admit it to outsiders. But they had agreed, claiming they wanted revenge for the way Zenobia's army had "brought them into" the Palmyrene Empire. A month later, a large band of bowmen from the Sarakene region of the Northern Sinai, whom the Romans called Saracens, had also wandered into camp seeking employment. The Sarakene were known to be an independent lot, more subject to their own whims than to the command of any master. The ragtag tribesmen and farmers were excellent marksmen who complained little, but were known to melt away quickly in melee combat. That was fine with Aurelian, as they might serve of some use and then disappear before he had to pay them. Ironically, King Shapur, known to have made an alliance with Assyria, had offered unlimited reinforcements from Persia, but had backed away when Aurelian could only offer delayed payments—which, as it stood, looked rather nebulous at best.

More to show that he was doing something than from any real strategic purpose, Aurelian had ridden out to study the walls. He was accompanied by General Domitianus and Captain Cimber, along with his adjutant, Captain Decius. General Mucapor had suggested that one of the senior men should stay behind just in case of a terrible disaster, and Aurelian had concurred without so much as a smirk. They trotted along at what he considered the safest distance: too close and he might be showered with spears or arrows, too far and he would be in danger of boulders from the springalds. He twisted his mouth ruefully as he looked at the battlements. Perhaps he should be praying to the gods that the vision of Apollonius would somehow create a miraculous weakness he could exploit.

To his surprise, the leader of the Saracens had requested to join them, claiming some vague knowledge of the fortifications from a visit many years before. Aurelian suspected the man wanted to solidify his position among his men, as the only qualification he seemed to possess as "leader" was the fact that he spoke traders' Greek, whereas none of the other Saracens spoke a word of either Latin or Greek. The request amused Aurelian, but he had no objection. A mule was found to accommodate the short and stocky Saracen, who called himself Khalil, on the circuit around the wall. They had halted when the man had bellowed out his mocking words.

"Well, Roman? Aren't you ever going to come and fight us?" The Palmyrene turned to those nearest him and laughed loudly at his empty challenge. Others joined in his merriment, offering their own insulting comments.

Aurelian stiffened, then sat back and rubbed at his left shoulder. There was nothing he could do about the man, so best to just let it pass.

"Would you like me to shoot the dog for his insolence?"

Startled, Aurelian looked back at the Saracen, who sat quietly on his mule. His Greek was a garbled version of the trader patois, but Khalil's meaning was perfectly clear. The distance must be sixty paces, and that did not take into account the elevation. The Palmyrenes had loosed a few arrows at them, but all had fallen short. Even without any wind, it would be a fantastic shot for a man twice the Saracen's size.

"You really think you could hit him?"

The little man gave a smug smile. "If he doesn't move."

"One gold piece if you can hit him, two if you kill him."

"Three would make my aim much better."

Aurelian leaned back and chuckled, impressed by the man's insouciance. He wondered if this was mere braggadocio. "Very well, then. Three if you kill him."

"Please move closer together in front of me, Highness." Khalil pulled an arrow from his quiver. "Block me from his vision."

Not at all certain this was a good idea, Aurelian nevertheless signaled for his officers to do as the Saracen had asked. Even as he moved to screen the man, Aurelian kept his glance sideways in case of treachery. With minimal motion, Khalil knocked an arrow and stretched his bow to its fullest. Aurelian found it hard to believe the Saracen had even taken aim before he let fly. Just turning back towards the riders from joking with his companions, the still jeering Palmyrene was taken full in the chest. Clutching at the arrow and gurgling blood, the soldier fell over the wall.

Aurelian turned to the Saracen and gave his first full smile for several months. "Truly, you and your men are welcome. You shall have your payment the moment we reach my tent."

Khalil gave a small salaam of acknowledgement. As the emperor and his escort cantered back to join the army, the Palmyrenes loosed a boulder from a springald. It missed so badly the riders paid it no heed.

As the little group rode back into camp, a great cheer went up from Roman soldiers who had witnessed the event.

* * *

Zenobia paced across the makeshift war room in the palace like a lion measuring its cage. The room looked much the same as when she had planned her campaign against Aurelian: a dozen large tables were covered with maps and other documents. Many officers and officials sat or stood within its spacious confines. This day had little of the controlled frenzy that had marked those heady months of preparation. A few small groups passed the time in desultory conversation. It had been a long siege, and boredom had long ago set in.

Her eyes widened in pleasure when Rasses entered the room, approached her on hushed feet, and salaamed to the waist. Zenobia's welcoming smile fled when she saw the scowl barely concealed on his weather-worn features.

"What troubles you, Shaykh?"

His eyes crinkled and the corner of his mouth twitched in mild amusement. "You know me too well, my lady."

"I hope by now I know my friend and the commander of my forces."

With Zabdas wounded and Artabanes dead, she had given Rasses had taken command of her army. His first act had been to take his Bedouins and harass Aurelian's army on its march from Emesa to Palmyra, giving her crippled infantry time to cross the desert. Sadly, Zabdas had died before they reached the walls of Palmyra. When the Romans were at last driven from their land, she intended to reward Rasses handsomely. However, that day seemed further away with each new sunrise, with each new piece of bad news.

"The Romans have been reinforced, while some of our allies seem to grow weaker in their support!" Small drops of spit flew from the shaykh's mouth.

"Reinforcements? I understood several of his mercenary legions had left him after Emesa."

"True, my empress. Several of them deserted, including those barbaric Palestinians, thanks be to Malak-bel." Rasses made a sign of a blessing. "However, a large band of mercenaries—our spies think they are Armenians—have recently joined him. Another large band of bowmen from the Sarakene arrived only yesterday."

"Armenians and Sarakenes!" Her hand flew to cover her gaping mouth. Not only had those tribes pledged allegiance to her, but some of them had joined her army early on in the siege.

"Yes, my lady. And one of the Sarakenes has already left his mark."

"In what way?"

Rasses scowled again. "Aurelian and a few officers made a tour of our walls this morning, keeping out of the range of our archers. One of our soldiers mocked him. He was felled by an arrow from the group. Only one of those cursed Sarakenes could have performed such a feat."

Zenobia nodded absently, still thinking of the betrayal of tribes she considered to be Assyrian. "They are great marksmen."

Rasses sniffed. "Perhaps. I prefer to think the gods repaid the fool for his disrespect and arrogance."

This was a very bad omen. Her men had felt completely safe within the great walls of their city, with more than adequate water and food for a prolonged siege, save only one as long as that of the fabled Ilion. But tedium could also be deadly, and being cooped up for months with an army waiting outside—and one that had already inflicted a shocking defeat on them—inevitably led to tension and dissention. Especially when they had been betrayed.

On the first day the Romans had marched to their doorstep, Zenobia promised her people that one of those other eastern kingdoms which had sworn alliance with them only a few years before—Armenia, Arabia, and even Persia—would soon keep their pledge of aid. The people had cheered with great gusto. Armenia had indeed sent a small army, and the Saracens had also come in some force. But the Arabs and Persians kept begging off, and now more Armenians and Saracens had come to Palmyra, but the damned traitors had joined the enemy, like hyenas slinking away from one pride of lions which had grown old or weak in order to join a younger, stronger pride. That's what they all were: hyenas, jackals, vultures—creatures that fed on the carrion left by the real hunters of the world.

Longinus appeared in the doorway, and her hopes soared once more. In the darkness of the night, a messenger had returned from the Sassanid Empire, bringing the answer to her latest plea for Persian reinforcements.

"Well?" She did not wait for her prime minister to bow. "What did that desert weasel say?"

"I regret, my lady, that King Shapur claims he is unable to spare any men whatsoever right now. He sends his best wishes instead."

"Shapur!" Her voice dripped with disdain. "I thought better of him than Darius. Are all men cowards and traitors?" Zenobia saw the hurt expressions on the faces of Longinus and Rasses, and immediately softened her tone. "My sincere apologies, gentle friends. I did not mean to include you."

"We understand your distress, Empress." Longinus bowed slightly. "I am truly sorry to be the bearer of such terrible news."

"'His best wishes,'" Zenobia hissed. "I only wish that, when my army was knocking on his door, we had kicked it in and sent the man to join his ancestors."

*   *   *

Aurelian stood immediately when Domitianus entered his tent. He clasped the returning general's forearm in a tight grasp, then clapped him on the shoulder, ignoring the pain it caused in his own limb. Mucapor and Decius greeted Domitianus warmly in their turn.

"Congratulations, Domitianus. You return victorious with even more men than when you left."

"Thank you, Caesar." Domitianus inclined his head briefly. "As you predicted, many of the former Egyptian corps were happy to return to the fold after we retook Al-Jizah and Memphis, granting them full amnesty. Many claimed that Firmus and Timagenes forced them to desert or die. Of course, after we retook Alexandria and beheaded those two, nearly all the rest suddenly saw the error of their ways."

Without being told, Mnestheus poured wine for all of the officers.

"So you brought some of those back with you to split them up and left the African province commander in charge of the rest." Aurelian lifted his cup in salute. "That was cleverly done, Domitianus."

"I only carried your orders to their logical conclusion." Domitianus tipped his cup in return. The men sat back down, and Domitianus took the bench that had been placed for him in advance. "If I may ask, how fares your arm?"

Aurelian shrugged. No doubt Mucapor had told Domitianus of the injury he had sustained in battle, and the man must have noticed the small wince when he congratulated him. It was like Domitianus to notice small details where he might take advantage. "It was a clean wound. It heals well."

"I'm pleased to hear it." Domitianus raised his cup in suggestion of a toast and drank some wine. "I understand your strategy against Zenobia at Antakya was also extremely clever, Caesar. You destroyed a much more powerful army."

Aurelian waved the compliment away. "The men fought bravely and well." He took a sip of wine, then added: "And they carried out their orders precisely."

"I'm sure."

Aurelian inspected his officers as they drank silently, perhaps contemplating the courage and discipline of their troops. Or perhaps not: Mucapor gave Domitianus a sideways glance, almost too subtle for Aurelian to notice.

"I was saddened to hear of Procus," Domitianus blurted out. He took a deep gulp of wine.

Aurelian looked at Domitianus with a slight narrowing of his eyes, then regarded Mucapor for several seconds. He decided to take the remark at face value. "Procus was a good soldier and a loyal friend. He shall be terribly missed. But many good soldiers died that day to grant us victory."

"And they shall be revenged just as soon as we've taken Palmyra," Mucapor interjected smoothly. "We should start with that traitor, Sefer. If he betrayed Zenobia, he may well betray us for the right price."

Aurelian set his cup down on a table at his elbow. "General Mucapor, I thought I'd made it clear we will not create any more enemies than we must. After Zenobia surrenders, Palmyra will once again be part of our empire. I intend to make a peace that will last, not cause endless bloodshed merely to gain revenge." He rubbed his shoulder, using the time to take the edge from his voice. "As we learned with Tyana, mercy often wins more loyalty than the fear of the sword."

Mucapor hesitated, then stood and saluted. "As always, your wisdom matches your valor in battle, my emperor."

After the general reseated himself, Aurelian contemplated the man's handsome features for a moment longer. Mucapor reminded him of a cobra, his hair glossy and sleek, his skin shining, the eyes just a trifle beady and heavily lidded, the tongue dripping with a sweet poison. Aurelian only wished he could prove his suspicions. However, the man's family was much too powerful for him to take any action without concrete evidence.

Aurelian forced his mind back to the situation over which he had control, planning his next move after the arrival of Domitianus and his additional legions. While it might not yet seem so to Zenobia, it was clear to him that this changed the balance of power. Not only had they been reinforced, but their food supply was now assured, while the stores within the city could do nothing but dwindle. The ultimate fate of Palmyra would depend on how long he stayed the course, and Aurelian was absolutely resolved on regaining his empire no matter how long it took. At this point, it was only a matter of how many more lives would have to be lost before that happened. Aurelian slammed his hand down on the table, sending his cup flying and startling his staff. He leaped to his feet, and his officers followed suit.

"Decius, take a small delegation to Empress Zenobia. Tell her what has transpired in Egypt." He paced with great agitation in the confines of his tent. "Tell her that, if she surrenders, all shall be spared. Zenobia will be given a safe place of exile, and all the Palmyrene laws and institutions will be respected. The only condition is that all valuables— silver, gold, silk, horses, camels, and so on—will become the property of the Roman treasury."

Decius saluted. "Caesar!"

"So." Mucapor drew the word out in a deliberate drawl. "You do not intend to go and make the demand yourself?"

Aurelian stiffened, tempted to backhand the man to erase that supercilious smirk off his face. He closed his eyes and drew in a sharp breath. Then he exhaled slowly and opened his eyes. He attempted a smile, but wiped it away when he realized from the tension in his facial muscles that it must look more like a snarl.

"I'm no more courageous nor foolhardy than any other man. Perhaps some harm might befall me if I were to enter the den of the lioness, but I think it more likely that they would honor an offering of peace." Aurelian swept his gaze across all of his officers, once again coming to rest on the face of Mucapor. "However, I have learned something of power over the past years. It will not do for me to make this offering in person—it would then seem more of a plea than a demand." He turned his eyes to Decius. "No. You shall go to Zenobia and present my terms. When you return with her answer, we shall know our course."

"Yes, Caesar." Decius turned to go.

"Oh, one more thing."

Decius turned back to his emperor.

"Tell her this will be the only time that I will offer terms. If she refuses, then what happens to Palmyra and all its inhabitants will be on her head."

*   *   *

"Well?"

"Queen Zenobia sent the following answer." Decius held out a parchment that was still sealed.

Aurelian did not move from where he stood, his hands clasped behind his back as he contemplated the banner that proclaimed him Emperor of the Eastern Roman Empire. "Read it to me, if you will."

Decius cleared his throat. "No man as yet except you has ever dared to make a demand of me. Yet you demand my surrender, as if ignorant that Cleopatra the Queen chose rather to die than to live with loss of dignity. You demand that I betray my family, my trusted advisors, my army, and my people. The Persian assistance which is pledged to us and which we await, cannot be long in coming. What then, if the forces we expect should arrive? Then you will assuredly lay aside the pride with which you now demand my surrender, as if you had already triumphed. This is not a fitting ending to our dispute. Whatever is to be achieved in war must be performed by valor alone. If you wish to rule Palmyra, then you must dare to come and take it."

More than a minute passed. Aurelian did not move, giving no indication that he had even heard the words.

Decius cleared his throat. "Bold words."

Aurelian gave a quick, slight nod. "Yes. Bold words. From a bold woman."

Another silence ensued. Again it was broken by Decius.

"What are your orders, Caesar?"

"Orders?" Aurelian shook his head. "There are no further orders. We continue to build siege engines. We look for any possible weakness in their walls. And we wait. We just wait."

*   *   *

Even during the brightness of day, the throne room was illuminated solely by candles and torches. But this was the time of Suen, although it was the night when the moon god rested from his efforts. Somehow, Zenobia found the room more dark and gloomy than usual. She slumped on her throne, her cheek propped up by one hand, the small muscles around her mouth constantly twitching with frowns that were broken by deep sighs.

In spite of the defiant note she had sent Aurelian, she understood that defeat was inevitable. In her flash of anger, however, she may have made the ultimate results much worse for her people—and especially her son. What would Aurelian do to this potential threat to his rule once the city was forced to capitulate? What would he do to her people? The only thing she was certain of was that the city itself would be spared. After all, Palmyra was still the jewel of Assyria, and the key to the Silk Road. It was the heart of the power and wealth of the entire kingdom. But she and all of those loyal to her…they could be replaced.

Zenobia shifted to the edge of her throne, exchanged the hand her chin rested on for the palm of the other. Her eyes saw nothing. She welcomed the darkness and silence of the room, like the tomb that might soon encompass her human form. Strange that such a thought could comfort her.

The faintest whisper of slippers on stone caused her to raise her head. Longinus stood before her, hands folded together as though a supplicant to mercy. She widened her eyes.

"My Empress, I'm afraid I have more bad news." His voice was like a faint breeze in a sepulcher

Zenobia roused herself. "Aurelian's army has gained more reinforcements, Egypt has been lost and Firmus and Timagenes beheaded. What can be worse?"

"I am very sorry to tell you that many of your allies have deserted, including the Saracens and the Armenians who had remained loyal. They obviously decided it was hopeless when those reinforcements marched in yesterday. And the devils took many of our reserve food supplies with them."

"You're right; that's worse."

"And there's more."

Zenobia threw her hands in the air. "Of course there is! The day would not be complete without another disaster. What now?"

"I have just received news from Persia. Rather than a refusal to aid you, it seems King Shapur was very ill. He is now dead. His youngest son, Hormizd, has taken the throne."

"Hormizd!" Zenobia thought back to what she knew of the man. Her words came slowly as she followed her thoughts. "I don't know if he'll be a friend to Palmyra. Young men are rarely philosophical about the loss of any portion of their empire, and I doubt he would be willing to give us aid."

"Willing or not, majesty, I suspect he's too busy consolidating his power right now to even consider sending any troops to fight the Romans on our behalf. No; I think we can expect no support from the Sassanids for quite a while."

Zenobia leaned back on her throne and sighed. She steepled her fingers. If possible, the darkness deepened as the silence lengthened. The shadows from flickering torches writhed across the walls like the tormented souls of those never allowed to rest in the afterlife.

"It seems the Palmyrene Empire is no more, Longinus."

Longinus bowed his head. "It would seem you are correct, my lady."

Silence reigned once again. After a brief eternity, another sigh escaped the lips of Zenobia.

"What do you advise, Prime Minister?"

Longinus did not hesitate. "You must surrender—or escape."

"Surrender!" Zenobia rose from her seat. "As I told that man, my great ancestor, Cleopatra, preferred death to surrender to the Roman conquerors. Can I do any less?"

"That depends on what future you want for your son."

Zenobia stood mutely for a moment, then sagged back onto her throne. "You're right. I must consider Vaballathus more than my own fate."

"The Sassanids have still offered refuge for you and your son—that is, if you can get to Emesa and take the royal treasure with you."

Zenobia frowned, but it was not Longinus who vexed her. "The price of sanctuary can be very steep."

"True. But I fear the price of being captured by the Romans will be much steeper."

Zenobia placed her elbow on an arm of the throne and tucked her chin between her forefinger and thumb. "So you advise me to flee and rob my own people?"

Longinus locked one hand around the other wrist and drew himself up to his full height. "I advise you to take a treasure you helped enrich before Aurelian steals it to raise more armies. I advise you to take your son and yourself to safety, even if Hormizd will demand most of the treasure as his fee for harboring you." His severe tone changed to one more cajoling. "Perhaps he might even send an army if you can promise him more gold if he defeats the Romans."

"Humph!" Zenobia leaned back once more, her hands resting on her thighs. "It's ironic, don't you think? My once ally chases me to my once enemy."

Longinus cocked his head. "Yes, my lady. Life can be very strange."

This time, Zenobia thought for only a few seconds. "Very well. Arrange it for tomorrow evening."

"It's already arranged, great queen. Auzaina will escort you. You'll travel on camels as a merchant family."

Zenobia offered a strained laugh. "A merchant. Yes, very fitting, as I flee to Persia to peddle my wares. But do you not go with us?"

Longinus folded his hands together once more. "No, my lady. It will be dangerous enough to smuggle the three of you and a couple of servants safely out of the city without an old man along. I'll stay here and try to provide enough time for you to reach Emesa, and perhaps even Persia."

Zenobia stood up and went to him. She placed an arm over his shoulder, and leaned in so that her forehead touched his. She felt him quiver at the familiarity.

"You've been a great friend as well as a wise prime minister. I shall miss you, Longinus."

Longinus swallowed several times. "And I you, my lady Zenobia."

CHAPTER NINETEEN

After months of boredom, Vaballathus believed they were embarking on some sort of quest, not an escape. He was not a child any longer, nearly twelve, but Zenobia made light of the danger. She did not want him to think this was anything but a great adventure until they were well away. Days of plodding across the desert on cantankerous camels would dispel most of his excitement. Zenobia would have preferred her horse, but smuggling a spirited Arabian out of the city would be like sneaking a spring lamb past a pack of ravenous wolves. Camels were much better for a long trek across the desert, and could bear the weight of both supplies and the treasure she hoped would still be hidden in Emesa.

Led by Amar and followed by Bella and one other serving woman, Zenobia and her son walked quietly through the dark halls of the temple of Malak-bel. Dressed in black robes with hoods drawn tightly over their heads, the five fugitives made for a small door on the east side of the great temple. The night sent faint echoes through her mind of a night some five years before, but she pushed the distracting thought away to focus on the task at hand. Even Vaballathus had to stoop to exit the small door. Its hinges, also made of stone, were kept well-greased to ensure silence. It had been cut so fine that it was hard to see its outline in broad daylight from more than a few paces away when it was closed.

Pale starlight illuminated the group's path. Messengers who had found this gap between the stretched lines of the Roman army had described every step to Amar, who now trod it with great confidence, but in absolute silence. Carrying little and keeping low, the boy and three women followed with careful steps. More than an hour passed before the party felt they were safely past the enemy soldiers, but the two serving women believed at least half their lives had been spent in mortal danger.

"Did you not fear we would be seen at any moment?" Bella's words were loud and semi-hysterical as she gripped Leah's arm.

"Hush!" Amar spun and hissed the words, his voice low but piercing. "They may have sentries posted out here."

The party trudged on for another hour without speaking again. At last they came to a small oasis, one of the countless springs of the Fertile Crescent region. Two other members of Zenobia's personal guard awaited them, having made the passage the previous night on the orders of Longinus. Eight camels were tethered to shrub trees, two of them weighted down with supplies.

"We're one short." Amar raised his chin toward Bella and Leah. "You two will have to share."

Bella looked at the large beasts with widened eyes. "But we've never ridden anything but a wagon. How would we manage?"

Amar frowned. "Well, I suppose you could ride behind Baltasar and Oommen. I had not considered that you were inexperienced riders."

"No," said Zenobia. "I will take Bella, and Leah will have to ride behind Vaballathus."

"But, Empress! I could not subject you to the indignity."

Zenobia made a very unladylike snort. "Amar, you and your men must be free to fight if we are attacked, either by the enemy or by bandits. Our lives will balance out my dignity."

Amar salaamed. "Yes, Majesty."

With help from the men, the two servants mounted behind Zenobia and her son. Before Ishum began to spread his light over the world, the small party circled wide around the besieging army and turned toward the northwest.

The obscured terrain kept the refugees from traveling more than ten miles before dawn lit the landscape. It was too dangerous to continue without knowing if Aurelian had regular scouting patrols out, whether or not they had been betrayed, or if some other band of mercenaries headed for Palmyra might spot them. Amar led them to a small copse of trees. Fed by only a tiny spring, a few scrawny date palms provided some protection from the blazing sun. Zenobia hoped the oasis was not large enough to attract roving bands searching for water or shelter.

Baltasar and Oommen took the first watch. Zenobia, anxious for the safety of her son, fell into a fitful sleep after an hour of sudden starts and thoughts of what the future held. Good soldier that he was, Amar fell asleep almost at once. She wished she had either the training or the peace of mind to perform such a miracle. She wondered if she would enjoy a restful sleep before they were safely in Persia.

A light touch on her arm brought Zenobia fully alert. She opened her eyes to see the brown, twinkling eyes of her captain of the guard gazing down at her. The sun high in the sky told her it was at least an hour after midday.

"You should have wakened me earlier."

"Yes, Empress." Amar inclined his head, but there was no regret in his voice. He had already relieved the relieved the tired guardsmen of their watch.

While the others slept on, they discussed their travel plans in muted voices. They agreed they would travel through the night in order to preserve water and run less of a risk of being seen. They would skirt any towns in their path. While certain her people remained loyal, Zenobia knew that rumors had a way of spreading more from a desire for gossip than maliciousness. By the time all had been decided, Ishum was once again well on his way to a deserved rest. It was time to wake the others and prepare to travel.

*   *   *

After a week of increased artillery fire from both sides, with a few lives and structures being lost, the Palmyrene forces unexpectedly stopped their barrage. For days no rocks, arrows or other missiles were fired from the Palmyrene walls toward the surrounding soldiers. The activity on the walls was also strange. Men in civilian clothes, some of them rich in appearance, had been seen arguing with senior officers, gesturing at Aurelian's command tent, and sometimes they just stood as though brooding. Finally, a white flag appeared over the main gates.

Aurelian and his general staff donned their armor and assembled formally at the edge of the encampment, at the point closest to the command tent. Two hours after the flag went up, a large delegation emerged from the city. Smelling his own sweat from standing in full armor in the summer heat, even under a light canopy, Aurelian decided to take a hard stand with the delegation. Before the group was halfway to where he stood, Aurelian noticed the conspicuous absence of Zenobia, Vaballathus, Shaykh Rasses and Cassius Longinus. At the head of the party rode a man he thought he recognized, but he couldn't place the name.

The man dismounted as soon as the group reached the welcoming officers. He was short, in a long, flowing robe with enough gold brocade to ransom a princess, and wore a sword that dragged on the ground as he walked toward the Romans. He placed one leg in front of him to salaam and almost fell over making his obeisance. Aurelian bit his inner lip to keep his features straight.

"Greetings, great emperor." With some effort, the man pulled himself erect again. His Latin was formal, his accent well trained. "I am Nobonidus Zohan, Lord Protector of Palmyra and Governor of the Emperor's Person."

Aurelian widened his eyes. "I did not realize an Assyrian had been appointed to protect my person."

The man flushed red. Aurelian's staff laughed loudly, and several of the Assyrians hid smiles or chuckles behind their hands or beards.

"I beg your pardon, great emperor. I meant that I was appointed to that position by the Empress…that is to say, Queen Zenobia, when she left Palmyra for…her campaigns."

Aurelian cocked his head. "I seem to recall you. Were you not prime minister under Septimius Odaenathus?"

Zohan bowed his head. "I had that honor, imperial majesty. Her majesty Zenobia chose to so honor Cassius Longinus."

"Yes. So I understand. But why is the prime minister, or Queen Zenobia herself, not with you?"

Zohan flushed again. He looked back at the men with him, but they all studied their feet or the desert surroundings. Zohan turned back to Aurelian, but could not meet his eyes.

"There have been rumors since Suen last hid his face from men. Within the past week, it has been said that the empress fled the city with her son the emperor in the middle of the night. When the citizens began to grumble at the diminished food supplies, I and some of these other officials begged an audience of the empress for an explanation." Zohan waved his hand vaguely at the men behind him. "Neither Prime Minister Longinus nor Shaykh Rasses would tell us of her majesty's whereabouts, nor explain why our rations had decreased." He drew himself up to his full height, his eyes still below Aurelian's chin. "It was only when the people came to me, clamoring for their appeals to be heard, that we were able to force our way into the royal chambers." The man paused for dramatic effect, but Aurelian only raised his brows. Frowning at his lack of impact, Zohan finished. "The rumors were true. The empress and her son the emperor have fled with the captain of her guard and two serving women."

Aurelian turned to scan the faces of his senior staff members. Only Mucapor showed any emotion, his usual smug smile of self-satisfaction. Aurelian turned back to the Palmyrenes.

"And what is it that you have come to ask of me, as your queen has deserted you?"

"We wish to surrender. Our people are half-famished, and our army no longer wishes to do battle."

"Do you seek any terms?"

"No, Imperial Majesty. We seek only to implore the clemency of the great Roman emperor, Lucius Domitius Aurelianus."

Aurelian paused and reflected on this moment, which he had sought for some sixteen months. It was bittersweet. He had regained his empire, but without the woman that he desired even being present, let alone kneeling before his feet. That stage of his conquest would have to wait. In the meanwhile, he knew it would be best to treat these people with generosity if he wanted to rule them as willing subjects.

"Have Prime Minister Longinus and Shaykh Rasses agreed to this surrender?"

Zohan looked uneasily toward his companions, as though for support. Finding none, he pulled back his shoulders and answered the emperor. "No, Majesty. They have sequestered themselves within the quarters of the royal guard, and are protected by those men who choose to remain the vassals of Emp—of Queen Zenobia."

Aurelian nodded. He had expected nothing less. He would not

bother to add any drama to his response.

"Very well. I shall spare the lives and property of every individual—except for those whom I find treasonous to the Empire."

Zohan gave a curt bow to his head, clearly relieved that this edict would not include him. The other delegates also exhaled and turned their eyes in his direction.

"But Palmyra must pledge its complete loyalty to Rome and to me, and the royal treasury shall be mine."

Zohan's face reclaimed its distraught appearance. "But, Majesty, the royal treasury is not kept within Palmyra!"

"I see." Aurelian's thoughts raced. Of course it would not be. "Then where?"

Zohan coughed. Once more he looked back to his fellow dignitaries, but their attention had again turned to other things. He squirmed as Aurelian maintained his steely gaze on the man; the emperor thought of a slug writhing in the sun when its sheltering rock had been overturned.

Finally, the man sighed and looked him in the eye, although for a second only.

"Emesa."

"Ah." Emesa. Aurelian had held the city in his palm, gone to pay tribute to Sol Invictus in the temple of El-Gabal, and perhaps walked within a few paces of the building that housed the wealth accumulated by Zenobia—his rightful riches. It was irritating. "Very well. I accept the surrender of Palmyra."

Zohan's shoulders slumped, and a sigh of relief escaped his lips. The other officials returned their eyes to the emperor.

"As a token of your submission, I command you to bring me all of the objects within the Temple of the Sun. None shall enter there without my express permission. I shall decide how to deal with the inhabitants on a case-by-case basis."

Zohan salaamed.

"Decius, take some of the excess grain Domitianus brought from Egypt and distribute it among the citizens of the city."

"As you command, Caesar."

Words of thanks flowed from the Palmyrene delegation, but

Aurelian waved them away. He turned to the general of his cavalry. "Domitianus, I'm sorry to have to send you off again so soon after a difficult journey, but I have a mission for you and all of your forces."

A hard smile came over the face of the general. "I await your instructions, Caesar."

*   *   *

As the small party descended the hills to their first destination, Zenobia breathed a sigh of relief. There had been no bandits, no scouting parties—in truth, no difficulties of any sort. This would be their first real test. As the towers of the city came into view, Zenobia reflected on why she had chosen this city to house the wealth that had poured in from allies and vassal states alike.

In many ways, the history of her city and Emesa were similar. Long ago, a tent-dwelling tribe called the Emesani settled the area along the Orontes River. Situated at a pleasant elevation between the coastland and the great Tadmorean Desert, it gained significance as the market center for the surrounding villages. Being in the hills and much more wooded than Palmyra, it soon became the source of the soft woods between the interior cities and the Mediterranean coast from trees such as cedar, pine, cypress, Kermes oak, and the occasional Aleppo and Black pines.

When the Imperator Pompey the Great began his incorporation of the Assyrian territories into the Roman Empire, the Emesani dynasty were confirmed in their rule as client kings of the Romans for providing aid in various wars, just as her husband's family, the Septimii, had done. Under the reign of Emperor Antoninus Pius, Emesa minted coins for the Eastern Empire, whereupon the city grew to rank with the important centers of Assyria. Another main stop along the Silk Road, Emesa grew nearly as prosperous and well integrated into the Roman Orient as Palmyra itself.

More so even than Palmyra, the city became a strong center of worship, primarily because of the Temple of El-Gabal. Only a few decades before, the Roman Emperor Elagabalus had claimed his hereditary rights of the Severan dynasty to become the high priest of the sun god El-Gabal. With the emperor leading Emesa in worship,

Assyrians and Romans alike considered the city sacred. With its combination of military and religious protection, Longinus had suggested that it would be an ideal location to house the new-found valuables: not so close everyone would know their location, but close enough to reach in an emergency. Zenobia blessed his foresight.

They waited until late afternoon to enter the city. Baltasar and Oommen went to the market place and made a show of searching for merchants who traded in pots, knives, carpets, clothing, and other goods that were needed by the Bedouin tribes. They let it be known on the following day they would be purchasing four full camel loads—enough for a small merchant band to make a profit, but not a rich enough cargo to entice an attack by any but the most desperate bandits. Before the market closed, they stocked up on food for the trip back across the desert. Bella and Leah made trips to the city wells to fill up every water skin they possessed.

Zenobia, Amar and Vaballathus walked the camels around as though searching for stabling. Their seeming meanderings took them through all of the streets around a small temple, of no significance, dedicated to a god that had not been worshiped since Rome had spread its influence over the city. Although Aurelian had left no garrison after his visit, it was clear the rulers had once more pledged their fealty to Rome. The guards at the gates and on the walls were on a higher state of alert than usual, but none were posted anywhere near the temple. Not used to subterfuge, the effort to appear casual while feeling like a cobra coiled inside a small basket wore on each of them.

When at last Ishum sank beneath the horizon to his rest, the others rejoined them at the front of the temple. Zenobia took a key from her purse and unlocked the heavy but well-oiled door. One last look around assured them they were not observed. They led the camels into the main chamber. There were no windows in the building, but the stealthy band of invaders risked lighting only a few torches. Zenobia triggered a cunning mechanism on the back wall, and the bolt locking the altar in place shifted. It took all three men to push the altar aside, revealing a narrow set of steps that descended into the bowels of earth below the building. The two serving women stayed above with the animals.

It was not long before Zenobia and her son, as well as the three men, reached a large chamber below. There they saw the trappings of the now neglected god, along with many objects of little value. Zenobia pressed another pedal that only a chosen few knew about. This time, the men pulled up a hinged block of the stone flooring. Another narrow flight of steps led to a smaller room below, and it was there they discovered the real valuables of the ephemeral Palmyrene Empire; all but Zenobia's eyes were wide with wonder at the incredible display.

Zenobia decided that only the lightest, most precious items would be taken: jewels, solid gold pieces, small ornaments that could be traded easily, plus a few larger objects of high value. It still took most of the night to transport the treasure up the two flights of stairs and bundle it up on the camels. The men took turns traversing the staircases while the women wrapped the booty into small packages and placed them into the travelling bags with great care. Vaballathus had been assigned to guard duty, and he took his charge as seriously as any watchman on the main gate. When they agreed the four pack camels carried all the weight they could bear without excess strain, they placed the few items of normal trade on top so as to pass any casual inspection.

First light found the tiny caravan already at the gate, eager to pay the tariff required of a merchant party leaving the city with a full load. Passing through the gates, Zenobia could see that the spirits of each of them soared as Ishum displayed his face in the eastern sky. Whatever the amount of caution they had taken in the passage to Emesa, it would be trebled on their journey to the eastern border of the empire. They skirted Palmyra many leagues to the south, hoping any search parties sent out by Aurelian would have gone east towards Persia.

Twice along the way they passed roving bands of Beduin. Zenobia sent Baltasar and Oommen into the camps to buy what food the nomads could spare, with instructions to pay a generous price both for the supplies and for any word concerning Palmyra. Neither band knew anything about the goings on of the Romans or Palmyra, other than the rumor that the empress had fled and the city had surrendered to the invading army. She and Amar agreed this was encouraging: news of Roman patrols scouring the country for them would have spread as quickly as a sandstorm. Still traveling by night and sending out one of the two guards as advance scouts, their progress slowed to half of that during the sojourn from Palmyra to Emesa. Now late in the summer, the heat of the night remained oppressive, so to travel quickly would be both dangerous and exhausting. Speed did not matter. Reaching Persia safely was her only concern.

At last the verdant strip of land that bordered the Euphrates River came into view. The lush scents of the vegetation assailed Zenobia's nostrils like the sweet perfume of freedom. They had chosen a little-used crossing much farther south than the metropolis of Dura-Europa, away from the routes preferred by merchant caravans. The barge was small, and even their modest number of people and animals would need to be ferried across half at a time. Once across, however, they would not be far from Babylon, now under the control of the new Sassanid king, Hormizd I, and from there it would be a short trip northeast to Seleucia. After that, they would be at the mercy of this man who was a virtual stranger to them. Zenobia could only hope they had secured enough treasure to convince him to lead an army against Aurelian and secure what was left in the hidden vault. Zenobia had every intention of exaggerating what Hormizd would find if he retook Emesa.

This time Amar acted as the scout. He took pains to ride first north some distance and then south along the wide, languid waters. The heavy spring snowmelt had long ago subsided, but so close to the delta of the Tigris-Euphrates triangle, flora both large and small were in full bloom. Seeing no signs of Roman patrols or encampments, Amar returned after several hours to rejoin the others.

"Is the way clear, Amar?"

"I saw no signs of any military forces, friend or foe," Amar answered carefully. "That is not to say what my eyes may have missed, my empress."

Zenobia gave a smile meant to give comfort. "We know how sharp are those eyes and mind, Amar. Did you speak with the ferryman?"

"Yes, my lady. He said a squadron of Roman cavalry rode by two weeks past, but he has seen none since then. There has been only one small caravan since then, most assuredly only traders, no soldiers other than the guards."

"Then lead us down to the water, and to the warm embrace of Shapur."

Amar salaamed. "Yes, my lady."

The group carefully picked their way down the slope to the edge of the heavy wooden platform. The barge was fastened to a small wooden ramp, so only one man and camel had room to move at one time from the shore to the open end of the simple craft. The three other sides were bounded by heavy railings.

Oommen led one of the camels that held treasure onto the barge. The craft shifted slightly in the still waters as he fastened the camel's lead to the back rail; the animal moved nervously at the unfamiliar motion and the strange sight of water nearly all around it. The bargeman steadied the craft with a practiced hand. As Oommen attempted to calm the beast, Baltasar led a second pack camel onto the barge.

Suddenly a loud shout came from the shore. All eyes turned as one to witness a squad of Roman cavalry break from the surrounding vegetation and gallop toward them, shouting and waving their swords. The soldiers formed a semi-circle, pinning the band of fugitives against the water. Amar and Oommen drew their swords, and Baltasar leaped back onto the shore to stand by the side of his empress. His poor camel, half on and half off the barge, stumbled at the sudden noise and movement, nearly falling into the river. The two serving women screamed, cowering behind Amar. Vaballathus also drew his sword as he jumped in front of his mother, the officer leading the cavalry nearly on top of him.

Zenobia pushed Vaballathus out of her way. "Hold!" She held up her arms, hands open to show they were empty.

The Roman officer skidded to a halt only a few feet away, and the rest of his men followed suit, their swords still menacing the people standing on the ground. Only the bargeman looked calm.

"Lower your weapons, all of you."

At her imperious command, both sides hesitated. Then Amar obeyed his empress, and the other Palmyrene men slowly followed suit. The

Roman officer, a low-ranking centurion by his markings, also lowered his sword, laying the flat of the blade across his lap. Most of his men did the same, although a few clenched the hilt as though eager to make use of it. The man grinned as he looked down at her.

"Queen Zenobia, I presume?"

"You know who I am." Zenobia did not bother to hide the disdain from her voice or glance. "You must have had a long, tedious wait here."

"Ah, but it is all worth it now that I have a queen to accompany me back to Palmyra." The centurion's grin widened. "Unless you choose to resist us."

Zenobia could hear the eagerness in his tone. She would no doubt be spared, but the Romans had little use for those with her, including her son.

"Unless your men are butchers, there shall be no blood spilled here today, centurion."

The centurion stiffened slightly at the insult, but it achieved Zenobia's desired effect. He adopted more formal tones. "Then do you surrender, Lady Zenobia?"

"I have no wish to see my son and faithful attendants slaughtered to appease your boredom. We shall offer no resistance."

The centurion tightened his mouth, but made no further comment.

Within half an hour, everyone was mounted and ready to ride. Amar and the other two guards had been disarmed and their hands tied behind their backs. Vaballathus was not tied, though his sword was confiscated. The centurion sent one rider south to inform other search parties their quarry had been found. Leading the way, the centurion pointed his horse north.

"So, now we return to Palmyra." Zenobia thought on the ignominy of being led back into the city that would no doubt consider her a coward and a traitor.

"Not yet. We head north to Mari, where General Domitianus awaits. He told all party leaders that, should we capture you, to take you to him first. He wants the honor of leading you back into the presence of Emperor Aurelian personally."

*   *   *

It was a sweltering day outside, but cool within the royal chambers of Palmyra. Aurelian sat at the private desk of his former governor. For the tenth time he stared down on Domitianus' report concerning the search for and apprehension of Queen Zenobia. It had been delivered by a courier the day before. The details of the long, elaborate account were all etched in his mind. Every syllable of it, every image, evoked the face that had haunted his dreams for years.

The door opened and Decius entered. As Aurelian's eyes focused on the face of the other man, Decius saluted.

"Yes?"

"Domitianus is back, Caesar. As commanded, she has been brought directly."

Aurelian nodded. He had waited for this moment so long that he could barely hear his officer's voice over the drumming in his own ears, the beating of his own heart.

"Have her brought in. Tell Domitianus to have the boy guarded, but not harmed."

Decius saluted again and exited. Aurelian stood and walked around, trying desperately to compose himself. Two soldiers entered with Zenobia, who had shackles around her wrists. They stood facing each other, neither moving for several seconds. Aurelian found it easier to control his other emotions by using anger.

"Who had her shackled? I gave no such commands."

One of the legionaries started at the sharpness in his voice. "I'm sorry, Caesar. General—"

"Never mind." Aurelian cut him off, assuming the obvious. "Remove them."

The guards jumped to obey. When the shackles had been removed, Zenobia rubbed her wrists.

"You may go."

The soldiers saluted and hastily left the room. Aurelian leaned slightly toward Zenobia and sniffed.

"You need a bath."

"I would prefer my freedom."

Aurelian smiled. She was ever the queen.

The look on her face softened. "But a bath would be welcomed."

Aurelian clenched both hands into fists. "Why did you not simply surrender? It would have saved a lot of grief."

"Whose grief?" When Aurelian made no answer, she shrugged. "Would you have surrendered?"

"No. But then, I probably would not have let myself be captured."

Fleeting emotions crossed her lovely features. Anger? Regret? Frustration? At last came resignation. "I had my son to think of."

"Ah, yes. Of course." Aurelian took a deep breath. "Well, then I'm thankful for your son."

"Thankful." Zenobia's voice was flat. She looked down at her filthy clothing, lightly rubbing her wrists as though to erase the chafe marks. Then her gaze swept over the contents of the sumptuous room, no longer hers.

"I saw you didn't sack the city. You seem to have taken very little revenge. I'm thankful for that."

"Don't be. Why should I destroy my own capital?" The look on her face told Aurelian how harsh his words and voice had been. He whirled away, took two paces, composed himself. He turned back to her. "That would have been a waste. I only had a few people beheaded who deserved it."

"What! Who?"

"That chieftain of yours, Rasses. He wouldn't quit fighting. And Cassius Longinus, of course."

"But he was an old man! He couldn't harm you."

Aurelian stiffened. Why did he feel compelled to offer an explanation? "Longinus was a Roman, and therefore a traitor. At least Rasses was Assyrian." He scowled and waved his hand, dismissing an unpleasant thought. "He was an honorable man. I regret his death was necessary."

The bitter look on Zenobia's face made his throat constrict, and he wanted to stroke her cheek to comfort her.

"So I suppose my son and I will be next."

"Don't be absurd!" Once more he heard his own voice, loud and harsh. The words hung in the air like the sound of a lash on bare skin. He reached a tentative hand, but withdrew it before he could touch her flesh "I'm sorry." He composed himself once more. "You know I could never hurt either one of you, him for your sake."

"Then what?"

"You know what, Zenobia. You've dared to insult Rome, from the emperors down to the lowest plebian. The senate could never forgive such an insult to the Empire, could they?"

"I acknowledge you to be emperor, because you're a great warrior and a conqueror. Those weaklings in Rome I do not acknowledge."

A smile almost broke his features, but he strangled it before it touched his lips or eyes. "It's of no matter. Gallienus told me to bring you back to Rome in chains. That's exactly what I intend to do. And I'll bring your former treasury with me."

CHAPTER TWENTY

The late autumn weather favored the celebration, or perhaps Sol Invictus smiled down on his favorite son. A slight breeze lent a crisp caress to the warm air. A perfect day for a triumph.

Aurelian wore a purple toga trimmed in heavy gold braid beneath the new *paludamentum* Gallienus had given him. A wreath of laurel rested on his head. Woven gold sandals encased his feet. He looked the very image of a man who might become a god. Aurelian grimaced at the thought, but, as the *vir triumphalis*, it was the role he was expected to play in this little farce. He rode in a chariot made entirely of bronze, with lapis lazuli set in gold trim adorning the sides and front of the carriage. From its height he flung pure silver *antoniniani* coins to the crowd, newly minted with his image and latest title. They roared each time he flung a handful, especially when he took care to send a coin in the direction of a child. The heavy vehicle took four horses, magnificent stallions all, to pull it up and down the hills of Rome. The driver, dressed in a plain white toga, had been trained in the *Colosseumludi circenses*, the chariot races that entertained the masses.

The procession began early in the morning outside the Servian Walls in the *Campus Martius,* on the western bank of the Tiber. The air carried more of a bite then, and Aurelian had been happy for the heavy cloak. The chariot entered the city through the *Porta Triumphalis*, which was opened only for these occasions. As he entered the city he was met by the senate and magistrates. The procession had stopped so Aurelian could legally surrender his army to their command, which had followed him to the gates. In earlier times, the entire army of the general would march in the triumph. Now wiser and more cautious, the senate allowed only a selected company of soldiers to follow their commander. Aurelian had chosen his cavalry for this singular honor, both because of their great sacrifices in the battle of Antakya and because they had been responsible for the capture of Zenobia. On foot and led by Aurelian's staff officers, the cavalry were clad in splendid togas and wore small wreaths.

Leaving the rest of his army behind—who, unarmed, would soon be given the run of the city in order to enjoy the feasting and public games that would follow the ceremonies—the senate, headed by the magistrates, led the procession through the streets of Rome. A corps of trumpeters marched next, blaring their music over the screaming, waving crowd who lined the streets and leaned from every building. Carts brimming with the spoils of war, most notably the royal treasury of Palmyra—including all that Zenobia had left behind in Emesa—trundled along behind the trumpeters. A herder led two white bulls, which would soon be sacrificed.

A few members of Aurelian's guard carried the banners and other insignia of the short-lived Palmyrene Empire. Behind these tokens and in front of Aurelian's chariot, Zenobia staggered along as best she could. Wearing a sackcloth dress, her lustrous, black hair hanging straight, she was weighed down by golden chains and jewels that she had been given by supplicants to her court. Vaballathus walked by her side, also wearing a sackcloth toga, but unfettered. The crowd screamed insults and hurled rotten vegetables at the Palmyrene queen, but, as she passed, the crowd became strangely quieted by her regal bearing. While some captured enemy rulers or generals might be paraded and then taken to the *Tullianum* for execution, it had already been whispered about that Zenobia would be spared.

When they caught sight of their hero, the crowd noise once again swelled. They cheered wildly for Aurelian and his chosen escort, and showered them with flowers. Immediately behind Aurelian's chariot, and just before his cavalry, marched the twelve *lictors* of the imperator, formed from a special class of civil servants who were assigned the task of attending and guarding magistrates of the Roman Republic and Empire whenever they were in the capitol city. The *lictors* were the only armed men in the procession: their *fasces*, a bundle of wooden sticks tied together to symbolize strength through unity, had an axe blade emerging from the center, thus representing the summary power and jurisdiction of the official. While the weapons were more ceremonial than functional, they were still deadly.

The parade had proceeded along the *Via Triumphalis* to the *Circus Flaminius* and then the *Circus Maximus*. At an agonizing pace, the entire group climbed the Capitoline Hill to the *Capitolinus*, the temple shared by Jupiter, Juno and Minerva. Before he entered the temple, Aurelian stepped down from his chariot and doffed his *paludamentum* to put on a priest's robe. Happy not to get blood on his expensive robe, he offered the white bulls as a sacrifice to the great god Jupiter.

As he gave the blood of the bulls to the gods, Aurelian thought it odd that, in the midst of battle, he took very little heed of the carnage he wreaked upon the enemy. Yet, pulling a knife across the throats of animals standing quiet and helpless in front of him, he felt some measure of guilt. The stench of their warm blood filled his nostrils, and the splashing of it on his hands felt sticky, almost repugnant. Without washing his hands, he offered the tokens of his victory on the altar. He then took the wreath from his head and also offered it to Jupiter as a sign that he had no intentions of becoming the king of Rome. Once that part of the ceremony was over, he rinsed his hands and exchanged robes, although the increasing warmth of the day caused him to regret the thick *paludamentum*. As he exited the temple, incense was lit at the altars to burn throughout the day and night.

Finally, the procession descended the Palatine Hill along the Via Sacra and approached the Forum. The greatest throng had gathered early by the senate building in order to hear the speeches—or perhaps to witness the humiliation of the rebel. The great Julius Caesar had built his new Forum on one side of the Via Sacra and the Basilica Julia on the other side, and citizens crammed themselves into every single space where a human could see or hear.

The driver stopped the chariot at the base of the senate building. Waving to the crowd, Aurelian dismounted and walked up the steps with measured strides. Ranged along the portico, Gallienus and the senate stood waiting to receive him. As Aurelian reached the top, Gallienus held out his arms. The two men embraced to deafening adulation. After several minutes, Gallienus broke the embrace and raised his hands.

The *praeco*, decked out in the impressive robes of his office as official herald, rapped his staff on the stones of the portico, calling for the people's attention. "Hoc age!" the herald boomed. His deep baritone voice, trained to carry above the babble of the masses, spread over the audience like oil over rippling waters. "Hoc age!" he intoned again, and the noise died almost completely. He looked around. Satisfied he had done his job, the *praeco* bowed to Gallienus and stepped back out of the way.

One by one, senior senators praised Aurelian, vilified Zenobia, and extolled the virtues of Rome and its great citizens. Almost every one of the speakers explained how he personally had played some significant role in the drama, or at least how he had kept the central Empire intact while all of this warfare was being waged in the outer provinces. At long last, it was time for Gallienus himself.

"Fellow citizens of Rome! Be still, and harken to me." There was total silence. The Forum had been built to enhance the acoustics, so Gallienus' normal voice could now be heard throughout it by all but the deaf. "You all know how my brother, the Emperor Lucius Domitius Aurelianus, recaptured our eastern empire against fierce and overwhelming enemies. Here...." Gallienus pointed downward, and two guards dragged Zenobia up a few steps so the crowd could see her. They hissed appropriately. "Here he has brought the renegade queen, who broke her faith with Rome. See how the fruits of treachery bring down those who would be mighty without the will of you, the people!"

The crowd cheered lustily. Aurelian was amused at the way his friend and mentor could discard his normal bluff, soldierly manner and adopt the oratory of a politician practiced in the art of addressing *hoi polloi*.

Again Gallienus raised his hands, and again all sound died away. "Therefore, at our request, and by order of the senate, Lucius Domitius Aurelianus is proclaimed *Parthicus Maximus* and *Restitutor Orientis*!"

The people renewed their applause, with many shouts of "Aurelianus!", "*Parthicus Maximus*!" and "*Restitutor Orientis*!" echoing from the marble walls. Gallienus placed a wreath made of gold on Aurelian's head, then leaned over to speak in his ear.

"You did as I asked, brother. I leave her fate in your hands."

Gallienus took Aurelian's hand in his and held it aloft to the crowd. He waved with his other hand to invite even more noise, and Aurelian thought his eardrums would burst. Then Gallienus released him and stepped back, allowing his fellow emperor to bask in the love of the masses all on his own.

Knowing the senate would now disperse, Aurelian descended, step by measured step, down to the same level as Zenobia. He stopped just a few feet away and raised both of his arms in greeting as the citizens redoubled their efforts. The sound flowed against him like the waves of an incoming tide, leaving him awash in a strange pleasure he had never felt before. Still facing the crowd, he had to shout to make himself heard by the chained woman at his side.

"Although you stand by my side as I begged you, this is what you gave up to defy me."

"The moment must be sweet for you indeed," she shouted back.

The ceremonies done, many of the crowd scurried away to be the first to partake of the banquet, or to get the best seats in the different venues where the public games would be held. The noise abated enough for Zenobia to speak more normally, although she kept her face to the people. Aurelian heard the bitterness of her humiliation.

"So, I have served your purposes. Now you will have me executed. I beg you to spare my son."

"I told you, I could never have you killed. Nor your son." He tried to smile at the people who remained, still cheering, but instead felt the side of his jaw tighten in a grimace. "No, you face a much worse punishment."

At last, Zenobia turned to face him. "Which is?"

Aurelian met her gaze. "I have a villa at Tibur, just northeast of Rome. You and your son will live out your days in exile, never to see your homeland again. I will return to my empire, and tell your people of my mercy. They will soon forget you." He delivered this last statement with such invective that she winced. He hardened his heart against her beauty and sorrow. "And I doubt if I will ever see you again." He started down the steps to touch hands with the multitude who held out their arms to him, but were restrained by his *lictors*. But another thought occurred to him, and he turned back to the woman once more. "Oh, and one thing more: I will have a servant deliver the Palmyrene robe that offended you. It will keep you warm on the cold winter nights of Italia, and no doubt will remind you of your husband."

That look she gave him! Did he misconstrue, or was it what he had sought for years? Regret, longing, desire…perhaps even love? Zenobia clearly fought back tears, but for what, and for whom? No matter; it was far too late.

Before he could relent, Aurelian waved his hand. Understanding the gesture, the guards escorted Zenobia and Vaballathus away, fighting their way through the people who surged forward to touch the conquering hero. Aurelian continued to clasp hands with and wave at the cheering crowd, although his eyes were on the departing form of Zenobia. When at last he could see her no more, Aurelian signaled to his *lictors*, who pushed their way through the adoring masses so he could remount his chariot and flee from his triumph.

*   *   *

Tacitus lazed back on his divan, staring at the ceiling of the large, ornate lounge in his house, perhaps seeking to divine answers from the erotic frescoes above him. His chubby fingers played lightly over the goblet of wine that rested on his prominent stomach. Mucapor reclined on his left side on another divan, although he stared into the golden goblet in his hand as though admiring the color of the excellent vintage. No servants were present, not even the man who had served them on Mucapor's first visit to this ostentatious palace.

It was late at night, but the faint sounds of revelry still going on outside penetrated the thick walls of the home of Tacitus like poison wending its way through the bloodstream of its victim. Neither man had enjoyed the triumph, although both were obligated to attend. For several minutes there had been no other sound, the heaviness of their conversation making its continuance too much to be borne other than in short bursts. Finally, Tacitus felt compelled to pick up the burden.

"If it's going to get done, it can't be in Rome. He's much too popular right now."

Mucapor wagged his eyebrows several times, although this signal of astute contemplation was no doubt lost on his host. "Well." He leaned forward and took a small sip of his wine, savoring the thick, sweet taste, barely diluted by water. "We march for the east in two days, you know."

"Splendid." Tacitus gave a satisfied grunt, as though one troubling matter had been lifted from his shoulders. "But it's got to be before he reaches Palmyra and solidifies his power."

Mucapor glared at the man for underestimating his intelligence, but the consul did not bother to notice. Mucapor followed his fat host's glance upwards, registering once again the paintings of older, corpulent men cavorting with young, comely lads, some of them engaged in blatant sexual positions. It was not that he objected to the concept, but that a high-ranking official of Rome would display so crudely the Greek version of eros. And why was it that an older man was always portrayed in such painting as enjoying the favors of young men, as opposed to.... A smirk thinned the curvaceous lips of the general. Yes, it was time to bring his carefully laid preparations to their fruition.

"Don't worry. I believe I have a plan."

Tacitus grunted, the goblet moving up and down on his stomach, dangerously near to spilling wine over his expensive toga. "I hope it's a good one."

The smile on Mucapor fully blossomed, illuminating his beautiful face. "Oh, I think it will work...splendidly."

CHAPTER TWENTY-ONE

Once again Aurelian's plans to march back to the east were delayed; it took two days just to round up all of his legionaires. Between wine houses, houses of the *prosituta*, and infirmaries where men were treated for cracked skulls, alcohol poisoning and other sundry debilitations, it was a challenge for his search parties to retrieve all of them. This time there was no great urgency to get back to Assyria, although patience was not in his nature. Aurelian had promoted Decius—the only high-ranking officer remaining that he could trust—to the rank of praetor and left him in charge of two legions in Palmyra. With the eastern cities vying to prove their loyalty to Rome and the Persian Empire facing turmoil within, he foresaw little danger of another uprising so soon.

By the time his army reassembled, grain arrived from Egypt on the ships formerly under the command of Admiral Probus. Therefore, the newly appointed "god" blessed his troops with one more chance to win the love of the citizens they protected. Every oven was used to bake bread, the staple of every meal, and the legionaires were allowed to distribute the fresh loaves. The people had happily cheered another victorious army. Yet the restoration of bread, so scarce for more than a year, brought tears to their eyes as they took the prize from the hands of their heroes. Aurelian did not dispense any loaves personally, but it pleased him to walk the streets in a plain toga and watch the reaction of the people.

A full week after his triumph, Aurelian's army marched away from Rome. However, they trudged due north, not east toward Asia Minor. After Tetricus had been ousted from the Gallic Empire, a man named Faustinus took the office of provincial governor of Gallia Belgica, the heart of the lowlands in Gaul. Now he had decided to rebel. Aurelian and Gallienus agreed that it was more an annoyance than a threat, but, if it wasn't squashed immediately, other remote *praeses* might get the same idea. So Aurelian marched his army north to Augusta Treverorum, the provincial capital of Gallia Belgica.

The Emperor made quick work of the latest rebel. The battle against Faustinus became a farce; quite laughable. His small force of mostly new local conscripts quailed visibly at the sight of seasoned legionaires. The scuffle barely started before most of them ran for their lives. But the annoyance became a major aggravation: news of the infighting had encouraged barbarian marauders to attack Raetia and Vindelicia, so Aurelian ordered Faustinus beheaded as an example to his successor. Only after defeating the new invaders would Aurelian feel confident about the security of the Gallic portion of the Empire once again. As he marched his army east to the Danube, his only comfort was that he knew Zenobia's exact whereabouts, and that she could no longer incite rebellion against him in the territories that waited for his return. Finally, things were going smoothly.

*   *   *

Only six leagues long, the Via Tiburtina, the road from Rome to the small town of Tibur in the Latium region, had several treacherous stretches. It took two days for Zenobia and her son to be escorted to their new home and prison by four of Aurelian's legionaires. She expected harsh treatment, but the men were courteous and considerate. They wore the uniform of his personal guard, so no doubt Aurelian himself instructed them on their duties and behavior.

They entered Tibur in the late afternoon, on a chilly day in early autumn. The town was well situated on the edge of the Sabine mountains, although well above sea level, at the point where the Anio River formed its beautiful falls. Nestled by the upper course of the river, the town commanded an extensive view over the rolling, verdant countryside below. Tall marble columns split the imposing stone wall that marked the boundaries of their destination.

In spite of herself, Zenobia was impressed by the estate. She assumed Aurelian would exile them to some small, dank dwelling where they would be miserable for the rest of their lives. As prisons went, the villa was large and opulent, with extensive gardens and beautifully sculpted statues scattered about.

A staff of two dozen stood on the front portico, ready to greet them. As Zenobia dismounted, a boy ran down the steps to take the reins of her horse. An older male descended the steps more sedately. He bowed deeply before speaking.

"Greetings, great lady. My name is Valen, and I shall serve as the majordomo for your household."

"My household?" Zenobia gave the man a withering look. "Is it not that of the emperor Aurelian?"

Valen bowed again. "I beg your pardon, my lady. I spoke as the emperor commanded. That is to say, that we should all treat you and your sons as our masters, and this household as yours."

"I see. How noble of him."

"Indeed, my lady. He has been a noble gentleman since first I met him."

Zenobia sighed. It was unfair to take out her vexation with her circumstances on this man, who clearly had a high opinion of Aurelian, and it seemed with great reason. She forced a small smile. "You have served him long, then?"

"Some years, my lady," Valen proudly proclaimed. "I was captured in a battle in Thrace when the emperor was still a cavalry officer. After years of serving the emperor faithfully in Rome, my master was gracious enough to declare me a free citizen in the last census. Before his latest triumph, Caesar desired that I come here to Tibur to make certain that the lady was made comfortable."

Zenobia closed her eyes and breathed deeply. Aurelian never ceased to amaze her in all aspects. She had to admit that he had been most gracious to her as well. She opened her eyes and broadened her smile.

"Then I am certain you will follow your master's orders just as faithfully. Please, introduce my son and myself to the rest of these good servants."

Valen stepped over to the first woman in the line. "This is Marta." The stout, middle-aged woman curtsied awkwardly. "Marta is in charge of the cooking and cleaning staff. Marta was captured in Andalusia, and she's still a slave."

The other staff members were introduced in turn. Valen described their duties as well as their status as slaves or freemen, much to Zenobia's amusement. When the short ceremony concluded, Valen ushered them inside.

The interior boasted costly foreign marbles and fine mosaic pavements, with tasteful frescoes and stucco decorations on the walls and ceilings. The largest work of art inside was a bas-relief of bearded Hercules, draped in a long tunic with a lion's skin on his shoulders. Zenobia felt her cheeks twitch, not at all surprised that Aurelian would display a great warrior so prominently.

In deference to their long journey, an early dinner was served. The soldiers ate with the servants, and immediately took their leave to return to their unit.

On the following day Zenobia unpacked her cases with the aid of a personal maid. When they finished with most of her belongings, Zenobia sent the young woman out to prepare a bath. Only then did she reach into a chest that contained the sword and the robe, both of which had been sent to her by Aurelian just before she left Rome. She glanced at the sword, still incrusted with dried blood. She wondered why Aurelian had insisted she have it. She wondered for an even longer time why she kept it. Then she re-wrapped the terrible instrument and placed it in the bottom of the chest.

As she removed the covering cloth, Zenobia shook the robe out carefully. She stroked the fine cloth with lingering caresses, pulling up memories with each touch. On an impulse she put it on, the large cloak hanging nearly to the floor. She felt tears flood her eyes, and fought to keep them from falling on the fabric.

"It's a bit cold, ain't it, m'lady?"

Zenobia whirled, blinking at the sudden interruption.

"Yes." She cleared her throat. "Is it always this cold here?"

The serving girl shrugged. "This ain't too bad. Gets right frosty in winter, but not much snow. Summers are real nice."

Zenobia nodded and removed the robe. The girl's halting vulgar Latin was difficult to understand. Greta, that was her name. A slave from the Alamanni. "I take it my bath is ready."

"Oh!" The girl gave a clumsy bow. "Sorry, m'lady. Yes."

The cold seeped into her bones even as the slow days passed pleasantly. The high mountains, the green valley below, intrigued her for a while, but it was not home. The staff comported themselves politely and with attention—Valen in particular took great pains to make certain her every want was fulfilled—but she felt like a pampered songbird trapped in a golden cage. Even Vaballathus chafed at his confinement. Maybe Aurelian had assumed she would miss the power, or perhaps her people, but it was the desert itself that she longed for: the pristine, open vistas; the flora and fauna that were scarce and hardy, rather than the life forms that teemed in this verdant country; but most of all, the heat.

Aurelian had been correct about her fate. This was indeed a terrible punishment.

*   *   *

Aurelian marched first against the invaders at Vindelicia, northeast of the Danube. They gave his men a tough battle, but retreated to their homeland when he showed no mercy to the survivors. Then he led his troops back down the Danube to meet the smaller force. After a great victory at Raetia, it seemed as though every barbarian in Gaul was flying eastward on the wings of Mercury. Aurelian felt that Gaul was safe enough to leave to once more take command in Palmyra.

On the march to Thrace, however, Aurelian received news from the east that changed his mind. After the death of King Shapur, his son, the great warrior Hormizd I, had died under mysterious circumstances within the year. In quick succession, Hormizd's older brother, Bahram I, took the throne. Persia churned in turmoil under Bahram's insipid hand. Aurelian decided that this circumstance offered the possibility to attack the Sassanid Empire.

With Egypt back under Rome's thumb, Aurelian dispatched a messenger to General Probus to send whatever legions he could spare to Palmyra. They would join the two commanded by Decius, who was sent word to prepare for an invasion. Jupiter and Sol Invictus favored him: all of the augurs were propitious to finally bring Persia into the Roman fold.

*   *   *

Mucapor lay on his comfortable, spacious pallet. The limp form of Mnestheus made it crowded. Their passion, brief and unsatisfying to him, had nevertheless captured the attention of the emperor's scribe. After all the dilly-dallying, the time to put his plan into effect had arrived.

If Aurelian succeeded in conquering Persia, there would be no limit to his power. Decius' appointment to temporarily govern Palmyra—a clear signal Aurelian had no intention of ever giving him that position or any other—did not bode well for future advancement under this emperor. Even worse, if Aurelian knew about the murder of Odaenathus—which Mucapor suspected he did—even his powerful family would not be able to save him from the emperor's wrath. He must strike, hard and fast, or all would be lost.

"I need you to write a letter for me, Mnestheus."

"Certainly, Bicius." Mnestheus' drowsy voice, satiated from wine and unusual exercise, proved exactly the mood Mucapor wanted him in. "To whom, and about what?"

"To the Emperor Gallienus, from Aurelian."

For a moment, there was no reaction. Then Mnestheus roused himself. He propped his body up on one elbow and gave the younger man a questioning look. "Pardon me?"

"You must write that Aurelian has discovered the murderers of Odaenathus." Mucapor's voice was smooth, no trace of excitement or doubt. He had rehearsed this many times, uncertain if he would ever say the words out loud. "It was a plot by the Praetorian Guard to discredit the new emperor and foment a revolt against him in Palmyra."

"It…what?"

Mucapor tolerated the man's baffled reaction. After all, it must be quite a shock to him. "In it you will name me, General Domitianus, Captain Lucresus Cimber and Centurion Marcus Gladius."

"But...but—"

"Further, you will inform Emperor Gallienus that he intends to have us all arrested and executed as soon as we reach Palmyra to further appease the Palmyrenes, as he already so graciously spared the life of their former queen and her son."

Mnestheus gaped at him. Mucapor coughed to keep from laughing.

"But none of this is true! Why would Aurelian do such a thing?"

"Actually, it's partially true," Mucapor said blandly. "I did have Odaenathus murdered."

"You...." Mnestheus gulped loudly. "You did?

Mucapor spoke as though discussing the price of buying wine. "Oh, yes. It cost quite a bit to arrange it, but I hope it will be well worth the effort."

Mucapor could see the mind of the man whirling. Give him that much: at least he wasn't stupid. Just weak and sycophantic. Perfect for being manipulated.

"But there's only one thing you could do with such a letter...."

Mucapor put a thoughtful expression on his face. "I suppose that's true."

Even in the low candlelight, he saw that Mnestheus paled. The man gulped several more times in a very annoying fashion, tempting Mucapor to slap him into getting a grip on himself. But, really, wasn't this exactly the reaction he had hoped for?

"But...he's my emperor. And my friend."

A sneer came to Mucapor's lips and a bite to his voice. "Your friend? He's your master, and he's never treated you like anything else. Has he?"

"But—"

"But who is your lover, Mnestheus?"

"But, he—"

Mucapor made his voice hard and demanding. "Enough of these 'buts'! Who is your lover?"

"You are, Bicius." Mnestheus shrank into himself.

Mucapor smiled at him. "That's right." He kissed the man, quickly but firmly. "Don't forget that. Now, you will write that letter for me, won't you, Mnestheus?"

The old servant stared at him for a moment longer, but Mucapor had no doubt of the answer.

"Yes. Yes, of course I will."

*   *   *

As far as Zenobia could tell, her movements went unrestricted so long as she did not leave Tibur. When she went out alone, such as to observe the town market, a woman went with her. It was usually Greta, who acted clearly as a servant, not a guard. When she and Vaballathus went out together, an unarmed male servant followed. She had not asked to go into Rome and had no idea of what the answer would be if she did. At any rate, the weather was not conducive to a trip along the Via Tiburtina during the winter.

There had been one festival in the town since their arrival, and Zenobia and Vaballathus had enjoyed watching the merriments of the people from a distance. The music was loud and enthusiastic, although it was clear not many of the musicians made their living with their instruments. The singing and dancing was much the same, although there was one clear voice that rose sweetly above all the rest. Zenobia thought of inviting the woman to entertain them at the villa sometime, but that must wait until lingering animosities toward them had waned. Knowing Marta would be upset if they did not do justice to her excellent cooking, Zenobia ignored the tempting odors of food wafting from buildings and stalls and pulled her son back to the villa.

On fine days, the two of them went out riding. This was the highlight of their existence; Aurelian had left two beautiful, spirited Arabians for their use, and they rode the countryside of Tibur until they knew it intimately. Sometimes the rich soil flew from the thundering hooves of their mounts. At other times they were content to canter along, enjoying the scenery and their conversations, which were filled with history and philosophy, the two subjects Vaballathus had enjoyed the most under the tutelage of Cassius Longinus. It still pained Zenobia to think of how the wise head of that gentle, patient man had been struck away on the orders of the man she thought of every day.

Before long, it became clear why Tibur was a favorite resort and summer home for many of the wealthy and powerful of Rome. The abundance of refreshing waters from aqueducts and springs and the falls of the Anio were among its chief attractions. There were several large, attractive temples, especially a large temple of Hercules Victor, the chief deity of Tibur, which featured lovely descending terraces. On the cliffs above the Anio stood a large building with a colonnaded courtyard that served as the meeting place of the *Herculanei*

Augustales. The region held two small temples—one circular, with Corinthian columns, the other rectangular with Ionic columns—that were dedicated to Vesta and the Sibyl of Tibur. It was to the temple of Vesta that Zenobia was drawn most often, but she did not stay long because it bored Vaballathus.

So popular was the area that both Augustus and Maecenas had built villas there. The largest estate in the district, situated in the low ground of Tibur and occupying an area of some sixty-five hectares, was once owned by the great Hadrian. Aurelian's villa occupied a space only half that size.

As did the other wealthy estates in Tibur, Aurelian's villa enjoyed the best wines from the fertile soil in Campania, and cloths and clothing made from the finest wool from Apulia, Istria, Padua and Parma, and colored at the famous dye works at Aquileia. It boasted bronze articles from Capua and Bergamo, terra cotta ware from Puteoli, Cumae and Ischia, exquisite glass from Cumae, Sorento and Pompeii, high-quality bricks from Modena, amphorae from Pola, and amber imported from as far away as the Baltic in northern Europe. In short, any luxury that a resident desired and could pay for was to be found in the country homes of the mighty Romans. It all meant nothing to Zenobia. She would have happily traded it for a tent in the Fertile Crescent.

On a particularly fine spring evening, Zenobia and Vaballathus went out riding. Trotting their horses through a grassy meadow, Zenobia witnessed a strange sight. An eagle, rare to the area, stooped on its prey. It came up from the ground with a snake grasped in its talons. However, in an incredibly rare instance, the predator must not have captured the reptile properly, and allowed it to turn on its captor. The snake bit the eagle, which flinched at the strike.

With a start, Zenobia recalled the words of Aurelian when he learned of the murder of Odaenathus: "I see, I see. So, I have a snake within my cradle."

The eagle struggled to fly on directly into the sunset, but it had clearly been poisoned. In the fading light above the hills, Zenobia saw it fall from the sky as though plummeting from the sun into the ground just before the great orb disappeared. Colder than the chill of the evening air, a sudden shudder shook her entire frame. What evil did this weird omen portend?

CHAPTER TWENTY-TWO

Aurelian's scouts rejoined the army in Perinthus, on the northern shore of the Propontus in Thrace. Every officer down to *hastatus posterior*, the lowest rank of centurion, attended a general staff meeting. Mucapor listened to the report with excitement and trepidation.

The Sassanid Empire was in Chaos. General Probus had sent three full legions from Egypt to meet them in Palmyra, plus another corps of cavalry. Their combined forces, including cavalry, mercenaries, and such *auxilia* as the archers, slingers and javelin throwers, would be nearly eighty thousand strong. Aurelian intended to reinforce that with units from Assyria who had sworn renewed loyalty.

Then the emperor stated the obvious objective. They would cross the Euphrates into Persia by the following autumn and expand the Roman Empire to unprecedented proportions. They would annihilate the Sassanid dynasty, and destroy the eastern threat forever. The jubilation within the command tent was palpable.

On the march to Caenophrurium, a minor staging post on the road from Perinthus to Byzantium, Mucapor made clever use of his time. When the army made camp outside of the little town, he prepared to strike.

*   *   *

"Caesar! Please, come quickly!"

Years of training allowed Aurelian to come from a deep sleep to full awareness, weapon in hand. He relaxed at the sight of Mnestheus…until he realized the man was fully dressed, unusual for that time of night. The man trembled and bit his lip, but then, he was nervous most of the time.

"What is it?"

"General Mucapor says another messenger has arrived from Palmyra. The news is…well, it's rather alarming. The general feels you must make a decision immediately."

"About our plans? Now?"

Mnestheus shrugged, in no state to give a clearer idea of what was happening. Aurelian gave an exasperated sigh and rose. He shrugged on a robe.

Mnestheus ducked through the curtain that served as a door from the emperor's bedchamber into the command tent. As soon as he passed through the curtain, Aurelian beheld Mucapor, Domitianus, and two other officers of the Praetorian Guard in full uniform. He frowned at the unusual meeting.

"General Domitianus. Captain Lucresus Cimber and Centurion Marcus Gladius. And General Mucapor." Their eyes were slitted, lips compressed, cheeks taut; none responded to his greeting. What awful news could have reached the camp in the past few hours? He tried to lighten the mood. "Mnestheus said it was urgent. We haven't been ambushed by barbarians again, have we?"

The two junior officers moved to stand in back of Aurelian, surrounding him. Mnestheus, hiding behind Mucapor, now cowered into a corner of the tent.

Aurelian narrowed his eyes. His hand automatically went to his side, but found no weapon hanging there. "What is this?"

Aurelian looked at Mucapor, who put his hand on the hilt of his sword. The emperor lowered his own hand, but stood straighter.

"So, Mucapor." His voice was soft, almost sad. "Are you my Brutus?"

He heard both of the officers behind him draw their swords. Domitianus did the same, but Mucapor just stood there, a strange half smile, half snarl upon his features. All of his reflections of Mucapor as a poisonous snake flooded back into his mind. Suddenly a sharp thrust ripped into his side, and then another, high up near his shoulder. His eyes flew wide and he gasped, sucking for air. For a second he thought of the arrow he had taken at Immae, but that was nothing compared with this. The pain locked every muscle in his body, shooting bolts of fire through his veins down to the soles of his feet. He tried desperately to pull away, but his attackers had all of the leverage. Then Domitianus lunged forward to puncture his body beneath his rib cage, and the agony doubled. He wanted to scream from the pain, but his lungs produced only enough air for a faint wheeze. Even as his body shuddered from the blows, Aurelian noted that Mucapor drew his sword with relish and stabbed him through the stomach. Blood fountained from his front, and he felt the warm fluid of life seeping down his back. The bitter taste of blood and bile spewed up from his throat, but he could not spit it out. He wanted to say one word of hatred for the man, but in an instant of clarity wished that he could be saying one more word of love to the woman he had left behind.

Skewered like a piece of meat ready for the spit, Aurelian glared into the eyes of his treacherous general. That was the only voice left for him to express his loathing. Then the men behind pulled their swords out of him. He listed heavily to his left, and Domitianus' sword pulled free of his body. As Aurelian's head sank toward his chest, Mucapor pushed his sword in up to the hilt. Aurelian felt himself falling, but the sensation lasted only an instant.

*   *   *

The heat of the summer was not oppressive. Tibur's elevation reduced much of the humidity of the lowlands, especially near the coast. Still, unexpected visitors to the remote villa in the middle of the day were rare, especially one who clattered into the courtyard on a horse and then pounded on the door so insistently.

Marta lumbered from the kitchens, interrupted from overseeing preparations for the evening meal. Valen was there before her, and the majordomo opened the door as she entered the hall. Both were surprised to see a young man wearing the uniform of an imperial messenger. His horse could be in no more of a lather than this panting, dripping courier. He held a scroll clutched tightly in one hand. Both of the servants bowed, Marta more deeply than her free companion.

"This is the villa of—" The young man's voice cracked. He fought to get his emotions under control. "Of the Emperor Lucius Domitius Aurelianus?"

"It is, sir." Valen bowed low and swept his hand toward the door. "Would you be so kind as to step into the reception room?"

The man swallowed several times. A tic in his eye beat a steady pulse, which Marta found odd in a young man who had no doubt been chosen for his duty because of his courage and resolve. This nervousness—almost as though he were afraid of something—would have been more understandable if he stood in front of the emperor. However, he most assuredly knew that Aurelian had advanced with his army into the Eastern Empire, perhaps even Assyria by now. The knowledge struck a chill into her heart.

"I bear a letter from Emperor Gallienus." The messenger did not step across the threshold. "Where may I find the lady Septimia Zenobia?"

Valen gasped. "From Emperor Gallienus? Not...my master?"

The messenger moved his head from side to side as though it weighed too much for his rippling muscles to control. Marta somehow realized that the messenger knew the contents of the sealed scroll.

"My lady...Zenobia is...is in the courtyard with her son."

Marta was startled by the sudden change in the majordomo. His voice was that of an old man, attempting to wheeze out his last words. She could see by the sagging face and body that she would have to manage this situation.

The messenger clasped the scroll more tightly in his hand and took a deep breath. He exhaled as though steeling himself. The tic in his eye throbbed faster. He stepped into the entryway and advanced towards the courtyard like one approaching the cross on which he would be crucified.

"Sir." Marta was unsure of her right to speak, but certain this messenger bore terrible news, and did not want to face her mistress. "Perhaps it would be better...that is, would you prefer that I deliver the message to her?"

The messenger halted in mid-stride. He turned back to face Marta. The gleam of gratitude in his eyes faded almost as soon as it materialized.

"It is...my duty." He blinked several times, and his mouth worked as though working up the saliva needed to speak again. "But, perhaps it is enough that I give it to you, and you give it to her."

Marta nodded. The messenger thrust the scroll toward her. Marta took it as though reaching out to pet a suspect dog, then walked out the door to the courtyard. The young man remained rigid, like the image of Hercules on the wall.

*   *   *

Marta stepped through the doorway. She squinted, adjusting her eyes to the sunlight reflecting off of the stone flagging and walls after the cool darkness of the interior. The rapid thud of wood on wood told her that the lady Zenobia and her son were once again practicing sword fighting. For a moment she just watched, wondering what she would say. Should she just hand the scroll to her and go back inside, as though she conceived no idea of its contents?

Marta observed how the boy, a frisky colt of twelve years, danced around his mother. He was nearly as tall as her lady already, and had clearly been given excellent instructions in the art of swordplay. Only Zenobia's superior skill prevented his quickness and his daring attacks from penetrating her defense. Children had such energy, such a zest for life. Marta felt that the only thing worse than becoming old must be when a person died before their time. She exhaled heavily, surprised that she had been holding her breath.

Zenobia either heard the sigh or caught a glimpse of her in the doorway, for she held up her left hand and lowered her weapon with the other. Instantly reacting to the unspoken command, Vaballathus turned toward Marta, who still stood quietly.

"What is it, Marta?"

Marta always wondered at the strength in that voice, the calmness. She took a step into the courtyard and held up the scroll. "My lady, I have...I fear there is terrible news."

Zenobia squared her shoulders as one who had borne terrible news before. "Yes?"

Marta licked her lips. "It's a letter from Emperor Gallienus."

"From Gallienus!"

Marta guessed the thoughts racing through the other woman's mind from the slight shifts that flitted across her features. Without witnessing the behavior of the messenger or Valen, the lady somehow possessed a strong idea of what this must portend.

Zenobia held out her hand. Marta took several more paces and gave her the scroll.

"Thank you, Marta."

Marta inclined her head in a slight bow.

"My lady."

Zenobia broke the seal and read the scroll. Marta observed her closely, but could read no signs of the woman's reaction. Vaballathus tugged at her sleeve.

"Can we practice some more now, Mother?"

Zenobia's face remained placid, almost serene. But her voice quavered enough for Marta to detect it.

"No, I think that will be all for today." She swallowed once. "Why don't you go prepare yourself for dinner?"

"Yes, Mother." Disappointed, but obedient, he walked inside, still holding the wooden sword.

Zenobia glanced up into the sky as though searching for something that was not there. "Please offer the messenger food and drink, and have Pietro take care of his horse. And ask Valen to gather the staff and inform them—"

Her lower lip trembled, and Marta could swear that moisture came to her eye. But her voice remained calm.

"That the Emperor Aurelian has been murdered."

In spite of everything, Marta went limp. "Yes, my lady." Her voice was a whisper in her own ears.

Marta turned to the villa. She took a few dragging steps to the doorway, but felt compelled to turn and look at her mistress before she went back inside. Zenobia stood like one of the marble statues, the scroll clenched in her hand, staring out into the distant hills.

*   *   *

That night Zenobia made her way to the temple of Vesta, the virgin goddess of the hearth, home, and family. Few people worshipped her any longer, since Aurelian had made Sol Invictus so popular with traditional Romans and the new religion of Christianity had begun to grow throughout the empire. Vesta was a goddess of and for women; few men had any regard for her gentle powers. Still, Vesta's sacred fire burned at the hearth inside the temple, and the temple was cleaned regularly by an acolyte or a priestess. Zenobia had placed a small statue of Malak-bel in a far corner, but no one had disturbed this strange, foreign god.

Zenobia slipped down from the horse. Her bare feet knew the sting of the pebbles beneath them, but she ignored the insignificant discomfort. She pulled the sword from the scabbard on the saddle—the sword that had caused her so much grief, having blinded her to the truth. As she glided into the center of the temple, Vesta's eternal flame illuminating her way, she reflected that perhaps she had not wanted to see the truth. All her life she sought to be a true daughter of Cleopatra, strong and powerful, shielding her deepest emotions from any man. Only now could she admit that she was a woman like many others, and regretted the love she had thrown away.

Had her parents been right, that power gave you control over your life? That it was a guarantee of safety? Now it seemed to be an illusion of control, of safety. She had never loved Odaenathus, had rejected Aurelian, and had even left her own son behind to seek conquest and empire. And what did she have now?

It was too late for regrets. Only penance remained. As if her future life of solitude would not be penance enough.

In front of the statue of Malak-bel, Zenobia bowed from the waist. She laid the sword gently down onto the cold marble floor. Standing erect once more, she took two steps back. Her hands went to the clasp of the robe her once husband had given to her once lover. With deft movements, Zenobia threw off the robe to reveal her naked body. She shivered slightly in the cool night air. Then she prostrated herself fully on the floor in front of the image of her god.

There would be no words this time. Malak-bel knew her thoughts, the sorrow she suffered since she had watched Aurelian walk away, vowing they would never meet again. She did not mourn for his death: all men died. She mourned for the loss of the chance to tell him what she had longed to cry out to him in that moment, what she wished with all her heart she had found the courage to say.

She did not know how long she lay there, wallowing in her grief.

Her body felt as numb as her mind, but she forced herself up to her knees. Almost without thought, her hands came up to touch her face, then trailed down her throat until they rested on the softness of her breasts. With sudden violent pulls, she raked her long, sharp fingernails down and across, again and again, scratching her breasts until they bled profusely. Somehow, she felt no pain. She scooped up the dripping liquid and smeared the blood over her face, painting it the color of death. Then she lifted her face and spread her arms wide, as though to welcome the embrace of a lover. The sound of her voice, so piercing, so filled with longing, startled her own ears.

"Aurelian!"

Afterword

Emperor Lucius Domitius Aurelian was buried with great honor and deeply mourned throughout the Roman Empire. The senate proclaimed him Augustus, and he was deified as Divus Aurelianus. His scribe, Mnestheus, was murdered shortly after the assassination of Aurelian.

General Bicius Nastrud Mucapor was never appointed consul and governor of Palmyra, and never rose further in rank. The reign of Emperor Marcus Claudius Tacitus lasted only nine months before he mysteriously died. On the death of Tacitus, General Marcus Aurelius Probus was immediately elevated to wear the purple.

Little is known of Vaballathus after the defeat of Palmyra.

Queen Septimia Zenobia lived well into old age as a respected citizen of Rome. For one hundred years after Zenobia's death, mighty women warriors continued to ride at the head of their armies and rule over Assyria.

Author's Notes

Because this is a work of fiction, I will not provide a Works Cited page. There were a great deal of incredibly informative texts that I consulted for the novel, but this is not a scholarly tome. However, I feel it is only fair to mention some of the major works that I referenced while researching the rather sketchy knowledge we have of this era, and these events in history.

Naturally, I start with "The Decline and Fall of the Roman Empire" by Edward Gibbon. All of the major characters in my novel are mentioned in his book, to some degree. While it is unclear how accurate his descriptions may be, they are very useful in understanding the politics and relationships of the era.

Unfortunately, Zenobia herself was a minor—perhaps a deliberately ignored—character in Roman history. As we know, the victors always get to write the history books. One source of information was "Zenobia, Queen of Palmyra" by Jone Johnson Lewis. Some mention was made of her in the Encyclopaedi Britannica, but not much. Sadly, I must confess that Wikipedia provided most of the alleged information about her, as several other books on the subject were no more informative than this one is.

On the other hand, Aurelian is quite a known figure in Roman history. One source I used both for his history and fighting techniques was "The Emperor Aurelian's Campaign through Anatolia: From Byzantium to Antioch in 272 A.D." by Emily Wagner. Both the Catholic Encyclopedia and Cyclopaedia Brittanica provided much useful information. The Brithish Museum in London also contained some useful information and artifacts.

While Prince Odaenathus, General Mucapor, Mnestheus, Cassius Longinus, General Zabdas, Emperor Gallienus, Shapur I, and most of the other significant persons in this story also existed, very little is actually known about their lives and deeds. I have tried to create them as faithfully to what I learned as possible, but there is no question that much factual knowledge eludes me. Still, I hope I have neither savaged nor elevated their memories too badly.

As to other details—the description of the city of Palmyra, the geography of the time, the battles that are described, and even the weapons and tactics of the combatants—all are as accurate as my research could make them. The goal of any dedicated writer of historical fiction is, to the greatest extent possible, put the reader into the lives and environment of the people who created the story. I hope I have achieved this goal.

Don Maker
November 2, 2013

About the Author

Don Maker is a credentialed teacher and a published freelance writer of short stories and poetry. He is a board member of the California Writer's Club, Mt. Diablo Branch. Don received his A.A. in Speech Arts from San Diego Mesa College, his B.A. in English and Comparative Literature from the University of California, San Diego, and his M.A. in Education from Chapman University.

From his teaching background, Don wrote a novel based around education (*The Grindstone*). He then wrote a surrealistic play based on the life of Sigmund Freud, (*Sigi and Carl*). He continues to teach and to write novels on a variety of subjects, including a sports comedy (*The Jersey Jupiters*), a YA fantasy (*Miranda's Magic*), an historical fiction (*Zenobia*), and a comedy screenplay (*Uplifting Thoughts*). He is currently working on another historical fiction novel (*The Shakespeares and the Crown*). In non-fiction, he is a featured writer for Yahoo Voices.

Contact Information

Website:

http://donmaker.yolasite.com/

Email:

metacognitionblog@yahoo.com

www.ingramcontent.com/pod-product-compliance
Lightning Source LLC
Chambersburg PA
CBHW060130130626
46556CB00006B/2297